"IT'S AN ANGEL," LENA CRIED. . . .

And because she believed it, it was.

The light took form.

And substance.

And became everything a not quite seventeen-year-old girl wanted in an angel.

In the moment of making, the door flew open and a large, dark-haired man, waving one hand in front of his face to clear the smoke, burst into the room. "Lena! how many times have I told you . . . ?" His eyes widened, and his bellow became a roar. *"What the devil are you doing in my daughter's room?"*

Lena knew that angels were sexless, but her father didn't know that the beautiful young man with the bicolored hair was an angel, and his belief in what he was seeing was as strong as hers.

The last little bit of substance formed out of a father's fears.

And, all things considered, it wasn't actually that little.

His expression a cross between confusion and panic, the angel ducked the first blow, slipped under an outstretched hand, and ran for the bedroom door. . . .

TANYA HUFF

The Second Summoning

The Keeper's Chronicles #2

DAW BOOKS, INC.
DONALD A. WOLLHEIM, FOUNDER
375 Hudson Street, New York, NY 10014

ELIZABETH R. WOLLHEIM
SHEILA E. GILBERT
PUBLISHERS
www.dawbooks.com

First Printing, March 2001
3 4 5 6 7 8 9

For Meg, who helped keep the teenagers
sounding like they were seventeen, not forty.

In Memoriam:
Austin, 1980–2000

ONE

For all intents and purposes, the motel room was dark and quiet. The only light came intermittently through a crack in the curtains as the revolving sign by the road spun around so fast it caught up to its afterimages and appeared to read Motel 666. The only sound came from the rectangular bulk of the heating unit under the window that roared out warmth at a decibel level somewhere between a DC9 at takeoff and a Nirvana concert—although it was considerably more melodic than either. The smell emanating from the pizza box—crushed to fit neatly into a too-small wastebasket—blended with the lingering smell of the previous inhabitants, some of whom hadn't been particularly attentive to personal hygiene.

The radio alarm clock between the beds read eleven forty squiggle where the squiggle would have been a five had the entire number been illuminated.

Both of the double beds were occupied.

The bed closest to the bathroom held the shape

of two bodies—one large, one small—stretched out beneath the covers.

The bed closest to the window held one long, lean, black-and-white shape that seemed to be taking up more room than was physically possible.

The light flickered. The heater roared. The long, lean shape contracted and became a cat. It walked to the edge of the mattress and crouched, tail lashing.

"This is pathetic," it announced, leaping upon the smaller of the two figures in the other bed. "Even for you."

Claire Hansen stretched out her arm, turned on the bedside lamp, and found herself face-to-face with an indignant one-eyed cat. "Austin, if you don't mind, we're waiting for a manifestation."

He lay down on her chest, assuming a sphinxlike position that suggested he wasn't planning on moving any time soon. "It's been a week."

Twisting her head around, Claire peered at the clock radio. The squiggle changed shape. "It's been forty-six minutes."

"It's been a week," Austin repeated, "since we left the Elysian Fields Guest House. A week since you and young Mr. McIssac here started keeping company."

The other figure stirred, but the cat continued.

"For the first time in that week, you two are actually in the same bed and what are you doing? You're waiting for a manifestation!"

Claire blinked. "Keeping company?" she repeated.

"For lack of a more descriptive phrase, which, I might add, is my point—there's a distinct lack of more descriptive phrases being applied here. You could cut the unresolved sexual tension between you two with a knife, and I, personally," he declared, whiskers bristling, "am tired of it."

"Just pretending for a moment that this is any of your business," Claire told him tightly, "a week isn't that long . . ."

"You knew each other for almost two months before that."

". . . we're in one bed now because the site requires a male and a female component . . ."

"You're saying you had no control over the last seven days?"

". . . and did it ever occur to you that things haven't progressed because there's been an audience perpetually in attendance?"

"Oh, sure. Blame me."

"Could I say something here?" Rolling toward the center of the bed, Dean McIssac rose up on one elbow, blue eyes squinting a little behind wire-frame glasses as he came into the light from the bedside table. "I'm thinking this isn't the time or the place to talk about, you know, stuff."

"Talk?" Austin snorted. "You're missing my point."

The young man's cheeks flushed slightly. "Well, it sure as scrod isn't the time or the place to *do* anything."

"Why not?"

"Because there's a dead . . . lady standing at the foot of the bed."

Claire craned her neck to see around the cat.

Arms folded over a turquoise sweater, her weight on one spandex-covered hip, the ghost raised an artificially arched ectoplasmic eyebrow. "Boo," she suggested.

"Boo yourself," Claire sighed.

Cheryl Poropat, or rather the ghost of Cheryl Poropat, hovered above the X marked on the carpet with ashes and dust, the scuffed heels of her ankle boots about two inches from the floor. "So, you're here to send me on?"

"That's right." Claire sat down in one of the room's two chairs. Like most motel chairs they weren't designed to be actually sat in, but she felt that remaining in bed with Dean, even if they were both fully clothed, undermined her authority.

"You some kind of an exorcist?"

"No, I'm a Keeper."

Cheryl folded her arms. Half a dozen cheap bracelets jangled against the curve of one wrist. "And what's that when it's home?"

"Keepers maintain the structural integrity of the barrier between the world as most people know it and the metaphysical energy all around it."

The ghost blinked. "Say what?"

10

"We mend the holes in the fabric of the universe so bad things don't get through."

"Well, why the hell didn't you say so the first time? If I wasn't dead," she continued thoughtfully before Claire could answer, " I'd think you were full of it, but since I'm not only dead, I'm here, my view of stuff has been, you know, broadened." Penciled brows drew in . . . "Being dead makes you look at things differently." . . . and centered themselves again. "So, how do you do it?"

"Do what?" Claire asked, having been distracted by the movement of the dead woman's eyebrows.

"Fix the holes."

"We reach beyond the barrier and manipulate the possibilities. We use magic," she simplified as Cheryl looked blank.

Understanding dawned with returning facial features. "You're a witch. Like on television."

"No."

"What's the difference?"

"She's got a better looking cat," Austin announced from the top of the dresser in a tone that suggested it should have been obvious.

Claire ignored him. "I'm a Keeper."

"Well, jeepers keepers." Cheryl snickered and bounced her fingertips off a bit of bouffant hair, her hair spray having held into the afterlife. "Bet you wish you had a nickel for every time someone said that."

"Not really, no."

"They've got a better sense of humor on television, too," the ghost muttered.

"That's only because Keepers have no sense of humor at all," Austin told her, studying his reflection in the mirror. "If it wasn't for me, she'd be so smugly sanctimonious no one could live with her."

"And thank you for your input, Austin." Shooting him a look that clearly promised *"later,"* Claire stood. "Shall we begin?"

Cheryl waved off the suggestion. "What's your hurry? Introduce me to the piece of beefcake the cat thinks you should do the big nasty with."

"The what?"

"You know; the horizontal mambo, the beast with two backs." Her pelvic motions—barely masked by the red stretch pants—cleared up any lingering confusions. "He a Keeper, too?"

Claire glanced over at Dean who was staring at the ghost with an expression of horrified fascination. Or fascinated horror, she wasn't entirely certain which. "He's a friend. And that was a private conversation."

"Ask me if I care?" Translucent hands patted ephemeral pockets. "I'd kill for a freaking smoke. Couldn't hurt me much now, could they? You oughta go for it, Keeper."

"I don't smoke."

A ghostly, dismissive glance raked her up and

down. "Not surprised—you've got that tobacco-free, alcohol-free, cholesterol-free—is that your natural hair color?"

"Yes." Claire tucked a strand of dark brown hair behind her ear.

"Hair-color free sort of look. Take my advice, hon, try a henna."

"I ought to go for a henna?"

"Yeah, in your hair. But that wasn't what I meant. You oughta go for *him*." She nodded toward Dean. "Live a little. I mean, men take their pleasure where they find it, right? Why not women? Your husband screws around, you know, and everyone thinks he's such a freaking stallion and all you get's a 'sorry, sweetie' that you're supposed to take 'cause he's out of work and feeling unsure of his manhood—like it's your freaking fault he got LAID OFF. . . ."

Claire and Austin, who'd been watching the energy build, dropped to the floor. Dean, whose generations of Newfoundland ancestors trapped between a barren rock and an angry sea had turned adaptability into a genetic survival trait, followed less than a heartbeat behind.

In the sudden flare of yellow-white light, the clock radio and the garbage pail flew through the air and slammed into opposite walls.

". . . but if *you* do it, just once, then BAM . . ."

The bureau drawers whipped open, then slammed shut.

". . . brain aneurysm, and you're stuck haunting this freaking DUMP!"

Both beds rose six inches into the air, then crashed back to the floor.

Breathing heavily—which was just a little redundant since she wasn't breathing at all, but some old habits died very hard indeed—the ghost stared around the room. "What just happened?"

"Usually, when you manifest, your anger rips open one of those holes in the fabric of the universe," Claire explained, one knee of her jeans separating from a sticky spot on the orange carpet with a sound like tearing Velcro. "I'm keeping you from doing that, so the energy had to go somewhere else, creating a poltergeist phenomenon."

Cheryl actually looked intrigued. "Like in the movie?"

"I didn't see the movie."

"Again, not surprised."

"Why? Don't tell me I've got that movie-free look, too."

"All right."

"All right what?"

"All right, she won't tell you," Austin snickered.

Eyes narrowed, Claire glared down at him. "*You* are supposed to be on my side. And as for you . . ." She turned her attention back to the smirking ghost. ". . . get ready to move on." She wasn't supposed to make it sound like a threat, but she'd had just about as much of Cheryl Poropat as she could handle. *I've got a life, lady. Which is more than I can say for you.*

The ghost's smirk disappeared. "Now?"

"Why not now?"

"Well, I'm still hanging here because I've got unfinished business, right?"

Claire sighed. She should have known it wasn't going to be that easy. "If that's what you think."

"And just what's THAT supposed to mean?"

There was another small flare of energy. In the bathroom, the toilet flushed.

"With metaphysical phenomena, belief is very important. If you believe you're here because you have unfinished business, then that's why you're here."

"Yeah? What if I believe I'm alive again?"

"Doesn't work that way."

"Figures." She looked from Claire to Dean and back to Claire again. "Okay. Unfinished business—I want to talk to my husband. You bring him here, you let me have my say, and I'll go."

"Bring your husband here?"

"Can I can go to him?"

Claire shook her head. "No, you're tied to this room."

"Doomed to appear to couples and give them unwanted advice," Dean added from where he was kneeling in the narrow space between the bed and the bathroom wall.

"No one *ever* wants relationship advice, sweet-cheeks." For the first time since she'd appeared, Cheryl looked at him like he was more than pretty meat. "But how did you know?"

He sighed and tried not to think about what he was kneeling in. "We spoke to Steve and Debbie."

"Nice kids."

"They're some scared."

"Yeah, well, death's a bitch."

"Can you believe that she died right after a nooner with my best friend?" Howard Poropat sounded more resigned than upset by the revelation, his light tenor voice releasing the words in a reluctant mono-tone that lifted slightly at the end of each sentence, creating a tentative question. "Did she tell you that?"

"No, she didn't mention it." Claire braced herself as the car turned into the motel parking lot, sliding a little in the accumulated slush. When she thought it was safe to release her grip on the dashboard, she pointed. "There. Number 42."

Jaw moving against a wad of nicotine gum, he steered the station wagon where indicated. "Let's just go over this again, can we? Cheryl's ghost is haunting the room she died in?"

"Yes."

"And she can't move on until she says something to me?"

"Apparently." It hadn't taken much effort to persuade him that it was possible. For all that he reminded her of processed cheese slices, he had a weirdly egocentric view of his place in the world.

"You think she wants to apologize?" The car slid to a stop, more-or-less in front of the right room.

"I honestly don't know," Claire told him, slamming her shoulder against the passenger side door and forcing it open. "Why don't we go inside and find out?"

While Claire'd been gone, the room had been redecorated in early playing cards. Most of them were just lying around, but several had been driven into the ceiling's acoustic tiles.

"What happened?"

Dean nodded toward the ghost and mouthed the word, "Boom!"

Brows drawn in, Cheryl folded her arms. "We were playing a little rummy to pass the time, but he cheats!"

"Dean? I doubt that. He spent six months living next to a hole to Hell, and the ultimate force of evil couldn't even convince him to drop his underwear on the floor."

"Not him, the cat!"

Austin continued washing a spotless white paw, ignoring both the conversation and the seven of spades only partially hidden by a fringe of stomach fur.

17

Claire snorted. "What did you expect? He's a cat." She had no idea how a cat, a ghost, and Dean had managed to play rummy when only one of them could actually manipulate the cards, nor did she want to know. Shrugging off her jacket, she moved farther into the room, pulling a suddenly reluctant Howard Poropat along with her by the pocket on his beige duffle coat.

The ghost's eyes widened. "I don't believe it! How'd you convince him?"

"I asked him nicely." She dropped down onto the edge of the bed, out of the reconciliation's direct line of fire.

"Cheryl?"

"Howard."

The bed dipped as Dean joined her. Claire leaned back and, when her weight pressed into his shoulder, turned her head to murmur, "You okay?"

"I got clipped by the six of clubs, but my sweater deflected it."

Dean's sweater was a traditional fisherman's cable knit. Handmade by his aunt from wool so raw it had barely paused between sheep and needles, Claire suspected it could, if not deflect bullets, certainly discourage them. "Thanks for staying with her."

His arm slipped around her waist. "No problem, Boss, always willing to help."

Austin's right, Claire thought as they turned their attention back to the couple staring into each other's

18

eyes in the center of the room. *It's been implied for a week, what are we waiting for?*

There'd been contact—touching, kissing, more touching, gentle explorations all crammed into those rare moments when they were actually alone and not likely to hear a speculative comment just as things got interesting—but somehow they hadn't moved on to that next step.

Maybe I should lock Austin in the bathroom.

The next level of intimacy.

Not that he'd stay there.

The horizontal mambo . . .

Stop it.

"Howard."

"Cheryl?" Pulling off his glove with his teeth, he held out his hand and stroked the air by her cheek. "The, uh, Keeper, says you got something to say to me?"

"That's right." She leaned into his touch. His baby finger sank into her eye socket. She didn't even notice, but Howard shuddered and snatched his hand away. "It's about me and Tony."

"Tony? My best friend who you betrayed me with?"

"Yeah. Tony. I got something I need to say."

Howard spread his hands, the picture of forgiving magnanimity. "What is it, babe?"

Cheryl smiled. "I just wanted to say—had to say— before I left this world forever . . ." All four of her listeners leaned into the pause. ". . . that Tony was a better lover than you ever were. Bigger, better, and he knew how to use it! We did it twice, *twice*, during his lunch hour, and he bought me a hoagie! He made me forget every miserable time you ever TOUCHED ME!"

In the silence that followed the sound of Howard slamming up against the inside of the door, the queen of hearts fell from the ceiling and Austin murmured, "I gotta admit, that wasn't totally unexpected."

Calm and triumphant, Cheryl turned toward the bed. "All right, Keeper. I'm ready."

"Dean . . ."

"I'll see that he's okay."

It only took a moment for Claire to send Cheryl on. Thinned by a distinct sense of closure, the possibilities practically opened themselves.

"Remember what I said, hon." Scarlet lips made a suggestive kissing motion. "You oughta go for it."

Keepers were always careful not to respond emotionally to provocation from metaphysical accidents. Unfortunately, Claire remembered that after she shoved Cheryl through to the Otherside just a little harder than necessary. A lot harder than necessary.

Howard seemed essentially unaffected by both his dead wife's parting words and the impact with the door. As Claire resealed the barrier and turned, blinking away afterimages of the beyond and of a translucent figure bouncing twice, Dean was helping him onto the end of the nearer bed.

"Is she gone?" he asked, searching through thinning hair for a bump.

"Yes."

"Is she in Hell?"

"Not my department." Grasping the soft lines of his chin lightly with one hand, Claire tilted his head up. "It's time you went home, Howard."

Pale blue eyes widened.

"You were thinking about your late wife and you couldn't sleep, so you went out for a drive."

"For a drive. . . ?"

"You found yourself outside the motel room where she died, and you got out of the car."

"Out of the car. . . ?"

"You stared at the door to the room for a long moment."

"Long moment. . . ?"

"Then you got back into the car and you went home."

"Went home. . . ?"

"You don't know why, but you feel better about her death and the way things were left between you. You're glad it's over."

"Glad to be rid of her."

"Close enough." It was the first definitive statement he'd made. She carefully used the new, more probable version of events to wipe out his actual

21

memories. Then, still holding his chin, she walked him out to his car where she released him.

"Is he gone?" Dean asked as Claire came back into the room and sagged against the door.

"Oh, yeah. I demanded to know what he was doing staring at my room and he, after telling me his wife had died there, asked me if I wanted to comfort him."

"He was sad?"

"Not that kind of comfort, Dean."

"What . . . oh."

"Lovely couple, weren't they?" Rubbing her temples, she walked to the end of the bed and scuffed out the X with the edge of her shoe. "Makes you want to swear off relationships for the rest of your life."

It took her a moment to figure out why the answering silence resonated like the inside of a crowded elevator after an unexpected emission. Then she realized what she'd said.

And who to.

"Open mouth, insert other foot," Austin advised.

"But they *were* nasty."

"No one's arguing. Although I can't understand why you're afraid that you and Dean will someday morph into them."

Claire had a sudden vision of herself in red stretch

pants and a turquoise sweater and shuddered. "I'm not."

"You're not?"

"No."

Austin snorted. "My mistake."

"You're not getting a . . . a *feeling* about it, are you?" No one had ever determined if cats were actually clairvoyant or if they just enjoyed being furry little shit disturbers. Claire usually leaned toward the latter, but tonight . . .

"It won't happen, Claire."

"You're sure?"

"Of course I'm sure. I'm a cat."

Claire used a finger to smooth down the soft fringe of hair behind Austin's ear. "Do you think I should wake him up and apologize?"

"You already apologized. He already accepted."

"Then why is he over there by himself and I'm over here with you?"

The cat sighed and shifted position on the pillow. "You know, maybe you should have hit the unpleasantly departed up for some relationship advice. You couldn't possibly do any worse."

"I'm not doing *anything*."

"Well, duh. I can't decide if you're more afraid that being his first time he'll expect all sorts of commitment that you're not ready for, or if you're afraid that being all of seven years older and practically decrepit you can't live up to his expectations."

"As if. I just . . ."

The silence stretched, broken only by the steady rhythm of Dean's breathing.

"You just?"

"Never mind. Let's just go to sleep."

"And the cat scores another point."

"Austin, what part of *go to sleep* didn't you understand?"

Hundreds of miles away, Diana Hansen woke up with a feeling in her gut that meant one of two things. Either she now had a hormonal defense should she waste her calculus teacher, or that dream hadn't actually been a dream.

The question now became: should she interfere?

There were rules about Keepers using knowledge of the future to influence that future. Specifically, there were rules *against* Keepers using knowledge of the future to influence that future. Which was a load as far as Diana was concerned. What was the point of having the ability and not using it? Seeing a disaster and not preventing it?

No point.

And Diana refused to live a pointless life.

But this particular future disaster involved her older sister, and that muddied the waters. Although she no longer adored Claire with the uncritical love of a child for a sibling fully ten years older and had become quite capable of seeing every uptight, rule-following, more-Keeper-than-thou flaw, she still loved her and didn't want her to get hurt. On the other hand, she still owed her for telling their mother exactly what had happened and to whom in the basement of the Elysian Fields Guest House. Once *what* and *who* were known, it was only a small step to *why*.

Oh, yeah. She owed Claire big time for that.

One more understanding, hip to the millennium, talk from the 'rents and she was going to misuse her abilities in ways previous Keepers had never dreamed. She had a notebook full of possibilities. Just in case.

But she really didn't want Claire to be hurt.

Much.

Scratching the back of one bare leg with the toenails on the opposite foot, Diana sighed, decided to worry about it in the morning, and went back to sleep.

When Claire woke up in the morning, Dean was gone.

"Relax. He went out to get breakfast."

She threw back the covers with enough force to practically strip the bed, dropped her legs over the side, and shoved her feet into waiting slippers. "I wasn't worried."

"Of course not," Austin snickered from the dresser. "That's why you were wearing your kicked puppy face."

"I don't have a kicked puppy face!"

"If you say so."

"And stop patronizing me!"

"Where would be the fun in that?" he asked the bathroom door as it closed.

She felt better after her shower. As soon as Dean came back, they'd talk about what had happened or not happened, and move forward. She'd explain that this whole having someone without fur and an attitude as a part of her life, was still new. He'd understand because he always understood. She'd reassure him she wanted their relationship to continue. He'd be pleased.

Then maybe they'd lock the cat in the bathroom. Checkout time wasn't until noon, after all.

She was packing her white silk pajamas—in a reluctant acknowledgment of the information age, Keepers were instructed to wear something that could appear on the six o'clock news in front of those unavoidable live camera shots of rubble—when the phone rang.

"Hello?" Expecting it to be Dean, she was more than a little surprised to hear her younger sister's voice.

"Whatever it is you're about to do, don't do it."

Claire sighed. "Good morning, Diana. Why aren't you in school? Stop calling me at work. And stop thinking you know how to run my life better than I do."

"I'm at school." A sudden rise in background noise suggested the phone had been held out for aural emphasis. "You're probably just packing. And I don't *think* I know how to run your life better than you do, I'm sure of it." She moved the phone not quite far enough from her mouth and yelled, "Gimme a minute!" before continuing. "Look, I had a major precognitive thing going on last night and you're about to make a huge mistake."

Claire sighed again. In the best metaphysical tradition, Diana, as the younger sibling, was the more powerful Keeper—unfortunately, Diana was well aware of that. Fortunately, she hadn't discovered that, as all the other Keepers had been only children, she was the *only* younger sibling any Keeper had. It gave her the wiggins. The very last thing Diana needed to know was that she, at an obnoxious seventeen, was the most powerful Keeper on Earth. "What kind of a huge mistake?"

"Beats me."

"Can you give me some idea of scale?"

"Nope. Only that it's huge."

"That's not very helpful."

"I do what I can. Gotta blow, calculus beckons."

"Diana . . ."

"Kisses for kitty. And you might want to help Dean with those packages."

Deleting a few expletives, Claire hung up and hurried across the room as Dean returned with breakfast, his entrance turning into an extended production bordering on farce as he attempted to deal with two bags of takeout, the room key, and a cold wind from across the parking lot that kept dragging the door from his grip.

"It'd be easier if you'd come farther into the room," Claire pointed out, taking the bags.

Flashing her a grateful smile, he gained control of the door. "I'm trying not to track slush on the carpet."

Claire glanced down. All things considered, she doubted that a little slush would hurt, but then she wasn't the person who'd borrowed cleaning supplies from the housekeeping staff at every cheap motel they'd stayed in. The strange thing was, given how paranoid many of them were about releasing an extra sliver of soap, he almost always succeeded.

By the time she returned her attention to Dean, he had his coat off and was bending over his boot laces. And that was always worth watching. Perhaps his success with various housekeeping staffs wasn't so strange after all.

"Are you okay?" she asked, wondering if he'd recently found a way to iron his jeans or if they'd been ironed so often the creases had become a structural component of the denim. "You're moving a bit tentatively."

"My glasses fogged," he explained straightening. With one hand he pushed dark hair back from blue eyes and with the other he removed his glasses for cleaning.

Austin muttered something under his breath that sounded very much like, "Superman!"

Claire ignored him and began unpacking the food, fully conscious of Dean walking past her into the bathroom. He smelled like fresh air and fabric softener. She'd never considered fabric softener erotic before.

"Sausages?" Whiskers twitched. "I wanted bacon."

"You're having geriatric cat food."

"We're out."

"Nice try. There's four cans left."

He looked disgusted. "I'm not eating that. Those cans came out of the garbage."

"Interesting you should know that since you were in the bathroom when I found them."

Drawing himself up to his full height, he shot her an indignant green-gold glare with his one remaining eye. "Are you accusing me of something?"

Claire looked at him for a moment, then turned to Dean as he returned to the main room. "Dean, did you put Austin's cat food in the garbage?"

He had the grace to look sheepish as he took both plates of food from her and put them on the table. "Not this time."

"Then, yes, I'm accusing you of something." She

popped the top of one of the cans, scooped out some brown puree onto a saucer with a plastic spoon and pushed it along the dresser toward the cat. "You're seventeen and a half years old; you *know* what the vet said."

"Turn your head and cough?"

"Austin . . ."

"All right. All right. I'll eat it." He sniffed the saucer and sighed. "I hope you realize that I plan on living long enough to see them feeding you stewed prunes at the nursing home."

Claire bent down and kissed the top of his head. "It wouldn't be the same without you."

They ate in silence for a few moments. It wasn't exactly a comfortable silence. Finally, Claire stopped eating and watched Dean clean his plate with the efficiency of a young man who hadn't eaten for over six hours. She usually liked watching him eat.

He paused, the last bite of toast halfway to his mouth. "Something wrong?"

Aren't we supposed to be talking about last night?
"Diana called."

"Here?" The last of his toast disappeared.

"Well, duh." *Why aren't we talking about last night?*

"Is she in trouble?"

"No, she just passed on a warning." *I have an explanation; don't you want to hear it?*

"About what?"

30

"She didn't know." *Why are we talking about my sister?*

"Helpful." Plate cleaned, Dean picked up his coffee and leaned back in his chair, carefully peeling back the plastic lid.

Things seemed to be going nowhere. Claire picked up her own cup and took a long swallow. She could read nothing from his expression, couldn't tell if he was just being polite—and Dean was *always* polite—or if he honestly wasn't bothered—and Dean was so absolutely certain of his place in the world that not a whole lot bothered him. This was one of the things Claire liked best about him although it did make him a little passive, secure in the knowledge that if he just waited patiently the world would fix itself. As one of the people who fixed the world, Claire found this extremely irritating. *And does everyone hold mutually opposing views about the people they're in . . .* Shying away from the "L" word, she settled for . . . *a hotel room with, or is it just me?*

She suspected she needed to watch more Oprah.

Although *women who save the world and the men who confuse them* sounded more like a visit to Jerry Springer—provided she gained a hundred and fifty pounds and lost half of her vocabulary.

Look, if he's not questioning, why should you? With that settled, she took another drink.

"So, where do we go from here?"

"Why do we have to go anywhere?" she de-

manded when the choking and coughing had sub-
sided and all of the remaining napkins had been used
to deal with the mess. "What's wrong with the way
things are?"

"I just wondered where you were being Summoned to," Dean explained, somewhat taken aback
by the sight of Claire snorting coffee out her nose.
"But if you don't want to talk about it . . ."

"About what?" She dabbed at the damp spots on
her sleeve, trying and failing miserably to sound anything but near panic. *Definitely* more Oprah.

"About the Summoning."

"Right." Of course, the Summoning. Deep calming
breath. "North."

"Back across the border, then?"

"Probably."

"Is it another metaphysical remnant causing localized fluxes in the barrier between actuality and
possibility."

That made her smile. "Another ghost kicking holes
in the fabric of the universe? I don't know." When
he smiled back, she covered an embarrassing reaction
with a brusque, "You're getting good at this."

"Two this week," he reminded her.

Claire was fairly certain that her current attraction
to the restless dead was merely leftover sensitivity
from spending so much time with Jacques, the
French-Canadian sailor who'd been haunting the Elysian Fields Guest House. But, because that previous

attraction had gone farther than . . . well, than things were going now, she wasn't going to mention it to Dean. With any luck the residual effects would wear off soon.

What she'd had with Jacques had been simple. He'd been dead. The possibilities between them had been finite. The possibilities with Dean, however, were . . .

She saw them suddenly, stretching out in front of her.

Driving together from site to site, squabbling over what radio station to listen to and/or listening in perfect accord to a group they both liked. And if anything was possible, there *had* to be a group they both liked. Somewhere.

Sharing endless hotel rooms like this one, same burnt-orange bedspreads in a vaguely floral pattern, same mid-brown stain camouflaging indoor/outdoor carpeting, same lame attempt to modernize the decor by pasting a wallpaper border just under the ceiling, same innocuous prints screwed to the wall over both beds.

Sharing one of those beds.

They'd work together. They'd laugh together. They'd clean up after Austin together—although the possibility of Dean doing the actual cleaning all by himself was significantly greater than them doing it together.

And one day, she'd forget he wasn't a Keeper, or

even one of the less powerful Cousins, and something would come through the barrier, and she'd forget to protect him from it. Or it would try to get to her through him. Or he'd try to protect her and get squashed like a bug. Okay, a six-foot-tall, muscular, blue-eyed, glasses-wearing bug from Newfoundland, but the result would be the same.

All of a sudden, the future with Dean seemed frighteningly finite.

I might as well just paint a target on him now and get it over with.

"Claire? Boss?" It took an effort, but Dean resisted the urge to wave a hand in front of her face. If she was in some sort of Keeper trance, he didn't want to disturb it.

He'd seen a number of amazing things during the three months he'd worked for her at the Elysian Fields Guest House—up to and including Hell itself—but nothing had prepared him for time spent on the road in Claire Hansen's company. He'd expected her to be a backseat driver, but that had turned out to be Austin's job. She didn't eat properly unless he placed food in front of her—he was beginning to understand both why Austin was so insistent about being fed and why Claire was so thin. And she actually preferred watching hockey with that stupid blue light the American television stations were using to help their viewers locate the puck. Trust the

Americans not to realize that knowing the position of the puck was the whole point of the game.

He liked the way she felt in his arms, and he liked the way her face lit up when she looked at him. He liked looking at her just generally, and he liked being with her. And he was becoming fairly certain that liked wasn't quite the right word. When he thought about his future, she was a part of it.

"We can't travel together anymore."

Or not. Dean looked around for help, but the sounds of vigorous excavation from the bathroom suggested Austin was in the litter box. "What did you say?" He felt as though he'd just been cross-checked into the boards and should be staring through Plexiglas at a row of screaming faces instead of across the remains of a takeout breakfast into a pair of worried brown eyes.

"We can't travel together anymore."

"But I though we were. . . ? I mean, aren't we. . . ?" he shook his head, trying to find a question he could actually articulate. "Why not, then?"

"Someday I'll run into something I won't be able to keep from hurting you."

He was about to tell her that he was willing to risk it in order to be with her when she continued, and the conversation headed off in a new, or rather an old, direction.

"It's why Keepers don't travel with Bystanders."

"I *thought* we'd moved past that Keeper/Bystander thing?"

"We *can't* move past that Keeper/Bystander thing."

The sudden quiet resonated with the sound of clay particles being flung all over the bathroom floor.

"Dean? Do you understand?"

"Sure."

She'd been working on the various meanings men gave to *sure* for some time now. This one escaped her. *Sure, I understand, but I don't agree with you* was way too obvious as was, *I've stopped listening, but since you're waiting for me to say something, sure.*

"Dean?"

When he looked up, it didn't help. For some strange reason he looked angry.

"What about us, then?"

"An *us* will end with you dead because of something I didn't do, and I won't allow that to happen."

"You won't allow?"

"That's right."

He folded his arms. "So there's no us, and we know where you stand. What about me, then?"

"You?"

"Or do I have no say in this?"

"I'm the Keeper . . ."

"And I'm not. I know."

"I'm doing this for you!"

"And because you know best, I'm supposed to just walk away?"

"I *do* know best!" Claire shoved her chair away from the table. "And it might be nice if you realized I just don't want you to get hurt." The scene should have played out as sad and tragically inevitable, but Dean continued to just not get it.

"You know what I realize?" He mirrored her motion. "I realize, and I'm amazed it took me so long, that it's always about you. You've got no idea of how to . . . to compromise!"

"A Keeper can't compromise!"

"And I suppose a Keeper can't wipe her feet either?"

"Unlike you, I have more important things to worry about than that, and," she added with icy emphasis, "I have more important things to worry about than you!"

"Fine."

"Fine."

Silence descended like a slammed door.

"Well, that doesn't get any easier as I get older." Austin jumped up onto the end of the bed nearest the bathroom and turned to face the table, swiveling his head around so he could look first at Claire and then at Dean. "So, what did I miss?"

TWO

"**B**ut I brought you into America, I should take you out."

"It's not necessary." Claire shoved her makeup bag into the backpack—she used to carry a suitcase as well until Dean had asked her why. If she could fit a desktop computer, a printer, two boxes of disks, and the obligatory stale cough drop in the backpack, why couldn't it hold everything else? She owed him for that as well as for a thousand other things her brain insisted on listing. For doing the driving. For giving her all the red Smarties. For cleaning the litter box. For patiently explaining the difference between offside and icing yet again. For being a warm and solid support at her back. For . . .

"This is upper New York State, not Cambodia," she continued, almost shouting to drown out the list. "Canadians come here daily to buy toaster ovens."

"Fine." Dean jerked the zipper shut on his hockey bag, suddenly tired of being shouted at for no apparent reason. "You can catch a ride with one of them, then." He swung the bag up onto his shoulder, but Austin stepped in front of him before he could make it to the door.

"I don't want to ride with a toaster oven," the cat declared. "I want to ride with Dean."

"Austin." Claire growled his name through clenched teeth.

He leaned around Dean's legs to glare at her. "Is the site you're Summoned to on this side of the border?"

"No, but . . ."

"Then he won't be in any danger giving us a lift. And that *is* why you don't want him around, isn't it? To keep him out of danger?"

"Yes, but . . ."

"And we're going to need a ride."

"I know, but . . ."

"So say thank you and go settle the bill while we load the truck."

"While *we* load the truck?" Dean asked a moment later, settling the cat carrier on the seat beside him and opening the top.

"Please." Austin poured out and arranged himself in the shaft of sunlight slanting through the windshield. "Like you didn't know I wanted to talk to you."

"You need to talk to Claire, not me." He started

the engine, checked that it was in neutral and the parking brake was on, took his foot off the clutch, then began polishing fingerprints off the steering wheel with the sleeve of his jacket. "I sure didn't expect to break collar so soon."

"Break what?"

"Lose the job."

"Job? You weren't doing a job, you were just living your life. If it was a *job*," the cat snorted disdainfully, "she'd have been paying you."

"Then I didn't expect this part of my life to be over so soon."

"It doesn't have to be."

"Yeah, it does."

"You're just going to let her tell you what to do?"

"No. But I'm not staying if she thinks she has the right to make decisions about my life as though I wasn't a part of it."

"Of your life?"

"Or the decision."

"So you're leaving not because she told you to but because she thinks she has the right to tell you to?"

"Yeah."

Austin sighed. "Would it make a difference if I told you she's honestly afraid of you having your intestines sucked out your nose because she was thinking about your shoulders and misjudged an accident site?"

"Well, I don't want my intestines sucked out my

nose either," Dean allowed. Then he paused and blushed slightly, buffing an already spotless bit of dashboard. "She thinks about my shoulders?"

"Shoulders, thighs . . . as near as I can tell, she spends far too much time thinking about most of your body parts—sequentially and simultaneously—when she should be thinking about other things."

"Like accident sites?"

"Like me."

"Oh." And then because the cat's tone demanded an apology, he added, "Sorry."

"*And* accident sites," Austin allowed graciously, having been given his due. "Look, Claire tends to see things in terms of what she has to do to keep the world from falling apart. Close an accident site here, prevent the movie remake of 'Gilligan's Island' there, keep you from being hurt, feed the cat—everything's an absolute. She doesn't compromise well, it's an occupational hazard. Stay and teach her to see your side of things."

"*Only* if she asks me to." The steering wheel creaked a protest as Dean closed his hands around it and tightened his grip. "And since I know for a fact that Hell hasn't frozen over, I'm not after holding my breath."

Austin sighed and turned so he could see Claire picking her way across the slush covered parking lot from the office. "She's getting her own way, you'd think she'd be happier about it, wouldn't you? She looks miserable. Doesn't she? You don't want her to be miserable? Do you?''

"She started this," Dean muttered, eyes locked on the oil gauge. "If she wants me to stay, she has to convince me."

"All right. Fine." He put a paw on Dean's thigh and stared beseechingly up into his face. "What about me? I'm old. It wasn't that long ago that I lost an eye."

"I thought it had mostly healed?"

"That's not the point. It's November, it's cold. I don't want to go back to using any old thing that happens by. I *like* being driven about in a heated truck! Okay, I would've liked a heated Lincoln Town Car with leather upholstery more, but the point is, what about me?"

"I'm sorry, Austin."

"Not as sorry as she's going to be," Austin muttered as the Keeper opened the passenger door.

"The booth on the right has a longer line."

"A *longer* line?" Dean had been avoiding conversation by maintaining the speed of the pickup at exactly fifty-five miles per hour regardless of the gestures other drivers flashed at him as they passed. He glanced down at the cat and tried not to notice the various bits of Claire that surrounded him. "Why do you want me to use the longer line, then?"

"It'll take more time. And the more time we're

all together, the greater the odds are that you two will make up and I won't be tossed out into the cold with nothing but a cat carrier between me and November."

"There's nothing to make up," Claire told him impatiently. "We didn't have a fight."

"We didn't?"

"No." She threw the word across the cat to Dean. "I, as a Keeper, made a decision."

"About *my* future without talking to me."

"Sounds like a fight," Austin observed.

Claire wriggled back in the seat and crossed her arms. "This doesn't concern you."

"Oh, no? I'm the one who'll be riding in the overhead luggage rack . . ."

"You've never ridden in the overhead luggage rack!"

". . . or the baggage compartment."

"*Or* the baggage compartment!" she added, voice rising.

He ignored her. "Once again, I'll be at the mercy of strangers. Forced to live from paw to mouth, dark corners as my litter box, cardboard boxes as my bed."

"You like to sleep in cardboard boxes."

"That's not the point."

"You have no point. And stop whining; you're beginning to sound like a dog."

"A dog!" He twisted around to fry her with a pale green glare from his remaining eye. "I have *never* been so insulted in my life. You're just lucky I can't operate a can opener." Moving slowly and deliberately, he stepped down off her lap, onto the center of the bench seat, and turned his back on her.

The smile his companions shared over his head was completely involuntary.

Suddenly aware of her reflection grinning out from Dean's glasses, Claire dropped her gaze so quickly it bounced.

Teeth clenched with enough applied pressure to make his lone filling creak, Dean steered the truck carefully into the shorter line. The sooner this was over, the better.

Only two of the five Canada Customs booths were open. Only two of the five booths were *ever* open. On a busy day, when the line of cars waiting to cross the border stretched almost all the way back to Watertown, this guaranteed short tempers and a more spontaneous response to official questioning by Canadian Customs officials. Occasionally, on really hot summer days, responses were spontaneous enough to get the RCMP involved.

The constant low levels of sharp-edged irritation would have poked multiple holes through the fabric of the universe had government officiousness not canceled it out by denying that anything was possible outside their own very narrow parameters. As a result, most border crossings between the U.S. and Canada were so metaphysically stable, unnatural phenomenon had to cross them just like everyone else—although it wasn't always easy for them to find photo ID.

Later, they'd swap stories about how custom officials had no sense of humor, about how someone— or possibly something—they knew had been strip-searched for no good reason, and how they'd triumphantly smuggled in half a dozen toaster ovens, duty-free.

As Dean pulled up beside the booth's open window and turned to smile politely at the young guard, Claire reached into the possibilities. When the guard looked into the truck, her gaze slid over Austin like he'd been buttered, over Claire almost as quickly, and locked itself on Dean's face.

"Nationality?"

"Canadian."

"Canadian," Claire repeated although she suspected she needn't have bothered as the guard's rapt attention never left Dean.

"How long were you in the States?"

"Four days."

"What is the total value of the purchases you're bringing into Canada?"

"Six dollars and eighty-seven cents. I bought a couple of maps and a liter of oil for the truck," he added apologetically.

"You're from back East." When he nodded, she continued, startling Claire who'd never seen anyone who worked for Canada Customs look so happy. "I'm from Cornerbrook. When's the last time you were back?"

"I'm heading back now."

Their discussion slid into shared memories of places and people. Newfoundlanders, chance met a thousand miles from home, were never strangers. Occasionally, they were mortal enemies, but never strangers. After it had been determined that Dean had played junior hockey against a buddy the guard's second cousin had gone to school with, she waved them on.

"You never told *me* you were going back to Newfoundland," Claire pointed out as they pulled away from the border.

"You never asked."

"Oh, that's mature," she muttered. Now they were both ignoring her, Dean and the cat. It was the sort of thing she expected from Austin, but Dean usually had better manners. *Fine. Be that way. I know I'm right.* A sideways glance at his profile showed a muscle moving along the line of his jaw. A sudden urge to reach out and touch him surprised her into lowering her gaze.

That didn't help.

Two spots of heat burning high on each cheek, she turned to stare out at the pink granite rising in mighty slabs up into the sky.

Neither did that.

Think of something else, Claire. Anything else. Three times nine is twenty-seven. Fried liver. Brussels sprouts. Homer Simpson . . .

The insistent under-tug of the Summoning suddenly rose to a crescendo. Claire's hand jerked up and pointed toward a parking lot entrance for the Thousand Islands Sky Deck and Fantasy Land. "Pull in there."

Responding to her tone, Dean managed to make the turn, back end of the truck fishtailing slightly in the light dusting of wet snow. "It's closed," he said, coming to a stop by the entrance to the gift shop that anchored the Sky Deck.

"Not to me." This was it. The end of the line. Claire felt strangely unwilling to get out of the truck. And not only because it was beginning to snow again. *You're doing this for him*, she reminded herself. *He's only a Bystander, and you have no business putting him in danger.*

When he moved to turn off the engine, she steeled herself and stopped him, restraining herself from keeping a lingering grip around his wrist. "There's no point, you won't be here long enough." She undid her seat belt, pulled her toque over her ears, and grabbed the cat carrier from its place behind the seat. "Come on, Austin."

His back remained toward her, rigid and unyielding. "Austin!"

47

He ignored her so completely she had a moment's doubt about her own existence.

"What's the matter with . . ." And then she remembered. "Oh, for . . . Austin, I'm sorry I said you were beginning to sound like a dog. It was rude."

One ear swiveled toward her.

"You have never sounded like anything but a cat. Cats are clearly superior to dogs, and I don't know what I was thinking. Please accept my abject apologies and forgive me."

He snorted without turning. "You call that groveling?"

"Yes, and I'm sorry if it falls short of your high standards. Unless you're planning to walk, I also call it the last thing I'm going to say before picking you up and stuffing you into the carrier."

Her hands were actually touching his fur before he realized she was serious. "Oh, sure," he muttered, tail scribing short, jerky arcs as he climbed into the case, "give a species opposable thumbs, and they evolve into bullies."

Dean watched without speaking as she opened the door, set the cat carrier carefully down on a dry bit of pavement up near the building, and finally lifted her backpack out from under the tarp. She paused as if she was trying to think of something to say. She was wearing some kind of lip stuff that made her mouth look full and soft and . . . He leaned over and rolled down the window. "Do you need any help, then?"

He hadn't intended to say it, but he just couldn't stop himself; his grandfather's training was stronger than justified anger, emotional betrayal, and the uncomfortable way the seat belt was cutting into his . . . lap.

An emphatic "Yes!" came out of the cat carrier, but Claire ignored it. "No, thank you." She swallowed around the kind of lump in her throat that Keepers were not supposed to get. "You'd better get going if you're driving all the way to Newfoundland."

"It's an island, Claire. I won't be driving all the way."

"You knew what I meant." Her gloves suddenly took all her attention. "This is for your own good, Dean."

"If you say so."

It was as close to a snide comment as she'd ever heard him make.

For a moment Claire thought he wasn't going to go, but the moment passed.

"Good-bye, Claire." He wanted to say something wry and debonair so she'd know what she was losing, but the only thing that came to mind was a line from an old black-and-white movie, and he suspected that "You'll never take me alive, copper!" didn't exactly fit the situation. This was clearly the day his aunt had been referring to when she'd said,

"Some day, you guys are going to wish you'd watched a couple of movies with more talking than hitting." He settled for raising his hand in the classic *whatever* wave.

He left the window rolled down until he reached the highway. Just in case she called him back.

Claire stood and watched Dean back up and drive away, realizing she should have wiped his memory with something more possible—although at the moment, she couldn't think of anything more possible than the two of them spending their lives together.

I did it for his own good.

It was colder than it should be, and the chill had nothing to do with standing in an empty parking lot beside a closed second-rate summer attraction while an early November wind stuffed icy fingers under her collar and threatened snow. She stared at the single set of tire tracks until she couldn't feel her feet.

In the summer, Fantasy Land consisted of mazes and slides built into child-sized castles scattered along a path that twisted through the woods and paused every now and then at a fairy-tale tableau constructed of poured concrete and paint. In the summer, the fact it was a convenient place for the children to run off some excess energy before they were stuffed back in the car to fidget and complain for another hundred kilometers, lent the place a certain charm. In the winter, when nothing hid the damage caused by the same children who could disassemble an eight-hundred-dollar DVD player armed with nothing more than a sucker stick and a cheese sandwich, it was just depressing.

The Summons rose from the center of the Sleeping Beauty display.

Five concrete dwarfs, their paint peeling, stood around the bier that held the sleeping princess—or at least Claire assumed that's what the bier *had* held. The princess and two of the dwarfs had been thoroughly gone over with a piece of pipe. Bits of broken concrete lay scattered around the clearing, and Sleeping Beauty's head had been propped into a decidedly compromising position with one of the dwarfs.

"I'm guessing these guys are all named Grumpy," Claire muttered, as she approached the bier. "None of them are smiling."

Austin sat down in the shelter of a giant concrete mushroom and wrapped his tail around his toes. And ignored her.

Which was pretty much the response Claire expected. That dog comparison would likely haunt her for a while.

The hole itself was centered on the bier—no surprise since the vandalism had probably opened it. It was larger than mere vandalism could account for, though, and it had been seeping for some time. Unfortunately, the seepage wasn't dissipating.

Which meant that something in the immediate area was absorbing it.

A quick search showed no wildlife, not even so much as a single pigeon although evidence of pigeons had been liberally splattered on all five dwarfs.

"I hope this isn't going to be another one of those possessed squirrel sites. They're always nuts." She glanced over at the cat and, when he didn't rise to the provocation, sighed. *Great, my cat's not even responding to bad jokes, Dean's gone . . .* Her attention elsewhere, she tripped over a piece of broken princess, barely catching herself on the shoulder of a stone dwarf. . . . *and now I've twisted my ankle. How could this day possibly get any worse?*

A small stone hand closed painfully around her wrist.

I had to ask.

Fortunately, the hands were more or less in proportion to the body, so although the grip pinched, it wasn't difficult to break. Jerking free, Claire stepped away from the dwarf and felt something poke her in the back of the upper thigh.

It turned out to be a nose.

Her anatomical relief was short lived as this second dwarf made a grab for her knee, muttering, "Write on me, will you!"

He was pretty fast for concrete.

They all were.

". . . rotten kids . . ."

". . . ice cream on my hat . . ."

". . . you want Happy, I'll tell you what'll make me happy, you little . . ."

". . . gonna pay for those malt balls . . ."

". . . I'll hi your ho right up your . . ."

"Hey!" Claire danced away from the last dwarf and glared down at him. "Watch it, buster, you're supposed to be a children's display."

Stone eyes narrowed. "Grind your bones to make my bread."

"Oh, great . . ." She leaped off the concrete pad and onto scuffed grass. ". . . now they're free-associating."

The dwarfs came to the edge of the concrete but no farther.

Claire would have been a lot happier about that had they not been between her and the accident site. A quick jog around the perimeter proved she couldn't outrun them and, as long as the site was open, they wouldn't run down.

Secure in the knowledge that the Keeper couldn't get past them, four of the dwarfs started a soccer game with Sleeping Beauty's head while the fifth kept watch.

Two feints, a dodge, and an argument over whether it was entirely ethical to use chunks of dwarfs six and seven for goalposts, Claire realized she wasn't going to get by without a plan. Or a distraction.

"Austin?"

"No."

"I just wanted . . ."

"Tough. I'm not doing it."

"Fine. Then what'll distract five of the seven dwarfs?"

"A trademarked theme song?"

"I don't think so."

"You could sing the short version."

"No."

"You don't think they'd be up to it?"

She sighed down at the cat. "Are you done?"

"I will be shortly."

"Austin . . ."

"Okay. I'm done." He took a quick lick at a flawless shoulder. "How about five concrete lady dwarfs?"

"Why not? I'll just put an ad in the personals." Claire shoved her hands into her pockets and glanced around at the broken bottles, the scattered garbage, the senseless vandalism. She didn't even want to think about what the inside of Peter Peter Pumpkin Eater's wife's house looked like—give some people a dark corner, and they'd do one of two things in it.

Well, maybe three things.

Or four.

"Ow!" Kicked a little too hard, Sleeping Beauty's head rolled off the concrete and clipped Claire's ankle. "Yuck it up," she snarled, scooping up the head and taking aim at the clump of snickering dwarfs. "It's about to be game over!" As she released her makeshift bowling ball, she had visions of a five/two split, an easy spare, and a quick end to the stalemate.

"You missed," Austin pointed out, his tone mildly helpful.

"I know!" She had to shout to be heard above the laughter. Two of the dwarfs were propping each other up as they howled, one had fallen to the ground and was kicking little concrete heels in the air, and the last two were staggering around in increasingly smaller circles as they mocked her athletic ability.

It wasn't what she'd intended, but it had the same effect.

A quick dash, a fast sidestep over a pile of stained feathers that suggested at least one of the pigeons had been slow to get away, and a graceless but adequate leap put her up on the bier.

Keepers learned early on that the repair didn't have to be pretty as long as it did the job. Claire had personally learned it while closing a site at a book launch for a writer who very nearly acquired a life as interesting as his fiction—although it wouldn't have gone on as long. In the end, she'd been forced to evoke the paranormal properties of a crab cake, two stuffed mushroom caps, and a miniature quiche. The caterer had been furious.

Though not as furious as the dwarfs.

Who were too short to climb up on the bier themselves. The stream of profanity this evoked made up in volume what they lacked in size. Claire assumed they'd learned the words from the vandals and not the children—but she wouldn't have bet on it. Fortunately, concrete dwarfs were not fast thinkers. She had the parameters of the site almost determined when one of them yelled, "Pile up the broken bits. Build a ramp!"

As the first of the little men rose into view, Claire pulled a stub of sidewalk chalk from her pocket and scrawled the site definition across Sleeping Beauty's one remaining smooth surface. Reaching into the possibilities, she closed the hole, turned, and came hip to face with the advancing dwarf.

"Before the energy fades," he growled, "we'll rip you limb from limb."

Had they not been fighting each other to get up the ramp, they might have. As it was, Claire jumped off the other side of the bier and sprinted to the safety of the grass unopposed. The first dwarf to leap off after her, stumbled and smashed.

They were visibly slowing.

"Gentlemen!"

Four heads ground around to face her.

"You've got less than thirty seconds left. If I were you, I'd arrange myself so that I was making a statement when I solidified."

*   *   *

"Who'd have thought those concrete breeches would even come down?" Austin murmured as Claire carried him back toward the parking lot.

She half expected Dean to be there waiting for them.

He wasn't.

Of course he isn't, you moron. You sent him away.

She could barely feel the beginning of the new Summons over the incredible sense of loss. "I feel like I'm missing an arm or a leg," she sighed as she set Austin down beside the cat carrier and turned up the collar of her coat.

He snorted. "How would you know?"

"What?"

"The only thing you're missing is a sense of perspective. Some of us are missing actual body parts."

"I'm sorry, Austin. I keep forgetting about your eye."

"My eye?" His remaining eye narrowed. "Oh, yeah, that too. Now, if you'll excuse me, I'm going to go behind this building where I believe I saw a litter box shaped like a giant plastic turtle."

"That's a sandbox."

"Whatever. While I'm gone, why don't you answer the phone?"

"What phone?"

The pay phone on the other side of the parking lot began to ring.

* * *

Weight on one hip, Diana cradled the receiver between shoulder and ear and rummaged in her backpack for a pen. The odds were extremely good that Claire had paid no attention to her warning, but—having given it—she was curious about the outcome.

"Hello?"

"So, did you do it?"

On the other end of the phone, she heard Claire sigh. "Did I do what?"

"Make the huge mistake." Moistening the tip of one finger, she erased the phone number at the end of the ubiquitous *for a good time call* and replaced it with the number of the original graffiti artist. Erasing it entirely would only leave a clear space for some moron to refill and it was balance, after all, that Keepers were attempting to maintain.

"I don't know what you're talking about, Diana. I've just closed a small site and I'm about to move on to the next one."

"I'm talking about my precog. This morning's phone call. My timely warning." Brow furrowed, she tapped the pen against her lip, then rubbed out the punctuation and added *forest fires* in the same handwriting as *Rachel puts out* changing it from nasty to inane and thus maintaining the high school status quo. If there was a place more inane, Diana didn't want to know about it. "I bet you didn't even take precautions."

"*That* is none of your business."

Diana shook her head. No one did self-righteous indignation at the mere possibility of a double-entendre as well as Claire. And no one gave away so much doing it. "You ditched Dean, didn't you?"

"I did not ditch him. We're just not traveling together any longer."

"Dork."

"A Keeper has no business involving a Bystander in dangerous work."

"Think highly of yourself, don't you? You didn't involve him, he got involved all on his little lonesome. And, as I recall, his lonesome ain't so little."

"Diana!"

"Claire!" Suddenly depressed, she hung up. In her not even remotely humble opinion, Dean had been the best thing that had ever happened to her older sister. Just by existing, he'd managed to shake up that whole lone Keeper only-I-can-save-the-world crap that Claire believed. Apparently, he hadn't shaken it hard enough.

Sighing, she filled in the last blank space on the wall by the phone with a quick *John loves Terri* in a somewhat lopsided heart. It wasn't her best work, but at least it would keep something harmful out of the spot.

"A word, Ms. Hansen."

Pushing a strand of dark hair out of her eyes, Diana turned and forced a fake smile. "Yes, Ms. Neal?"

The vice-principal's answering smile had a certain sharklike quality about it. "If you think the school needs adornment, why not put your talents to use on the decorating committee for the Christmas dance."

"I'd love to, Ms. Neal, but I just don't have the . . . that wasn't a suggestion, was it?"

"Actually, it was an alternative to a month's worth of detention."

After the incident with the football team, her parents had forbidden her to open anyone's mind to new possibilities—although to give them credit, they'd admitted that two of the linebackers and a defensive end had been significantly improved.

"The committee has their first meeting tomorrow at lunch, on the stage. Be there."

"Yes, Ms. Neal."

"Now, if you're finished for the day, go home."

"Yes, Ms. Neal."

She could feel the vice-principal's gimlet gaze on her all the way to the door. *This bites. Save the world evenings and weekends and the rest of the time I'm at the beck and call of every petty dictator who works for the school board. I'm a Keeper. Why am I still here?*

As the door closed behind her, two confused teenagers walked in slow motion toward the phone from opposite ends of the hall, music from a modern love song growing louder and sappier the closer they got. When their hands touched, the music reached a crescendo, then faded as Ms. Neal confiscated the boom-box from a group of students on the stairs.

"John?"

"Terri?"

On the wall, the heart glowed.

"Well, gee, this is just so much better than sitting in a warm and comfy truck with someone who cares about you." Shooting the darkening sky a disgusted look, Austin picked his way between wet snowflakes to where Claire was sitting on a parking lot divider and jumped up on her lap. "I personally think it's pathetic that you'd rather face a quintet of evil gnomes than a normal human relationship."

"I'm not a normal human."

"Who is?"

"Diana thinks I've made a huge mistake with Dean."

"And this is the same Diana who very nearly released the hosts of Hell?"

Claire smiled and buried her face in the back of his neck. "You're right. She's been wrong before."

"First of all, of course I'm right. Secondly, she's not wrong this time. And thirdly, stop sighing like that, you're getting me damp."

"I know my responsibility as a Keeper."

"Responsibility?"

"Yes."

"That and three seventy-five will get you a mocha latte. Speaking of which, when do we eat?"

"Soon." Claire nodded at the late model sedan pulling into the parking lot. "There's our ride."

"Oh, great. She brakes for unicorns. And hobbits." Leaping down, he headed for the cat carrier, muttering, "I only hope she brakes for stop signs." Settling into the sheepskin pad, he glared up at Claire. "You know she's going to spend the whole trip telling us cute stories about her three cats."

"I know." Closing the carrier, Claire turned to face the conscripted Bystander's cheery wave and wondered if maybe Hell hadn't gotten free after all.

THREE

It was possible to drive from Kingston, Ontario, to Halifax, Nova Scotia, in seventeen hours. Dean knew someone who'd done it—admittedly in the opposite direction, but the principle was the same. It did, however, require a number of factors working in the driver's favor.

First of all, the varying police forces in charge of the highways stretching through Ontario, Quebec, Vermont, New Brunswick, and Nova Scotia needed to be off the road. Second, nothing could go wrong with the vehicle. The glove compartment inexplicably deciding not to close was one thing. Dropping the entire exhaust system onto the asphalt just outside of Fredericton was something else again. But then, it usually was. Thirdly, the driver had to be so pissed off at an ex that his anger would keep him awake and alert to the dangers of the Canadian highway system—which was pretty much like the American system only with more moose—for the entire seventeen hours.

Fortunately, government cutbacks on both sides of the border had accomplished what a Tim Hortons on every corner hadn't, making the odds of being stopped by a moose were significantly higher than being stopped by the police. And Dean's truck might be pushing the ten-year mark, but both muffler and glove compartment were in top condition although the latter now held a hairbrush, two lipsticks, seventeen packets of artificial sweetener, a fast food child's toy, a pink plastic pouch he thought held a pressure bandage until he realized to his intense embarrassment that pressure bandages didn't have wings, half a bottle of water, and an open can of geriatric cat food.

He just wasn't angry enough at Claire to drive for seventeen hours straight, although it had been a narrow miss when he'd found the cat food. Until they'd parted ways, he'd assumed the smell had been coming from Austin who was, after all, a very old cat.

Kingston to Halifax could be done in seventeen hours, but the trip took Dean three weeks. Just across the border into Vermont, he stopped to help a stranded motorist and ended up with a job in his diner while the regular cook worked out a small problem involving a cow, two liters of ice cream, and a tourist from New Hampshire. Dean didn't ask for details; he figured it was an American thing. He thought about Claire every time he saw a young, dark-haired woman, or a cat, or anything weird on the news. He thought about her when he picked up after the waitress, when he told customers to wipe their feet, and when he went to bed alone at night.

He thought about her when the waitress suggested he didn't have to go to bed alone at night. He thought about her as he thanked the waitress politely for the suggestion but declined. He wasn't actually thinking about Claire when the waitress asked if he was gay.

"No, ma'am. I'm Canadian."

That seemed to explain things to everyone's satisfaction.

He thought about her pretty much all the rest of the time, though, and when the regular cook returned, he actually paused for a moment before getting back on the highway, wondering if maybe he shouldn't head back into Ontario and try to find her. Didn't leaving make him as incapable of compromising as he accused her of being?

The shriek of brakes from the semi coming up behind him not only ended the moment but very nearly solved the problem. Heart pounding, he put the truck in gear and continued east.

He'd seen Claire deal with Hell. And Austin. If she wanted to, she could find him.

It was mid-December by the time he arrived at his cousin's apartment in Halifax. He'd intended to stay only until he could book passage on the ferry home, but for one reason or another, many of them having to do with beer, it didn't happen.

*   *   *

Austin stretched out his paw and neatly hooked a French fry from Claire's fingers. "You're thinking about Dean, aren't you?"

"No." Except that the truck that had very nearly run her over as she closed a site at Highway Two and King Street in Napanee had been just like Dean's. Except it hadn't been a Ford. And it was red, not white. And Dean's truck just had a standard cab. And was clean. But other than that . . .

The bed sagged under Claire's weight, then kept sagging as the mattress came to an understanding with gravity. It wasn't the most uncomfortable motel bed she'd ever slept in, but it was close. It reminded her of the bed in the motel just outside of Rochester. The bed that she and Dean had so briefly and so platonically shared. If she put out her hand, she could almost feel the heat of . . .

. . . a seventeen-and-a-half-year-old cat.

"You're thinking about Dean, aren't you?"

"No."

* * *

"You okay?"

"I'm fine." Having reassured the dark-haired, blue-eyed, glasses-wearing young waiter, Claire put her fingers back in her mouth.

"Bar's been almost shut down twice, you know, but I never seen a rat in here before."

He still hadn't seen a rat, but Claire had no intention of telling him that.

"Good thing you had your cat with you, eh?" Dark brows drew in. He scratched at stubble. "Actually, I don't think you're supposed to bring your cat in here."

The possibilities were adjusted slightly. "It's okay."

"Cool. You want another drink?"

"Why not." Since she'd already been distracted enough to nearly lose a finger, Claire figured she was entitled to watch as he walked away from her booth in the darkest corner of the nearly empty bar.

Austin horked a dark bit of something up onto the cracked Naugahyde seat. "You're thinking about Dean, aren't you?"

Fingers in her mouth, Claire ignored him.

He snorted. "Good thing you had your cat with you, eh?"

Just outside of Renfrew, Claire stood on a deserted stretched of highway and stared at the graffiti spray painted twenty feet up a limestone cliff. The hole, situated between the "u" and the "c" had turned the most popular of Anglo-Saxon profanities into a metaphysical instruction.

Before Austin could ask, she shoved frozen fingers deeper into her coat pockets and sighed. "Yes. I am. Now, drop it."

"I was only going to mention that Dean would know exactly what cleaning supplies you're going to need to get that paint off the rock."

"Sure you were."

On the opposite shoulder of the road, someone slapped a handprint into the condensation covering the windows of their parked Buick.

* * *

Against all expectations, Diana enjoyed the decorating committee meetings.

"So it's settled; for this year's Christmas dance we use a snowflake motif." Stephanie's smile could cut paper. "And, Lena, I don't want to hear another word about angels."

"But angels . . ."

"Have been done to death by all and/or sundry. Get over it."

Watching Stephanie cut through the democratic process with all the precision of a chainsaw sculptor was significantly more amusing than watching the cafeteria's hot lunch gel into something approaching a life-form.

"Diana . . ."

Jerked out of her reverie, Diana fought the urge to come to attention. Tall and blonde, Stephanie wouldn't have looked out of place in jackboots, provided she could find a purse to match, and someday she'd run a Fortune 500 company with the same ruthless élan she used to run Medway High. Unfortunately for the world at large, Keepers weren't permitted to make preemptive strikes.

". . . since we're trying to make this place look less like a gymnasium, I want you to make a snowflake pattern out of white-and-gold streamers about five feet down from those incredibly ugly ceiling tiles."

Diana glanced up at the ceiling, then over at Stephanie. The gym was probably thirty feet high, and it would take scaffolding to reach anything higher than the tops of the basketball backboards. The odds of the custodians building that scaffolding were slightly lower than the odds of any member of the senior basketball team being picked up by the pros. At zero and thirteen, the senior basketball team couldn't even get picked up by the cheerleaders. "You want me to what?"

"Try to pay attention. I want you to hide the ceiling behind a crepe-paper snowflake." Stephanie met Diana's incredulous gaze with a level blue stare, assuming compliance.

Although not the uninvolved stick in the mud Claire had been during high school, Diana had tried to give the whole Keeper thing the requisite low profile. Given how generally pointless she found the whole public school system, it hadn't always been easy, but she'd made it to her final year without anyone pointing and screaming "Witch!" Well, no one anyone who mattered listened to, anyway.

So what had Stephanie seen?

And bottom line, did it matter?

"A crepe-paper snowflake?"

"Yes."

"Okay."

It *was* an ugly ceiling.

Meeting over, Lena fell into step beside her as they left the gym. "*You're* the *senior* student on the committee, *not* Stephanie, so if *you* wanted *angels* . . ." Her voice trailed off suggestively, having applied the maximum emphasis allowed.

"It was the committee or a month of detention," Diana reminded her. "But I don't think angels are a good idea."

Lena looked crushed. "Why *not*?"

"Flaming swords, smiting the ungodly . . ."

"Angels aren't *like* that!"

"Maybe not the ones you run into, but the problem is, you can never be sure."

"Of *what*?"

"Of what kind of angel you're running into."

Lena thought about that for a moment, then, as Diana headed into the first of her afternoon classes, muttered, "My mother's right. You're *weird*."

*   *   *

With over three million people, Toronto had two working Keepers, one very elderly Keeper plugging an unclosable site out in Scarborough, and half a dozen Cousins monitoring the constant metaphysical flux—one of whom had made a small fortune following the stock market in his spare time. He said he found the relative calm relaxing.

The Summons took Claire to the College Park subway station on the University line where ninety-six hours previously a government worker from one of the nearby offices had been pushed from the platform. At the time, the old Red Rocket had been three hundred meters away grinding its slow way north. The intended victim had plenty of time to dust himself off, climb back onto the platform, and threaten the man who'd pushed him with an audit—but that was moot. Inept evil was still evil and a hole had opened at the edge of the platform.

For the next three days, it spewed bits of darkness out onto commuters in the morning and gathered them up again in the evening larger and darker. It was probably a coincidence that members of the Ontario government, arriving daily at the legislature building only a block away, proposed a bill to close half the province's hospitals and cut education spending by 44% during those three days since it was highly unlikely that any member of the ruling Conservative party took the subway to work.

By the time Claire got to the site, the hole was huge and thousands of government employees had arrived at their jobs in a bad mood and left in a worse one—which was pretty much business as usual only more so.

Just after midnight, the platform was essentially deserted. A group of teenagers, isolated in headphones and sunglasses, loitered at one end and an elderly woman wrapped in at least four layers of clothing and surrounded by a circle of grimy shopping bags glared at her from the other.

With a sigh, Claire shifted the cat carrier to her other hand and walked reluctantly forward, wondering why she couldn't see through the glamour. When she got close enough, and the scent of unwashed clothing and treasured garbage overwhelmed the winter-chilled metal, machine scent of the subway, she realized that she couldn't see through the glamour because there wasn't one.

"Hey, tuna!" A black nose pressed up against the screen at the front of the carrier, then suddenly recoiled with a sneeze. "Six days old, wrapped in a gym sock previously worn by someone with a bad case of toe rot, and I'd rather not be any closer." He sneezed again. "Can we go now?"

"No. And keep your voice down. We're in a public place."

"I'm not the one talking to luggage."

At the outer edge of the shopping bags, her eyes were watering. Nothing could smell so bad on its own, it had to have been carefully crafted. Claire was thankful she'd never had to study under this particular Keeper. *This afternoon we'll be combining the scents of old cheese and the stale vomit/urine combination found in the backs of certain taxis . . .* Like life wasn't already dangerous enough?

"You Claire?"

"Yes." At least the other Keeper wasn't insisting on using the traditional and ridiculous "Aunt Claire."

"Are you Nalo?"

"I am. So, where is he?"

Claire blinked at the other Keeper. "Pardon?"

"Your young man. I heard at Apothecary's that one of us made an actual connection with a Bystander." She craned her neck, showing a remarkable amount of dirty collar. "Did he have trouble finding parking?"

There was absolutely no point in suggesting it was none of her business.

"We're not traveling together anymore."

"You're not? Why not? I heard he was a looker and pure of heart, too." One eye closed in an unmistakable wink. "If you know what I mean."

Claire made a mental note to smack Diana hard the next time she saw her. "We're no longer together because I decided that he wasn't safe traveling with me."

"First of all; you decided? And second, he'd already been to Hell, girl. What did you think could happen that was worse?"

"How about asphyxiation?"

Nalo pointed a long, dark finger in a filthy fingerless glove at the cat carrier. "If you can think of a better way to keep Bystanders far away from this hole, then I'd like to hear it. Until then, I don't take attitude from no cat."

It was probably fortunate that the approaching subway drowned out Austin's response.

The teenagers got on, and out of the door closest to the hole stepped a large young man in a leather jacket, a tattoo of a swastika impaled by a dagger nearly covering his shaved head. Pierced lip curled, he swaggered toward the two women. He sucked in a deep breath, readying himself to intimidate, then looked appalled, and choked.

"You know what I think when I see a tattoo like that?" Nalo murmured as the sound of violent coughing echoed off the tiles. "I think, he's gonna look like a fool when he's eighty and in a nursing home."

"Maybe he'll regrow his hair."

"Won't help, he's got male pattern baldness written all over him."

Claire couldn't see it, but she could see the words

"hate" and "kill" written into the backs of his hands. Reaching into the possibilities, she made a slight cosmetic change. Then she reached a little farther.

His eyes widened and, still coughing, the hand that said "male pattern" gripping the crotch of his jeans and the one that said "baldness" outstretched to clear the way, he ran for the stairs.

"Will he be back?"

"Depends on how long it takes him to find a toilet."

"He could just pee in a corner."

"That'll take care of half the problem."

Nalo grinned. "Very clever. You're subtler than your sister."

"Public television pledge breaks are subtler than my sister."

"True enough. Well, that was the last regular train past this station, so let's get to work before the maintenance trains hit the rails." Nalo shrugged out of her coat, peeled off the gloves, and was suddenly a middle-aged black woman in a TTC maintenance uniform. A lot of her previous bulk had come from the tool belt around her waist.

"You do a lot of work in the subways?" Claire asked, setting Austin's carrier down and opening the top for him.

"Hundreds of thousands of people ride them every day, what do you think? Most of the holes close on their own, but enough of them needed help that it finally got easier just to buy the wardrobe—we've got a Cousin in the actual maintenance crew who picked it up for me."

"Was he monitoring the site?"

"This one and a couple of others." The older Keeper glanced at her watch. "Security'll be here shortly. I've dealt before, so I'll deal again; why don't you and your younger legs jump down on the track and map the lower parameters."

Yes, why don't I? Although she tried, Claire couldn't actually think of a good reason, so she stalled. "What about the camera? I should adjust it to show a different possibility."

"Already done."

So much for stalling. Pulling her kit from her backpack, she walked over to the edge of the platform and sat, legs dangling. "You coming, Austin?"

"Not likely."

"There's mice down there."

"I should care?" But he trotted over for a closer look. "Not *just* mice."

A group of tiny warriors no more than two inches high, their dark skins making them almost impossible to see, were silently surrounding an unsuspecting rodent. The kill was quick, the prey lifted in half a dozen miniature arms and, to Claire's surprise, thrown against the third rail. There was a sudden flash, a wisp of smoke, and tiny voices chanting, "Bar. Be. Que! Bar. Be. Que!"

"What's the delay?" Nalo asked, walking over. "Oh, Abatwa. I don't know when they came over from South Africa, but they've adapted amazingly well to the subway system. You know what to do if you're challenged?"

As far as Claire could tell, they all seemed to be males. "Flattery?"

"That's right. Watch where you're stepping, it makes them cranky."

Given the nature of some of the debris, Claire figured stepping on one of the Abatwa would be the least of her problems. She didn't even want to consider how some of it had gotten down there. About to push off, she caught a memory and froze. "You said something about maintenance trains?"

"You've got lots of time."

"But we don't know how long this will take."

"Girl, you worry too much." Nalo's pat was almost a push.

Claire took the hint and dropped down onto the greasy ties. As she turned toward the job, heavy footfalls heralded the approach of Transit Security. They seemed perfectly willing to believe that both Keepers were maintenance workers and that Austin's carrier was a toolbox, making only a cursory check and leaving quickly. Claire suspected that the collection of filthy shopping bags discouraged suspicion. And conversation. And breathing.

Her suspicions were confirmed when one of the

guards promised to tell the cleaning crew about the mess. "They can get them ready for the garbage train."

"Garbage train?" Claire asked when they were gone. "Is that the maintenance train you mentioned?"

"One of them," Nalo allowed, pulling a piece of chalk from her tool belt and squatting by the upper edge of the hole.

"One of them? How many of them are there?"

"Depends."

"On what?"

"On how many of them there are."

"Wonderful."

The cleaning crew arrived before they finished mapping. None of them spoke English, two of the three couldn't speak to each other. They all made their feelings quite clear about the bags.

"I don't know about you," Austin muttered when they left, "but I've just learned a few new words." He wandered over to the edge of the platform and peered down at Claire. "How's it going?"

"Fine." The hole came over the edge of the platform, wrapped around the lip, and extended two feet down a blackened concrete block wall. It took a liberal application of nail polish remover to get even small sections of the concrete blocks clean enough to take a definition. And her fingers were getting cold.

"Dean could get that clean in no time."

"And if Dean were here, that would be relevant."

"Hey, *I* didn't chase him away."

"Shut up."

"Almost done?"

"Almost."

"Good."

She glanced up at his tone. "Why good?"

"Well, I don't want to rush you, but there's something going on just down the line."

"Going on?"

He cocked his head, ears pointing south. "Sounds like a train."

"Great."

"But it's stopped now."

"Fine. Let us know when it starts moving. Nalo?"

"I'm ready. If you're not sure you can finish before the train gets here, hop out and we'll redo after."

Claire glanced down the tunnel. She couldn't see a light, she couldn't feel the wind of an approaching train, and she just wanted this whole thing to be over. "There's one last definition; I can finish." The concrete wasn't exactly clean, but it would have to do. A little extra pressure on the chalk got the symbol more-or-less inscribed. "That's it." A movement in the air lifted her hair off the back of her neck as she straightened. "Let's go."

Because of the bend in the site, it was impossible for a single Keeper to see the entire perimeter. While Nalo pushed her edge in, Claire reached into the possibilities and lifted.

The movement in the air became wind.

Claire could feel the vibrations of the approaching train in the soles of her feet.

The hole fought to stay open.

As the bottom edge reached the tricky turn at the lip, she could see a small light growing rapidly larger in the corner of her eye.

Rapidly larger.

It became a train.

I might just as well throw myself under it. I can't believe I screwed things up so badly with Dean. How can I miss him so much and keep on living? What's the point of a life without someone to share it wi . . .

A sudden multiple puncture through the skin of her hand jerked her back to herself. Grabbing possibilities, she tightened her grip on the definitions, flung herself up onto the platform, and slammed the hole shut just as a three-car train roared through the station, lights blazing and Christmas music blaring.

Lying flat on her back, she lifted her injured hand up into her field of vision. "I'm bleeding."

"You're lucky that's all you're doing; that cat just saved your life. What happened?"

"I was . . ."

"Thinking about Dean."

She turned her head until she could see Austin, opened her mouth to deny it, and sighed.

"*Were* you thinking about this boy?"

Another turn of her head and she could see Nalo

frowning down at her, hands on hips. "It was more like a bad soap opera than actual thought," she admitted reluctantly.

"Get up," the older Keeper instructed. "We need to talk."

Her tone left no room for argument. It barely left room for vowels.

As Nalo made sure the hole was truly sealed, Claire got slowly to her feet then bent down and picked up the cat. "Thank you."

He rubbed the top of his head against her chin. "Same old, same old."

". . . and being without him is affecting the way you're doing your job. Not to mention putting your life in danger. And what do you think would have happened if that train had killed a Keeper while you were under the influence of darker possibilities? I'll tell you what, we'd have had a repeat of that whole Euro Disney thing!"

Claire shuddered.

"The powers that be clearly want the two of you together, or you wouldn't be in such lousy shape without him." Nalo handed her a glass of eggnog and set a saucer of it on the coffee table for Austin. "Drink this. You'll feel better."

"There's rum in it."

Austin lifted his head, a fleck of foam on his muzzle. "There's no rum in *mine*."

Both Keepers ignored him.

"Do you love the boy?"

A mouthful of eggnog came back out Claire's nose. "He's not a boy!"

"Pardon me, Miss Defensive, and use the napkin, not your sleeve. Do you love the man, then?"

"I just want what's best for him."

"How about you let him decide what's best for him and you answer my question." Nalo settled into a wing-back recliner and stared at Claire over the edge of her glass. "Do you love him?"

"Love." She tried for nonchalance and failed dismally. "What is love anyway?"

"Claire . . ."

There was power in a name. In this particular instance, there was also a warning.

The depths of the eggnog held no answers although the rum made a couple of suggestions Claire ignored. Sighing, she set the empty glass down on the coffee table next to a crocheted Christmas tree. "Since he left, I've felt like there's a part of me missing."

"Close but not good enough. Do you love him?"

"I . . ."

"Yes or no."

Yes or no? There had to be other options. When none presented themselves, she sighed. "Yes."

"Yes, what?"

"Yes, I love him." The world stopped for a moment, and when it started up again, Claire felt a little light-headed. "Shouldn't there be music or something?"

"The world stopped. That wasn't enough? You want a sound track, too?"

"I guess not."

"Good. Does he love you?"

"I don't know."

Austin looked up from the bottom of his saucer. "He does."

"How do you know?" Claire demanded, leaning forward to stare into his face.

"He told me."

"No, he didn't."

"Are you calling me a liar?"

"I'm calling you a cat."

Austin thought about that for a moment. "Fair enough," he conceded.

"It's obvious you and Dean should be together," Nalo declared, drawing the attention of both Claire and the cat. "So what are you going to do about it?"

Claire shook her head. "Keepers don't . . ."

"Don't tell me what Keepers don't; I've been one a lot longer than you have. Keepers don't deny the truth when it jumps up and bites them on the ass, that's what Keepers don't. If it helps, think of the space between you as an accident site you have to close."

"But the danger."

ment that Keepers
have the only power. If you love him, you find that
boy then you trust in the power of love to keep him
safe. And if that cat doesn't quit making gagging
noises," she added with a dark look at Austin, "I'm
going to use him to line a pair of slippers."

"She didn't tell you anything you didn't already
know."

"I know." Bedded down on Nalo's couch for the
night, Claire stared out the window, past the lights
of the city at points farther east. Dean was out there,
somewhere, and as much as it was going to cost her,
she could think of only one way to find him.

Austin kneaded her hip, his claws not quite going
all the way through the duvet. "So what *are* you
going to do about it?"

"Go home for Christmas."

"Diana?"

"Diana."

"And if you're Summoned somewhere else?"

"Then I'll know that Dean and I aren't supposed
to be together and I'll be miserable and unhappy for
the rest of my life."

"That's your entire plan?"

Claire sighed and stroked her fingers along his
spine. "That's it."

"You know, you guys really need a union."

*   *   *

The Christmas dance was Diana's first. She hadn't planned on attending but when her parents had discovered what she'd done too late to have her undo it, they'd insisted she be there just in case. They'd said rather a great deal more as well, but she'd stopped listening to the lecture early on.

Standing against the wall of the gym, arms crossed, a cardboard cup of punch in one hand, she watched twinkling bits of light falling gently through the central hole in the crepe-paper pattern. It was working exactly as designed; the weave captured good feelings rising up from the crowd, filtered and purified them, then sprinkled them back down like metaphysical snowflakes through the center hole. And in spite of minor panic from the 'rents about the dangers inherent in too much of a good thing, the inevitable counterbalance of teenage angst insured that the system didn't spiral up and out of control.

It was probably going to be the first high school dance in history where everyone had a good time and no one had *too* good a time.

As ordered, the pattern even looked like a snowflake from below.

She was remarkably pleased with herself.

Draining the cup, she set it down and walked across to where the senior basketball team were standing morosely by the wall. They were now zero and nineteen. The chess club was more popular.

"Joe, dance with me!"

He looked startled but took her hand and allowed her to lead him out onto the floor.

As the music started to slow, Diana reached into the possibilities and changed the CD before he could pull her close.

Everyone *was* going to have a good time, but there were limits to even the most selfless charity work and Joe *had* missed his last five free throws.

Just after one a.m., Diana slipped off boots and coat and padded upstairs in her socks, reaching just far enough into the possibilities to muffle the sound of her arrival. She didn't actually have a curfew—there was a certain inane sound to *you can only save the world until ten on a school night*—but she liked to keep the parental units guessing. Fully aware of this, they set certain metaphysical traps, which she easily deflected, and all parties remained secure in the knowledge that they were holding up their respective ends of the teenager/parent relationship, Keeper/Cousin variety.

Diana suspected her parents didn't think of it that way, but as long as they were happy, she didn't really mind.

She waited until she had her bedroom door closed behind her before she turned on the light.

"I need a favor."

The possibilities muffled her startled shriek and Claire easily fielded the candle she threw. "Don't you have somewhere to be Summoned to!"

"No." Claire set the candle on the stack of paperbacks piled by the bed.

"No?"

"How loud was the music at that dance? No. I am, at the current time, not being Summoned anywhere."

Her heartbeat beginning to return to a more normal rhythm, Diana crossed over to the beanbag chair, scooped Austin up into her arms, and settled them both, the cat on her lap. "Whoa. You do know what that means?"

"How many more years have I been doing this?" Arms crossed, Claire paced the eight steps to the wall and back. "It means I'm supposed to be here. I'm supposed to do what I'm doing."

"You don't look very happy about it. What are you supposed to be doing that's got you so nervous?"

Dropping onto the end of the bed, Claire picked a tuft of fuzz off the folded Navaho blanket. "Like I said, I need a favor."

"You're supposed to ask me for a favor?"

"No. I *need* to ask you for a favor."

"Me?"

"Do you see anyone else in here?" Claire demanded, nostrils pinched. "If I could do this any other way, I would, but I need a favor only you, my only sister, can provide."

"Only me?" The grin became a smirk as she stroked a thoughtful hand down Austin's back. "In all my life you have never come to me for counsel or help. You have never invited me to be a part of what you do. Now you come to me and say you need a favor." She stroked the cat again. "Now you call me sister."

Austin stretched out a paw, and pushed against her lap. "Hey, Godfather, behind the ears."

"You're sure you know the number?"

"Always." Diana poked at the phone.

"That's too many numbers!"

"Relax and tell me again how I was right and you were wrong."

"Just dial."

"I've dialed; it's ringing." The look on Claire's face evoked an involuntary smile—which slipped as Claire stood motionless and stared at the receiver. "Hey? Are you going to take this thing from me or . . . too late. Hi, Dean."

Dean pushed himself into a sitting position on his cousin's sofa bed. "Diana?" He slid on his glasses and glanced over at the VCR for the time. The piece of black electrical tape was no help at all. "How did you get this number?"

"If I told you that, I'd have to kill you. There's someone here who wants to talk to you. Someone who's very, very sorry she sent you away and . . . ow! What's your damage? It sure seemed like you didn't want to . . . okay, okay, stop pinching!"

During the pause that followed, he dug for his watch. Two forty-one. a.m.

"Dean?"

Remember to breathe, he told himself as the room started to spin. "Claire?"

Fingers gripping the plastic so tightly it creaked, Claire had a sudden flashback to the hotel room in Rochester.

"Howard?"

"Cheryl?"

And we all know how well that turned out. She swallowed, unable to actually say the words. If Dean had said something, anything, but he didn't—although she could feel him waiting.

Diana rolled her eyes. Leaning forward, she caught her sister's gaze and held it. "Tell him, Claire." The she reached into the possibilities and added the magic word. *"Please."*

Resistance was futile. The words spilled out before Claire could stop them. "Dean, I'm sorry. I was wrong to just arbitrarily decide we shouldn't be together anymore. I should have told you about the danger and let you . . ." When Diana scowled, she wet

89

her lips and made a quick correction. ". . . trusted you to make your own decisions. I want us to be together."

"Why?"

"Why? I . . . um . . . Diana, if you *please* me again, I'm going to smack you!" Having glared down her sister, she took a deep breath.

"If it helps, think of the space between you as an accident site you have to close."

Moving the phone away from her mouth, she growled, "Would a little privacy be asking too much?"

Diana, secure in the certain knowledge that Claire owed her big time, snorted. "Well, duh."

Austin ignored the question as it clearly did not apply to cats.

Neither response surprised her. She tucked the phone back up to her mouth and lowered her voice. "Dean, since you left, I've felt like there's a part of me missing."

She could still feel him waiting.

"Close but not good enough."

"Look, I love you. Okay?"

She loved him. Over the thundering of his heart, Dean could hear music. It filled the apartment, thrummed in his blood, and just about made his ears bleed.

In the next room, his cousin banged on the ceiling.

"It's almost three o'clock in the freaking morning, butthead!

"Dean?" Claire frowned at the phone.

"What's happening?" Diana demanded, reaching for the receiver.

Claire smacked her hand away. "I don't know. It sounds like Bon Jovi."

The music stopped.

"Dean?"

She loved him. The words echoed in the sudden silence.

She loved him.

Now what? Was he supposed to say he loved her, too, or would she think he was just saying it because she'd said it even though he did, and had known it since he drove away and left her standing all alone in that parking lot even though he hadn't realized he'd known it until this very moment?

And then what?

"Dean?"

"What's the matter?" Diana made another unsuccessful grab for the receiver.

"He's not saying anything."

"Give me the phone."

Claire stared down at the cat. "What?"

"The phone, give it to me." When she hesitated,

he sighed. "Trust me, it's a guy thing. You need to break this up into bite-sized pieces."

As the silence from the other end of the line continued, she laid the phone down on the bed beside Austin who cocked his head so that his mouth was at the microphone and one ear pointed at the speaker.

"Dean, you still there?"

That wasn't Claire. Where had Claire gone?
"Claire?"

Austin's tail tip flicked back and forth. "She's here, but right now, we need some answers. Do you love her?"

Dean sighed in relief. That, he didn't have to think about. "Yes."

"Do you want to be with her?"

"Yes."

"Write down these directions."

He shook his head to clear some of the adrenaline buzz and grabbed a pen off the end table beside the sofa bed. Paper. He had no paper. Pulling the fabric tight over his leg, he wrote the directions on the sheet, repeated them, and hung up.

"Well?" Claire demanded as Austin lifted his head. "What did he say?"

"He said yes. Hang this up, would you. If you're

thinking of what to get me for Christmas, I'm fairly certain I could manage one of those large-buttoned phones they have for seniors."

"Austin."

"Just think of the time you'd save if I could order my own food."

"Austin!"

"What?"

Claire managed to avoid throttling him but only just. "He said yes, and?"

"And I expect he's folding his underwear into his hockey bag even as we speak."

"He folds his underwear?" Diana snickered.

"He folds everything," Austin told her, fastidiously smoothing a bit of rumpled fur.

"Austin . . ." Claire ground the cat's name out through clenched teeth. ". . . what does Dean's underwear have to do with *anything*? And you . . ." She turned a warning glare on her sister. ". . . can just shut up and let him answer the question."

"It has to do with packing." When she continued to glower, Austin sighed. "Packing to come here. And you're welcome," he gasped as jubilant Claire scooped him up into her arms. "But I'm old, and you just drove a rib through my spleen."

"Do cats have a spleen?"

"I think you're missing the point."

"Sorry." She set him back on the bed and, suddenly conscious of her sister's smug expression, stiffened. "What?"

"Don't you have appreciation to show to someone else? Someone who, oh, made the initial contact?"

"Thank you."

"You're welcome."

"And I would have told him without your help."

"Oh, sure. And *Babe* would've been nominated for that best picture Oscar without my help."

"Diana!"

"I was a lot younger then! And it's not like it won . . ."

It was not possible to drive from Halifax, Nova Scotia, to Kingston, Ontario, in seventeen hours. For reasons unknown to mortal man—although most mortal women were aware of them as they involved asking for directions when trying to get out of Montreal—the trip from east to west took eighteen hours. Dean actually had to drive past Kingston through Toronto, to London, then north to Lucan. The whole trip took him twenty-three hours. He saw one police car parked at a doughnut shop. He saw no moose.

FOUR

"That's his truck. He's here!"

"Claire . . . can't breathe . . ."

"Sorry." She loosened her grip on the cat, who squirmed out of her arms and stalked to the other end of the couch, tail lashing from side to side. Brushing drifts of cat hair off her sweater, she murmured, "I can't believe how nervous I am."

"I can't believe how nerdy you are," Diana sighed. "You love him, he loves you, yadda, yadda, yadda. Now haul ass out there and let him know he's at the right house."

"Keepers don't . . ."

"What? Make spectacles of themselves with Bystanders in public?" Diana's mimicry of her sister was cuttingly accurate. "If you wait until he comes up to the house, you'll have to invite him in. If he comes in here, he'll have to make nice with Mom and Dad. If, on the other hand, you meet out there, you can take him directly to your place and make nicer with each other. Your choice.''

Eyes locked on the figure getting out of the truck, Claire hesitated . . .

"You know Dad'll want to show him the photo album.''

. . . and decided.

"Now haul ass out there and let him know he's at the right house?'' Austin snorted as he walked over to stand beside Diana at the open door. "I never knew you were such a romantic.''

Fireworks! Claire thought with the small part of her brain still functioning. Then she realized it was just the Christmas lights on the front of the house reflecting in Dean's glasses. He tasted like coffee and toothpaste. Or coffee-flavored toothpaste.

After a moment, she pulled her mouth far enough away from his to sigh, "You're here.''

He smiled down at her, finding it just a little difficult to focus. "I'm here.''

"I'm glad you came.''

"I'm glad you called.''

"I can't hear them.''

"Lucky you,'' Austin muttered, moving away from the open door. "If I have to hear any more, I'm going to hork up a hairball. That dialogue is so banal she should have run into his arms in slow motion.''

"There's a foot of snow on the path," Diana reminded him. She took another look. "Or rather there was." The snow beneath Dean's work boots and Claire's running shoes had melted and the cleared area was spreading fast. Peering through fog created by the sudden, localized heat, she grinned and yelled, "Get a room!"

"Diana?"

"Mom." Diana pulled the door closed as she turned. There were some things that shouldn't be shared across the generations. *Third Eye Blind* and bicycle shorts topped the list, but watching Claire suck face with a hunka hunka burning love in the front yard followed close behind. Most of the time, Diana tried to be sensitive to parental feelings. "What can I do for you?"

"Was that Dean's truck I heard?"

"Yes, it was."

"Has Claire gone out to meet him?"

"Yes, she has."

"Is she going to bring him inside to say hello to the rest of us?"

"I somehow doubt it."

Martha Hansen studied her younger daughter's expression. "I see. It's like that, is it? Well, good."

"Good?"

"Yes, good. I like Dean, and I hope he and Claire will find happiness together. Not many Keepers manage to find someone to share their lives with," she added, shooting a pointed look at her younger daughter. "Most of you are such arrogant know-it-alls that you end up old and alone."

"Yeah, yeah, if we end up old at all." Diana waved off the warning. Since she had every intention of going out young in a blaze of glory, it was moot. "So you don't mind about the hot monkey sex in the front yard?"

Martha's smile grew slightly wistful. "Your father and I were like that when we first got together. We couldn't keep our hands off each other."

"Eww, gross!" The list of *not to be shared* was hurriedly revised, parental coupling confidences now moved into the primary position.

"Shouldn't I go in and say hello to your parents?"
Dad'll want to show him the photo album.
"No."

Dean pulled back reluctantly, tracing a line of kisses up her face as he lifted his head. "Claire, it's polite."

He was never impolite. Claire didn't think he could be. "If a little old lady showed up right now," she murmured while nibbling on his chin, "would you help her across the street?"

"What little old lady?" Although cognitive thought was becoming increasingly difficult, he was fairly certain they hadn't been talking about little old ladies.

"Any little old lady."

Now he was confused. Separating his chin from her mouth with a soft sucking sound, he looked around, wondering where the fog had come from. "I don't see a little old lady."

"There *is* no little old lady." Claire made a mental note to be more specific in the future. "I was just making the point that there's a time and a place for everything, and this is not the time to be with my parents." She glanced down.

Dean's cheeks flushed crimson. He grabbed her wrists and pulled her hands away from his jeans. "Claire, I . . ." Then the length of her thigh brushed against his, and he made a sort of choking noise deep in his throat as he bent his mouth back to hers.

"I have my own apartment over the garage," she murmured against his lips. "It's not actually part of my parents' house. Technically, we can go directly up there without being rude."

"Claire . . ."

"If we go up there now, I can give you your Christmas present."

"Christmas isn't until tomorrow," he protested weakly.

Twisting free of his grip, she slid her hands up under his sweater until she could feel his heart slamming against his ribs so hard that the muscle sheathing them shivered under the impact. She shivered a bit herself and murmured, "Do you *really* want to wait?"

"Way to go, Dean! He's carrying her up the stairs. Ouch, that had to hurt. Hit her head on the side of the garage." Shaking her own head in sympathy, Diana shifted position slightly to get a better angle on the scene. "She seems to be okay—they're carrying on. Probably has so many endorphins in her system she can't feel a thing."

"Diana!" Her mother twitched the curtains out of her grip. "That's quite enough of that!"

The garage having just cut off her line of sight, Diana shrugged and stepped away from the window, raising both hands in exaggerated surrender. "Not a problem, Mom, your wish is my command."

"Good." Martha tucked a strand of graying hair back behind her ear and folded her arms. "Then let me make that wish just a little more specific—no more spying on your sister, period. No hidden microphones. No web cams. No scrying in any form; no mirrors, no bowls of water, and especially no entrails. I need those giblets for the gravy. You will leave Claire and Dean alone while they . . ."

Diana's eyebrows rose to touch her hairline.

"Yes, well, just never mind what they're doing. They're adults, and it's none of your business. Or mine or your father's," she added before Diana could speak. "When you're out on your own, we will extend the same courtesy to you, so there's no need to look at me like that."

"Like what?"

"Like your life is a never-ending battle against personal oppression. You're seventeen, Claire's twenty-seven."

"And Dean's twenty-one."

"Which means?"

"Absolutely nothing. I'm happy she's happy. I'm happy they're happy. I'm happy *you're* happy. But, all things considered, you might want to have the fire department on standby."

"The fire department *is* on standby," her mother pointed out dryly. "Or have you forgotten what happened last Christmas when the star of Bethlehem went supernova."

Diana had long since stopped protesting that they'd have won the Christmas lighting contest had the fire department simply damped down the crèche like she'd asked them to instead of putting the whole thing out because her parents always answered with irrelevancies. The roof had been perfectly safe. Essentially safe. Slightly scorched . . .

A short time later, having been forced to eat a piece of fruitcake and talk to Aunt Corinne on the phone, she straightened up from the wall that separated her room from Claire's apartment, set the empty glass down on her desk, and sighed. "That works on television."

"So does David Duchovny but he's got just as slim a connection to the real world," Austin reminded her, eye narrowed as he watched her push a handful of pencils one at a time, into a mug. "I thought your mother told you to leave them alone."

"She didn't specifically say no eavesdropping." Picking a pair of sweatpants off the floor, Diana poked her finger through a ragged hole in the knee.

"She didn't specifically tell you not to feed the cat, but I notice you've managed to resist."

"You just ate some fruitcake."

"Your point?"

"Do cats even *like* fruitcake?"

"Does anyone?"

She threw the sweatpants into the laundry basket and dropped into her desk chair, spinning herself petulantly around and around. "You're being awfully understanding considering that Claire's shut you out, too—after *we* got them together."

"If you think I'm interested in watching talking monkey sex," Austin snorted, "think again."

"That's *hot* monkey sex."

"You're all talking monkeys from where I sit. And I've seen that friction thing; it never really changes."

A six-car passenger train roared across the room and into a tunnel.

"Okay," he said thoughtfully when the noise had died. "*That* was different."

"Diana!"

Waving away the lingering scent of burning diesel, Diana opened her bedroom door, fingers hooked in the trim as she leaned out into the hall. "Yeah, Dad?"

"What the bloody blue blazes was that?"

"I think it was a euphemism." The vibrations had knocked askew a set of family photographs hanging on the wall across from her. A previously serious portrait of Claire had developed a distinctly cheesy grin. "Or maybe a metaphor."

"Well, don't do it again!"

"It wasn't me!" She closed the door, not quite slamming it, and walked to the bed. "Why does he always assume it's me?" she demanded, scooping Austin up into her arms.

"It always *is* you."

"Not this time."

"Natural mistake, though. Close your eyes."

"Why?"

"Trust me. Three, two, one . . ."

The possibilities opened.
Wide.

"Holy shit!" One hand pressed against the glass, Brent Carmichael turned away from the window and stared at the half dozen firefighters standing behind him. Behind them, the cards they'd abandoned lay spread out on the table. "Did you see that?"

"I'm still seeing it," one of the others muttered trying to blink away afterimages.

"It came from the direction of the Hansen place." Someone whimpered.

The silence stretched past the point where it could be comfortably broken and then went on a little longer. Finally, the shift senior, a man with eighteen years experience and two citations for bravery, cleared his throat. "I didn't see anything," he said.

A mumbled chorus of, "Neither did I," followed the collective sigh of relief.

"But . . ." Brent looked out into the darkness of Christmas Eve, at the starlit beauty of the velvet sky above, at the strings of brightly colored Christmas lights innocently mirroring that beauty below, and remembered other visits to the Hansen house. Or tried to. Most of the memories were fuzzy—and not warm and fuzzy either, but fuzzy like trying to pull in the WB without either a satellite dish or cable, picture skewed, one word in seven actually audible. And the harder he tried, the less he could remember.

Except for the incident with the burning bush. That, he couldn't forget.

Denial became the only logical option.

Happy to have that settled, he turned back to the game. "What moron just chose Charmander against Pikachu?"

*   *   *

The light should have dissipated.

Should have.

Didn't.

Instead, it found itself in an empty, cavernous room in a large, two-story brick building. Caught by the power woven into the snowflake pattern, it rose up through the crepe-paper streamers toward the ceiling, was filtered and purified, and poured back through the center hole.

More now than merely a glorious possibility, it hovered for a moment above center court, then, following the pull of need, it passed through the window, and out into the night.

Lena thoughtfully flicked her lighter on and off. She'd already taken the batteries out of the smoke detector in the hall, but after a certain point that became moot and her father would come charging down into her room demanding to know if she was trying to burn down the house.

There were six candles burning under her angel poster, nine among the angel figurines on her dresser, three votive candles in angel candle holders, and one in a souvenir Backstreet Boys mug on the bedside table.

Close to the limit.

One more, she decided, and started searching through the stubs of melted wax for something worth burning. Nothing. Unfortunately, that *one more* had gone from being an option to being a necessity during the search. Slowly, she turned to her bookshelf.

The angel standing beside her CD player was an old-fashioned figure about a foot high in long flowing robes and wings. He was even carrying a harp. His gold halo circled a pristine white wick.

Heart pounding, Lena approached with the lighter. This had been her very first angel, plucked out from between a broken Easy-Bake oven and a stack of macramé coasters at a neighborhood yard sale. *Oh, please*, she thought as the flame touched the wick. *Let this sacrifice be enough to make it happen!*

There was no need to be more specific about what it was. *It* was always the same thing. She'd wished for it on a thousand stars, her last three birthday cakes, the wishbones of four turkeys, Christmas and Thanksgiving, and with a penny in every body of water she passed. The school custodian had fished enough pennies out of the toilets in the girls' washrooms that he'd treated himself to a package of non-Board of Education toilet paper—the kind that couldn't be fed through a laser printer.

The wick darkened, a bit of wax melted on the top of the golden head, and then the flame roared up high enough to scorch the ceiling, filling Lena's basement bedroom with light.

The light moved slowly away from the candle, into the center of the room.

"It's an angel," Lena cried, eyes watering, eyebrows slightly singed.

And because she believed, it was.

The light took form.

And substance.

And became everything a not quite seventeen-year-old girl wanted in an angel.

In the moment of making, the door flew open and a large, dark-haired man, waving one hand in front of his face to clear the smoke, burst into the room. "Lena! How many times have I told you . . . ?" His eyes widened, and his bellow became a roar. "What the devil are you doing in my daughter's room?"

Lena knew that angels were sexless, but her father didn't know that the beautiful young man with the bicolored hair was an angel, and his belief in what he was seeing was as strong as hers.

The last little bit of substance formed out of a father's fears.

And, all things considered, it wasn't actually that little.

His expression a cross between confusion and panic, the angel ducked the first blow, slipped under an outstretched hand, and ran for the bedroom door. He would have made it except that he hit a bit of unexpected anatomy on the edge of a chair and the sudden pain dropped him to his knees. The second blow connected.

Lying on the floor, hands clasped between his legs,

he stared blearily up at the angry man standing above him, and wondered just what exactly was going on.

He wasn't the only one.

"What do you mean, he had no clothes when he got here?"

Diana, heavily shielded and doing her best impersonation of nothing at all, waited in the triangle of deep shadow behind the love seat, determined that this would be the year. From where she crouched, eyes grown used to the dark could see the entire fireplace—top to bottom, side to side—and, beyond it, the lower curve of the Christmas tree. On the mantel, beside the cards, was a glass of milk and three cookies. Homemade chocolate chip cookies, with the chips still soft from the oven. Only the best bait would slow him down.

She'd almost caught him a couple of times, but something had always distracted her at the crucial moment. When she was younger, she'd wanted to see him just for the sake of seeing him. Now, after so many failures, it had become a point of pride.

The instant camera she held had been in her stocking three years ago. She suspected he was taunting her.

A sudden clatter up on the roof brought a pleased smile—earlier in the day, she'd cleared away the snow that might muffle the first sounds of her quarry's arrival.

A bit of soot fell from the chimney onto the hearth.

Show time.

Then something slammed against her shields and exploded into a rainbow of metaphysical light.

Blinded by the brilliant yellows and reds and greens, Diana stood, tipped a lamp over with her shoulder, caught it before it hit the floor, and stumbled out from behind the love seat. She could hear nothing over the thrumming of frustrated possibilities but when one hand brushed for an instant against fur trim, she took three quick pictures with the other.

Then the moment passed, and she could both see and hear.

The milk glass was empty, the cookies were gone. The stockings bulged.

Austin was lying on the hearth, a brand new calico square stuffed with catnip under one front paw. "Aren't you getting a little old for this?" he sniffed.

"Isn't he?" Blinking away the last of the after-images, Diana dropped onto the sofa with a frustrated groan. "He's never done *that* before." Bending forward, she scooped the developing evidence up off the rug. "At least I . . ."

A familiar black-and-white face stared up at her from all three photographs.

Leaping up beside her, Austin nodded toward the

middle picture. "Could I get a copy of this? You've caught my best side."

It was the self-satisfied "Ho Ho Ho" drifting down the chimney that really hurt.

Head pillowed on Dean's chest, Claire half woke to a sudden metaphysical prod. Still wrapped in a warm cocoon of exhaustion and fulfillment, slightly smug from having lived up to the expectations of all parties involved, she shunted it off into the barricade she'd set up years before when Diana had decided privacy was a relative term and then went back to sleep.

Every year, at the moment Christmas Eve became Christmas Day, a miracle was said to occur—animals were given a chance to speak.

In a cream-colored bungalow just outside Sandusky, Ohio, a small gray tabby with a white tip on her tail woke, stretched, and walked up the length of the body under the covers until she could poke a paw into a half-opened mouth.

Midnight. And the miracle.

"Hey. Wake up and feed me."

Father Nicholas Harris stood in the open doorway of St. Patrick's, shaking hands and wishing his parishioners would just go home. He loved celebrating the Midnight Mass on Christmas Eve—it was one of the few masses in the year where the verb celebrate actually seemed to apply—but he'd been up early after a late night, and he was so tired he actually thought he'd seen the silhouettes of flying reindeer and a heavily laden sleigh cross the high arc of the window over the door during the second soloist's somewhat shrill but enthusiastic rendition of "The Holly and the Ivy."

"Father Nick, I'd like you to meet my sister Doris and her family. . . ."

He smiled, shook hands with a dozen strangers, declined his fourth invitation to Christmas dinner, and tried not to think of what the open door and the December night were doing to his heating bill. Finally, the end was in sight, only two more hands to shake.

"Father . . ."

One of Frank Giorno's hands enclosed his in an unbreakable grip while the other grabbed a bit of jacket and dragged a young man forward.

". . . this punk who showed up naked in my daughter's bedroom believes he's an angel, so I brought him to you."

He didn't know why he was in a small book-lined room, but since no one was yelling at him, or shaking him, or hitting him, things were looking up. Adjusting bits he wasn't used to having pressure on, he studied the man behind the desk, recognized him as another servant of the light, and hoped that Lena's father had been right during all the shouting and that this was where he was supposed to be.

Trying not to fidget under the searchlight intensity of his unwanted guest's gaze, Father Harris shuffled a few irrelevant papers around and wondered irritably why Frank Giorno hadn't just called the police. He had to be in denial about finding the young man in his daughter's room. Granted the boy deserved points for originality in a bad situation, but what angel ever had bleached blond tips on short dark brown hair? Or managed to slouch in such a convincingly adolescent way? Or looked quite so confused? The boy's eyes were . . .

. . . were . . .

Gold flecks in velvet brown brightened, merged, and became a window into . . .

. . . into . . .

Father Harris rubbed at his own eyes. He was far too tired to do any kind of counseling when he was not only seeing things but smelling grilled cheese sandwiches—his favorite food. Far, far too tired to wait for a stubborn teenager to speak first. "What's your name, son?"

Name? Did he have a name? Everything had been named in the beginning so it was entirely possible. He started from the top, hoping something would sound familiar. There were only 301,655,722 angels after all, he'd have to reach it eventually.

"Son, your name?"

Startled, he grabbed one at random. "Samuel?"

"Are you asking?"

"No." It had become his name. Whether it had been his name before was immaterial—he hoped.

"Samuel what?"

Was there more? He didn't think so. "Just Samuel."

Father Nicholas sighed. At this rate they'd still be sitting in his office on New Year's. "What are you on, Samuel?"

That was easier. He glanced down. "Laminate." When the priest made an unhappy face, he took a closer look. "Laminate flooring, in medium oak, three ninety-nine a square foot, twenty-year warranty."

"No . . ."

"No?"

Something in the young man's expression insisted that the question be answered, as asked. "Well, yes. How did you know?"

He shrugged matter-of-factly. "I have higher knowledge." It was in the original specifications; higher knowledge, mobility, great hair, and he was supposed to have brought a message, although he didn't actually know what the message was. Lena Giorno's shaping had been a little vague about everything except the great hair. That, she'd been quite definite about.

"Higher knowledge about flooring?"

"Yes." He waited for the priest to ask about other

topics, but Father Harris only sighed again and ran a hand back through his hair.

"Okay, Samuel. Let's start over. What did you take?"

He straightened, appalled at the question. "Nothing!"

"Nothing?"

"Nothing. I swear to . . . you know." One finger pointed toward the ceiling. "These clothes were given to me." He glanced down at the front of his sweatshirt then back up again. "I don't even know who Regis Philbin is."

"Well, you're probably the only person in North America who doesn't," the priest muttered. Then, raising his voice, he added, "Why were you in Lena Giorno's bedroom?"

"She called me."

"On the phone?"

"On a candle."

"She called you on a candle?"

"Yes."

Knowing Lena as he did, Father Harris took a shot in the dark. "An angel candle?"

"Yes."

"And now you're an angel?"

"Yes."

Feeling as if he'd just won a game of twenty questions, Father Nicholas sank back in his chair. "You're an angel because Lena wanted you to be an angel?"

Samuel nodded, happy that someone finally understood. "Yes. But her father expected me to be something else, so . . ." He spread his hands and looked down the length of his body. " . . . things got confused."

"I'm sure they did."

"I have genitalia, and I don't know what to do with it. Them."

"Genitalia?"

"You know, a . . ."

A hurriedly raised hand cut off the details. "I know."

"It's making everything . . . strange."

Now that was a complaint the priest had heard before. While he'd never heard it put quite that way, a good ninety-nine percent of the teenage counseling he did involved raging hormones. It felt so good to be back on familiar ground, he thought he might as well start off with a few stock platitudes. "If you want to maintain your self-respect, it's important to fight the temptations of the flesh."

"Okay. But what do I do with them during the battle?"

And the familiar ground shifted. More tired than he could ever remember being, Father Harris rubbed at his temples and muttered, "Try tucking left."

Fabric rustled.

Fine. I surrender. I don't know what he's on, but I'm going to let him sleep it off. In the morning, when we're both coherent, I'll find out just who he is and what I should do with him.

Next morning . . .

"Merry Christmas, Dean." Hurrying across the living room to take his free hand in hers, Martha Hansen reached up and kissed him on the cheek.

"Mrs. Hansen . . ."

"Martha. We're glad you could join us."

Holding his other hand, Claire smiled up at him. "Told you."

"You told him what, Claire?"

She switched the smile to her mother. "That he had no reason to be nervous."

"It wasn't your mother . . ." Dean began in a low voice, but Claire cut him off before he could finish, adjusting her grip to drag him across the room.

"Dad? This is Dean."

John Hansen balanced his mug on the arm of the sofa, stood, and shook Dean's hand. "I'm pleased to finally meet you, son. The rest of the family has had only good things to say."

"Not quite true. *I* told you I thought he had a lot of nerve telling me how to behave and that, even though he may be woogie, I couldn't see what Claire saw in him. OW!" Diana glared across the room at her sister.

"Context, dear," her mother admonished. "You'd

almost got him sacrificed. And, Claire, you know better than to use the possibilities like that."

"Which is why I threw a hazelnut."

"I apologize; your aim is improving."

"What about me?" Diana demanded, dropping down on the floor by the Christmas tree.

"You should also apologize. Dean's a guest in this house, and you're being deliberately provoking."

All three women turned to look at Dean, whose ears darkened from scarlet to crimson. "That's okay. It's . . . uh . . . I mean . . ."

"Dean?"

He turned toward Claire's father wearing the same desperately hopeful expression as a Buffalo Bills fan during NFL playoffs. "Yes, sir?"

"Would you like some coffee?"

"Yes, sir."

"Come on, the pot's in the kitchen. We'll go get some for everyone." Detaching Claire's hand from Dean's arm, he drew the younger man out of the living room, saying, "I have this sudden urge to build a workshop. You've got no idea how great it is to have a little more testosterone in this house."

"Like some of us had a choice about that," Austin snorted from the top of the recliner as they passed.

Dean had been a little unsure of what to expect when he walked into the Hansens' living room with Claire that morning. After all, everyone in the room would know exactly how they'd spent the night. He didn't regret any of it—although his memory of times five and six had grown a little hazy—and he felt as though things were now back on track, that he was doing exactly what he was supposed to be doing with his life.

But he could see how things might be awkward.

It didn't help that both Claire's parents were Cousins, less powerful than Keepers but still among those who helped keep the metaphysical balance. Dean had learned from experience how painful an unbalanced metaphysical could be.

He was fairly certain Mrs. Hansen had liked him when they'd met back at the guesthouse, but Mr. Hansen was a total unknown. Following the older man into the kitchen, he searched for the right thing to say. Found himself saying, "I really love your daughter, sir."

"John."

"Sorry?"

"If you're going to be a part of Claire's life, and all signs seem to indicate you are, you might as well call me John."

"Yes, sir. John. Signs?"

"You know . . ." He set down the coffeepot and waved his hands around in the universal symbol for spookiness. ". . . signs: bright lights in the sky, heart-shaped frost patterns on the windows, K-Tel's love songs of the '70s mysteriously cued up on the CD player."

"I see."

"Really?"

"No, sir. But I know how I feel and I know how Claire feels, and that's what matters."

Claire looked more like her father than her mother, Dean realized as the older man's mouth curled into a familiar smile and he clapped him on the shoulder. "Good man. Give me a minute to finish up here, and we'll get back to the ladies."

"Women," corrected a bit of empty air over the sink.

John raised a hand and there was a muffled, "Ow!" from the other room. "And don't ever expect any privacy," he sighed.

"No, sir."

Glancing around the kitchen, Dean noted the juvenile artwork framed and hung in the breakfast nook, the souvenir tea towel stamped with the ubiquitous *My daughter closed a hole to Hell and all I got was this lousy tea towel*, the simmering pot of giblets, the mess. . . . His eyes narrowed. The early morning stuffing of the turkey had left bread crumbs and less easily identifiable debris scattered along six feet of counter. It looked as though the turkey had put up a fight. And very nearly won. He picked up the dishcloth without thinking and by the time the tray of coffee was ready, the counter was spotless.

As John handed Dean the tray, he nodded approvingly. "If you ever stop loving Claire, feel free to keep coming around."

"With a little scouring powder, I could get those stains out of the sink."

"Later, son."

Back in the living room, Dean had barely handed the tray in turn to Martha when Claire stuffed a large, lumpy, striped sock into his hands. It took him a moment to realize what it was. "There's a stocking for me?"

"Hey, the big guy doesn't make mistakes." Diana smashed a chocolate orange apart against the side of the fireplace. "Five people in the house, five filled stockings."

"The big guy?"

"Santa. St. Nick. Father Christmas."

"Is real . . ." And then he remembered the sound of Hell arguing with itself. " . . . ly efficient."

Claire patted his arm as he sat. "Nice recovery."

"Thank you."

A couple of hours later, after the stockings were emptied and presents had been unwrapped and exclaimed over and rather too much chocolate had been eaten for the time of day, Claire took a long swallow of lukewarm coffee and sank back against Dean's arm. "This has been the best Christmas ever. It's been . . ." She cocked her head and frowned. ". . . quiet."

Diana looked up, started to protest, paused, and nodded. "Too quiet," she agreed.

Austin dove under the couch.

"Do you feel any kind of a Summons at all?"

"No. You?"

"No. Not since last night. I felt the prod and . . . Of the Summons, you deviant!"

Diana raised both hands. "Hey. Didn't say anything."

"I *saw* your face."

"We'll deal with Diana's face later, Claire," their mother sighed. "Right now, what happened last night?"

Claire chewed her lower lip, trying to remember. "It woke me and I . . . oh, no. I shunted it into the privacy barrier. It must still be there."

Martha Hansen shook her head. "Claire, I realize you were a little preoccupied last night, but that was very irresponsible of you. Release it at once." As Claire reached into the possibilities, she added a worried, "Let's just hope it wasn't urgen . . ."

Every light on the Christmas tree exploded, and as brightly colored shrapnel ricocheted off hastily erected shields, the angel on the top of the tree broke into a loud chorus of "Day Dream Believer."

"That," Austin observed from under the couch, "doesn't sound good."

FIVE

"Claire!"

It was a voice that required a response regardless of circumstances. A voice that could be heard across a crowded shopping mall, that could blow past headphones, and could cut right through indifference. Had Hannibal used it on his elephants, he'd have not only made it across the Alps and conquered Rome but he'd have done it with clean dishes and folded laundry.

Claire recognized it in spite of the Summons careening around inside her skull like roller derby on fast forward. "Mom?"

"Uncross your eyes, dear. You don't want your face to freeze like that."

After a long moment, Claire figured out just where her eyes were attached to her face, and a moment after that she got them working again as a set. Gradually, the multiple images of her mother merged and nodded approvingly.

Worry lines pleating his forehead, Dean leaned into her line of sight. "Claire, are you okay?"

"I . . . I can't feel my fingers."

"Sorry." He loosened his grip. "What happened?"

Shaking the circulation back into her hand, she sat up. "It was a Summons. *Is* a Summons."

"Do Summonses usually . . . ?" His gesture took in the fine patina of broken glass that covered the carpet three feet out from the Christmas tree creating a perfect reproduction of "The Last Supper" with the Teletubbies replacing four of the Apostles.

"No."

"Thought not."

Tinky Winky appeared to be arguing with St. James.

Gripping Claire's chin between the thumb and forefinger of one hand, Martha turned her daughter's face up into the light. "Your pupils are dilated, and your pulse is racing."

"Mom, I'm fine. The Summons has blown off its stored energy and is settling down to same old same old. Give me a minute or two and I'll have totally recovered."

"Really?"

"Yes."

"Good." Straightening, she folded her arms and frowned. "What were you thinking? How could you have trapped a Summons in a privacy barrier!"

"How could she?" John repeated thoughtfully before his elder daughter could muster a defense. "That's a good question. It shouldn't have been possible, not even for Claire."

Martha turned to face her husband, brows lifting as she reconsidered all the implications. "Do you think the resolution of the situation with Dean has actually added to her power?"

"It's possible. I'd like to run some tests."

"But it could have just been the timing. I doubt that she deliberately tapped into the sexual energies."

"True, and an accidental surge would be harder to reproduce under measurable conditions, but . . ."

"Excuse me?"

Both Cousins turned.

Claire was on her feet, arms folded. "No one is running any tests."

"But . . ."

"No, Dad; I have a Summons to answer. And I only knocked it aside because it felt like Diana."

All heads turned.

Diana pulled a candy cane out of her mouth and shrugged. "I don't know what she's talking about. I had better things to do last night than . . . wait a minute. Santa!"

Her father sighed. "Diana, are you suggesting that Santa was spying on Claire and Dean?"

"No!" And then less emphatically. "Although there is that whole sees you when you're sleeping, sees you when you're awake schtick, which I strongly suspect is not entirely legal."

"Diana."

"And he does know," she added, "if you've been naughty or nice. Or specifically in this case, if Claire's been naughty or nice."

"Diana!"

"Okay. Something hit my shields just as Santa showed up. I figured it for his annual distraction and flipped it . . ."

"To me." Claire nodded. It was all beginning to make sense. "When I felt your touch, I leapt to an understandable conclusion . . ."

"Hey!"

" . . . and trapped it in the barrier."

"So!" Diana bounced to her feet. "This is really my Summons."

"Are you feeling it now?"

"What difference does that make? It hit me first."

"Perhaps . . ."

"Perhaps?"

Claire ignored her protest. ". . . but it hit me last and besides, from the intensity of the thing we're practically on top of the site. I can run out, close the hole, and be home before the turkey comes out of the oven."

"And don't you think highly of yourself," Diana snorted. "You think because you can find it, you can close it. You've forgotten what it's like around here."

"I've forgotten more than you know." Claire tossed a superior smile across the room.

Diana tossed it back.

When the smoke cleared, Martha had her right hand clamped on Claire's left shoulder and her left on Diana's right. "Both of you answer it."

"But . . ."

"No buts. While I'm willing to regard your childish behavior as an inevitable result of the amount of sugar ingested this morning, I am not willing to see it continue. You are both far too old for this."

"But . ."

"What did I say about buts?" She turned them toward the door. "Claire, try to make it a learning experience for your sister. Diana, try to learn something. Dean, I'm very sorry, but you'll have to drive them. As long as you're here, I suspect no other transportation will make itself available."

Trying to hide a smile, Dean murmured an agreement.

"Austin, are you going or staying?"

A black-and-white head poked out from under the front of the couch and raked a green-gold gaze over the tableau in the doorway. "Let me see, stuffed into the cold cab of an ancient truck with tag teams of young love and sibling rivalry or lying around a warm kitchen on the off chance that someone will take pity on a starving cat and give him a piece of turkey. Gee, tough choice."

"You're not starving," Claire told him, rolling her eyes.

"I'm not stupid either. Have a nice time."

"Diana, stop shoving."

"Oh, yeah, like you care. You're practically on his lap. Moving that stick shift ought to be interesting."

Thankful that he'd taken the time to back in—reverse would have approached contributing to the delinquency of a minor—Dean slid the truck into gear, eased forward, and jerked to a stop at the end of the driveway.

A lime-green hatchback roared past, the driver's gaze turned toward the Hansens' house, whites showing all around the edges of his eyes.

Diana waved jauntily.

"Diana!" Claire reached into the possibilities just in time to keep the small car from going into the ditch as it disappeared around a curve on two wheels. "You know how nervous Mr. Odbeck is, why did you do that?"

"Couldn't resist."

"Try harder. We need to go left, Dean."

"I don't know about nervous," Dean observed as he pulled out, "but he was driving way too fast for the road condition, and he wasn't watching where he was going."

"That's because Diana keeps things interesting around here."

"Interesting how?"

"Strange lights, weird noises, walking trees, geothermal explosions."

"Hey, that geothermal thing only happened once," Diana protested. "And I took care of it almost immediately."

Almost. Dean considered that as he brought the truck up to the speed limit and had a pretty fair idea of why Mr. Odbeck was so nervous. "Is that what you meant when you told Claire she's forgotten what it's like around here?"

"It's not her," Claire told him, "it's the area."

"He asked me."

"Sorry. Turn right at that crossroads up ahead."

"The area?" he prompted, gearing down for the turn and trying unsuccessfully not to think about the warm thigh he couldn't avoid rubbing.

"Is he blushing? Ow!" Diana rubbed her side and shifted until she was up as tight against the passenger side door as she could go. "Mom's right, you're too skinny. That elbow's like a . . . a . . ."

"Hockey stick?"

"The area," Claire said pointedly—Dean realized a little too late that was not a blank he should have helped fill—"is covered by a really thin bit of barrier."

"The fabric of reality is T-shirt material where it should be rubberized canvas. Your mother told me that back in Kingston," he added when the silence insisted he continue. "She told me that's why they're here, her and your father, because stuff seeps."

Diana snickered as she exhaled on the window and began drawing a pattern in the condensation. "Jeez, Claire, and I thought *your* explanations were lame."

"At least I haven't turned the McConnells' fence posts into giant candy canes."

"Oops." She erased the pattern with her sleeve and reached into the possibilities.

Claire squinted into the rearview mirror. "Now they're dancing."

"It's not my fault! It's Christmas. There's so much peace and joy around it's messing everything up!" This time when she reached, she twisted. "There, those are fence posts."

"Definitively," Claire agreed. "You do know you've anchored them in the barysphere?"

"At least they're not dancing."

"Yes, but . . ."

"Why don't you finish telling Dean why closing this site may not be a piece of fruitcake. Not literally fruitcake," she amended, catching sight of Dean's profile. "Although fruitcakes have punched holes through to the dark side in the past."

"You're not helping," Dean pointed out, and turned left following Claire's silent direction. "There's a hole in the T-shirt fabric . . ."

". . . and because the fabric's so thin you can't just pinch the edges together nor will it take anything but the most delicate of patches. It can be tricky, but it's nothing I can't deal with."

Driving left-handed, he caught Claire's fingers and brought them to his lips. "I never doubted you for a moment."

She smiled and rubbed her cheek against the shoulder of his jacket. "And why's that?"

"I've seen you in action."

"Oh, barf." When two pairs of narrowed eyes glanced her way, Diana shrugged. "Austin's not here. Someone had to say it."

"True enough." Claire straightened as Dean murmured an agreement. "Stop there, at the gray brick house."

As Dean brought the truck to a stop, Diana squinted at the mailbox through a sudden swirl of snow. "Giorno."

"You know them?"

"I go to school with a Lena Giorno. She's a year behind me, though. I've never been to her house."

Seat belt unfastened, Claire turned slowly on the seat, feeling the summons pulling at her. "Well, you're about to."

"Mr. Giorno, hi, Merry Christmas. I'm Diana, a friend of Lena's, and this is my sister Claire."

Even standing out of the line of fire, Claire could feel the charm Diana was throwing at the glowering man in the doorway. The air between them practically sparkled, but it didn't seem to be having much effect—the glower never changed, and he remained standing squarely in the doorway as though defending the house against all comers.

"Francis! We can't afford to heat the whole world! Close the door!" Mrs. Giorno's shout carried with it the distinct odor of burned turkey.

"Don't you start!" He turned his head just far enough to bellow his response back over his shoulder. "I'll close it when I'm good and ready to close it! Lena," he said, facing the porch again, "is not going out. Maybe when she's thirty, I'll let her out, but not until. You kids shut up in there!"

The background shrieking changed pitch.

A little worried about all the head swiveling, Diana cranked it up a notch. "We didn't want Lena to come out, Mr. Giorno. We were kind of hoping we could come in and see her."

"I don't . . ."

"Please."

His expression changed so quickly it looked as though his cheeks had melted. "Of course you can come in. Girls like you should not be left standing on the porch unwanted. You're good, nice girls. Good girls. My Lena's a good girl." He sniffed lugubriously and rubbed the palm of one hand over his eyes. "You come in." The now damp hand gestured expansively as he moved out of the way. "You come in, you talk to my girl, and you find out why she

131

should break her father's heart. Come." He squeezed Diana's shoulder as she passed and beckoned to Claire. "Come."

It looked as though a bomb had gone off in the living room and the debris field had spread through the rest of the house. That it was Christmas Day in a house with three children, two teenagers, a cat, and a pair of neurotic gerbils might have been explanation enough another time, but *this time*, neither day nor demographic came close to explaining the level of chaos. The Christmas tree was on its side, half the lights still on, the cat—wearing a smug smile and a half-eaten candy cane stuck to its fur—curled up in the broken branches. Nonfunctioning toys and run-down batteries were scattered throughout, two AAs had been hammered into the drywall of the hall as though someone at the end of their rope had tried every battery in the economy-sized package and these were the last two and they still didn't work. The gas molecule racing around turned out to be the five-year-old with a stripe shaved down the center of his head.

"Lena's downstairs in her room," her father told them, pulling a handkerchief out of his pocket and blowing his nose on the bit that wasn't covered in melted marshmallow Santa. "Go. Talk to her."

Diana glanced at Claire from the corner of her eye. When Claire nodded, she smiled. "Thank you, Mr. Giorno."

"No, thank *you*."

As they started down the stairs, he turned away, hand over his face and shoulders shaking.

"I didn't mean to make him cry," Diana murmured, as the two Keepers picked a careful path down through the mess.

"You didn't. The energy seeping from the site is warping the possibilities. Can't you feel the fine patina of darkness?"

"Yeah, but I figured it was smoke from the turkey. Or maybe the Christmas tree—it seems to be smoldering in spots." As they stepped down onto the painted concrete floor, she looked expectantly toward her sister. "Well?"

There were two bedrooms and a bathroom to their right. Laundry room, furnace room, and wine-making equipment to their left.

Following the Summons, Claire turned right.

The door to the front bedroom was shut. Claire knocked.

"Go away! I *hate* you!"

"Wow." Diana took half a step back. "She really does hate us."

"What do you expect? She's in there with the site. You try," Claire suggested when her second knock brought no response at all.

"Lena? It's me, Diana. From the decorating committee, remember?" She jiggled the knob. The door was locked. "Let me in."

"No!"

It was one of the most definitive "no's" Diana had ever heard, and she'd heard her fair share. "You sure it's in there?"

Claire nodded.

"Then it'll take more than a cheap lock to keep us out." Diana reached into the possibilities. The door came off in her hand. "Okay." She staggered back under its weight. "I didn't mean to do that."

"You never do," Claire sighed, "but that's not important now. Look."

"Oh, man, I knew she was into angels, but this is just too much."

"Not that. Look down."

The hole had opened just off the corner of Lena's bed; a dark, ugly, metaphysical blemish on the pale pink carpet.

Lena lifted a blotchy face from her pillow and glared out into the basement. "Put that door *back*! I am *not* coming out! I don't care *what* my father says!"

"Look, Lena, you don't have to come out. We're not here to . . ." Realizing a little late that she wasn't going to get into the room while holding the door, Diana leaned it against the opposite wall and stepped over the threshold. "We're here for you." Skirting the hole, she circled around to the far side of the bed and sat down. "We want to help."

"You *can't* help me."

As she turned her head toward Diana, Claire came

into the room, knelt by the hole, and used her finger-tip to brush a symbol against the nap of the carpet.

"*No one* can help me," Lena continued, rubbing her nose on the back of her hand. "My father took my angel away!"

Wondering how she could tell there was an angel missing given the number remaining in the room, Diana patted her shoulder in a comforting sort of a way. "Well, you've got more . . ."

"No! He was a *real* angel. He came out of the light last night when I lit my candle! And I don't *care* if you believe me."

"I believe you. Did your father happen to hit this angel?" Claire asked in such a matter-of-fact tone that Diana swiveled around on the bed to stare at her.

"Yes. He just *barged* in like he does, all mad, and when he saw him, he like totally lost it and he hit him and took him away, and I am *never* speaking to him again."

"Where did your father take the angel, Lena?"

"To the priest! I so totally *hate* him!"

"The priest or your father?"

"*Both* of them!"

"Diana." Bending, Claire traced another symbol, then hurriedly erased it as a bit of the carpet melted. "I think Lena would feel better if she got some sleep."

"No! I don't *want* to . . ."

Diana adjusted Lena's head on the pillow, then turned back to her sister. "Are you suggesting that Lena actually got visited by a real angel?"

"I'm not suggesting anything. You heard her: a Bystander can't lie to a Keeper."

"But they can lie to themselves. Lena once honestly believed she saw an image of Leonardo Di Caprio in a bowl of butterscotch pudding, throwing the female half of the ninth grade into hysterics for the remainder of lunch."

"Really?"

Diana nodded. "It wasn't pretty."

"Well, this time she isn't lying to anyone, herself or us." Claire sat back on her heels and waved a hand around the room. "There's distinct residue under the darkness. It's obvious once you know to check for it."

"Oh, yeah. Obvious angel residue. That's something you don't hear everyday."

"Diana, this is serious."

"Okay, I'm being serious." Picking up the Backstreet Boys mug, she made a face and put it down again. "Question is, why would an angel appear to Lena? Obsession isn't enough to open the possibilities that wide. You think it was sent with a message?"

"Can't have or it would have vanished once the message was delivered, and she said that her father took it away."

"Maybe it got taken away before the message got delivered."

"No, it would never have allowed that to happen. A message from the light gets delivered, regardless. An angry father would've stood about as much chance facing down a determined angel as he would have facing down a runaway transport with pretty much the same result. Here's a better question: how could the possibilities have opened that wide without me noticing?"

"That's easy. If they opened last night, you were busy." Eyes narrowed, Diana grinned suddenly. "Are you blushing?"

"No." Claire didn't even try to make the denial sound convincing. Given the heat of her cheeks, there didn't seem to be much point. "So why didn't you notice?"

"Beats me. Must've gotten lost in that whole peace-and-joy stuff. You know what it's like around this time of the year."

"True enough."

"And since it was from the upper end of things, it's not really our problem anyway."

"True again." She traced a third symbol, and the noise level upstairs began to fall off. "That's put a temporary cover over the site, but I'm going to need details to actually seal it."

"Like?"

"Like why would a basically decent man take a swing at a messenger of the light."

"Is that what opened the hole?"

"Diana, Mr. Giorno punched an angel; what do you think?"

"Just checking." Leaning forward, Diana brushed a bit of thick, dark hair back off of Lena's face and softly called her name. "Don't wake up," she instructed when the sleeping girl began to stir, "just tell me, without getting angry, why your father hit the angel."

"He was naked."

"Your father?" Given the amount of hair curling up through the opening of Mr. Giorno's collar and right down to his knuckles, that was an image Diana quickly banished.

"Not my father. The angel."

"The angel was naked?"

"Uh-huh." She smiled slightly. "I saw his thing."

"Lena, angels don't have things."

"I know *that*." Even asleep she managed the emphasis. "But he did. I think . . ." Her brow furrowed. "I think my father gave it to him. It was big."

"And your basis of comparison would be?"

"Diana!"

Without turning, she flapped a hand at her sister to shut off further protests. "You can get back to me later on that, Lena. Right now, you drift off again and I'll call you if I need you."

"O . . ." A long sigh. ". . . kay."

After checking to see that she'd gone deep again, Diana stood and spread her arms triumphantly, modifying the gesture somewhat to catch the cherub she'd knocked off a shelf. "Tah dah. Her father burst into her room as Lena's obsession was manifesting a naked angel, jumped to the fatherly conclusion, and slugged the guy."

Claire rolled her eyes and added a little more power as the cover shifted. "Only a teenager would manifest a naked angel."

"Get over it. You manifested a naked Dean all last night."

"That's not the . . ."

"And ignored a Summons—this Summons—while you were doing it. And I'm not saying I wouldn't have done the same thing under similar circumstances. All I'm saying is that you have no cause to be pointing the finger at someone else's hormones."

After a long moment, during which several high-pitched voices could be heard insisting that they hadn't touched the gravy and they didn't know what was floating in it, Claire sighed. "Okay. You have a point. And since he might have had clothing had things not been interrupted and since her father seems to have added the . . . uh . . . thing . . ."

Diana snorted. "You know, Claire, if you're playing with one, you really should be able to name it."

This was more than Claire could take from a sister ten years younger. "Good," she snapped, "because I was thinking of calling it Floyd!" She regretted the words the moment they left her mouth and snapped her teeth closed just a little too late to catch them. From the way Diana's eyes lit up, she knew she'd be paying for that comment for the rest of her natural life. And possibly longer. "Let's just get back to work," she suggested sharply, her tone a preemptive strike. "I'll seal this. You clear the hatred out of your friend."

"Sure."

"Diana . . ."

"Don't worry, I'll be careful."

"That wasn't . . ." When Diana lifted an eyebrow in exact mimicry of Claire's best sardonic expression, Claire had to laugh, in spite of what would be inevitable later. ". . . what I meant, as you very well knew."

"Yeah. But I'll still be careful." She sat back down on the edge of the bed and gently turned Lena's face toward her. "Although the urge to do something about her decorating is extreme."

". . . but did you ever stop to think that perhaps they didn't want quite so many chestnuts in the stuffing?" Claire asked as they picked their way up the icy front path to the truck.

Diana shrugged. "Beats what was in there before I fixed it. And *that*, by the way, is why you should never keep the litter box in the kitchen."

Things were back to normal in the Giorno household. Tree and dinner had been restored, gifts repaired, the cat appeased, and family tensions resolved.

The site it had involved considerably more cleanup than a Keeper would normally perform, but—as Diana pointed out just before the cat knocked the tree over again with no help at all from the dark possibilities—it *was* Christmas.

Dean jerked awake when Claire opened the passenger door. "Everything fixed, then?"

"Everything we could fix," she acknowledged as she kicked the snow off her boots and slid over beside him. "Sorry it took so long."

"That's all right. Your thing kept the truck warm."

"Her thing?" Diana snickered, climbing in. "Got a name for it?"

"Ignore her," Claire advised, hoping Dean would assume her ears were red from the cold.

From the look in his eyes, he didn't.

He glanced at Diana, then back at her, but only said, "Where to now?"

"Back to pick up our stuff and then south, we've got another Summons."

"Another Summons?" Martha Hansen set the roasting pan on the stove top and lifted an indignant Austin down off the counter before she turned to face her daughters. "Do you think it concerns the angel?"

"Unlikely. Mr. Giorno took him to Father Harris over at St. Patrick's, so that should be the last we see of him."

"Him?"

Claire shot a look at Diana, saw she had a mouthful of dill pickle, and reluctantly continued. "Apparently, he somehow acquired gender during the manifestation."

"Gender?"

Diana swallowed and snickered. "Means just what you think, Mom."

"Oh, the poor boy! He must be so confused."

"Confused? Surprised maybe," Diana allowed, perching on the corner of the kitchen table and tossing a hot roll from hand to hand. "But it's not like they're that difficult to operate. It's pretty much point and click." She glanced around the suddenly silent kitchen. "You know, metaphorically speaking. Okay," she sighed, "they don't actually click, but you've got to admit they point." Catching her parents exchanging a meaningful look over the mashed potatoes, she tossed the roll to Dean and spread her hands. "What?"

"We'll talk later," Martha said tightly. "Right now," she turned to Claire and gathered her into her arms, "you'd better get going."

Austin's head snapped up from where he was investigating a bit of spilled grease. "Excuse me? I have been waiting five hours for that bird to come out of the oven; that Summons can just wait for twenty more minutes."

"We don't know how long it's been waiting already," Claire reminded him as she crossed the kitchen to hug her father. "Things got a little stacked up, remember?"

"So I should suffer?"

Martha bent and stroked his head. "Don't worry, I'll pack up a box of food while Claire and Dean are getting their things together."

"You know that this is your second Summons this morning," Diana complained, sliding to her feet as Claire stopped in front of her. "You've had two today and I've had none. How unfair is that?"

"You're not on active duty yet."

"But I'm on vacation. And I'm so available."

"And if something opens up that's serious enough to need you, you'll be Summoned. Just like you were when I needed you in Kingston." Reaching out, Claire touched her sister on the cheek. "Everything'll change once school's over in June. I know it's hard when there's so many more important things you feel you should be doing, but you'll get through it. I did."

"Don't patronize me." The answering shove rocked Claire on her feet. "And don't forget your presents. And be careful. And let Dean help. Really help, not just hang around and pick up after you."

"I will."

"I doubt it."

"I'll try."

"Good enough." She stepped back. "Well; go."

About to turn for the door, Dean found himself pulled into a motherly embrace. He hesitated for a moment, then he returned it and was curiously reluctant to let go when Martha pulled away. Although his mother had died when he was a baby, he'd always felt her love in his life. He'd had no memory of ever feeling her arms, though. Until now.

As though she could sense his reluctance, Martha reached up and touched his cheek. "I'm very glad that you and Claire have found each other, Dean McIssac. You're a good man; strong, steady . . ."

"Mom," Diana interrupted, sitting back on the edge of the table and picking up another roll, "Claire's trying to answer a Summons. This isn't the time to write Dean's eulogy."

He shot a questioning glance at the younger Keeper. "Eulogy?"

"You'll be fine." Martha patted his arm.

"I know." He shifted his weight. "I just wondered what eulogy meant."

"Obituary."

"Oh."

She patted his arm again. "You'll be fine."

"Sure."

"As long as he's ready for what he's dealing with," John Hansen reflected, putting down the carving knife and wiping his fingers on a dish towel.

One hand still outstretched and hovering over Dean's sleeve, Martha turned toward her husband. "Won't it be what he's *been* dealing with?"

"That's not a certainty. Thing's have changed between them. Probably for the better, but he'll be in some unusual positions for a Bystander."

Dean's ears were suddenly so hot he was afraid they'd ignited. Unusual positions? How had Claire's father found out about . . . then he realized he'd misunderstood.

"Well, they're not going to run into anything he can't handle," Martha declared. "I can't imagine anything worse than what he's already faced in the Elysian Fields Guest House."

"I can."

"Austin, be quiet." Claire bent, scooped up the cat, and handed him to Dean.

"Hey! Support the back legs!" Hooking his front claws into a flannel collar, Austin heaved himself into a more comfortable position as Dean adjusted his grip. "I'm old. I don't dangle."

"Sorry."

"Dangling! Honestly."

Claire smoothed the ridge of fur along his spine. "Let it go, Austin."

"He was holding a roll. I have crumbs in my tail."

"I'll brush them out as soon as we're on the road." She hooked two fingers in behind the faded blue of Dean's waistband and tugged him toward the door. "Say good-bye, Dean."

"Good-bye, Dean."

At least he made the cat laugh.

It isn't fair. Diana ran the vacuum at the bits of broken glass and felt a sulky satisfaction as Laa Laa and Saint Matthew disappeared. *I should be out changing the world like Claire—not going to stupid school. Stupid, useless waste of time.* A swath of clean carpet appeared, bisecting Jesus and Po. *I'm so tired of Claire getting to do everything first.* Got to get her ears pierced first, got to graduate from high school first, got to travel to a tropical island and narrowly avoid having the entire place follow Atlantis to the bottom first. *No, wait, that was me.* And in the end, the whole thing had been nothing more than a damp misunderstanding.

The head of the vacuum cleaner was too broad to reach the last few pieces of glass. Realizing that she needed an attachment, Diana bounced it impotently against the hearth instead. *My life sucks. Claire gets a Summons. Lena gets an angel. What do I get? A bunch of burst lights.*

And let's not forget Claire also gets Dean. And Floyd. Snickering to herself, she started on Dipsy and St. Peter. *A memorable Christmas Eve for all three of them. Which may not be what I want from life, it's just . . .*

. . . just . . .

Something lingered at the edge of memory, almost but not quite dredged up by her train of thought. Absently running the vacuum over the same bit of carpet, she started working back.

Christmas Eve.

Claire gets Dean.

Burst lights.

Lena gets angel.

She stepped on the switch and shut the vacuum

off and could just barely hear Dean's truck starting up over the sudden pounding of her heart.

Her mother hurried into the front hall as she yanked open the door. "If you're going out to the truck, take this with you."

The smell of turkey rising from the box made questions about contents redundant. She snatched it up without breaking stride.

"Diana, your boots!"

"No time! I've got to catch Claire before she leaves." As Claire would say, Keepers didn't keep vital information from other Keepers. Which was not to say that Diana ever actually listened to what Claire said or had any intention of telling her what had actually happened to that *Best of John Denver* CD. Box tucked under one arm, she sprinted forward.

"Yes!" Austin jumped up onto the top of the seat where he had an unimpeded view through the back window. "Here comes the food!"

Claire twisted around until she could see Diana racing down the front path. "How can you tell what she's carrying from here?"

"I'm a cat."

A vein began throbbing on Claire's forehead. "Why do I even ask?"

Wondering that himself, Dean rolled down the

window as Diana hit an icy patch and slid to a sudden impact against his door.

"I know where the angel came from," she announced before anyone in the truck could speak. "I was right, Lena's obsessions didn't open the possibilities, and I was also right about you being distracted."

"What are you talking about?"

Diana grinned, passed the box to Dean, and poked the forefinger on her right hand through a circle made by the thumb and forefinger on her left. "You opened the hole and Lena's desire to see an angel was strong enough to define what came through."

"No." Claire shook her head. "Even if we did open the possibilities . . ."

"You did."

She looked down at the cat. "Excuse me?"

"Way open. Way, way open." He scratched his shoulder. "It was pretty impressive actually."

"So much for all those safe sex lectures, eh?"

"Get stuffed. And stop making that disgusting gesture. It wasn't like that."

"Was it like this?" Diana barely had time to change the position of her fingers before Dean reached out and enclosed both her hands in one of his.

"No," he said quietly, ears scarlet. "It wasn't like that either."

Suddenly feeling both embarrassed and mean and not much liking the feeling, Diana pulled free. Teasing Dean was somehow not the same as teasing

Claire. *But I'm not apologizing. I mean, if he can't take a joke . . .* "Look, I saw it, too, what Austin saw, but I never connected it with Lena because that kind of thing always dissipates after, giving everyone in the immediate area a happy."

"It should have dissipated," Claire agreed. Her eyes narrowed as she read her sister's body language. "Why didn't it?"

"My bad. Sort of."

"Sort of?"

"Okay, jeez. Totally. I made this decoration for the school's Christmas dance that would gather up all the good feelings and spit them back out intensified to make more good feelings, and I think I made the attraction too strong . . ."

"Quel surprise," Austin muttered.

". . . and it pulled in the light, giving it sort of a proto-form that kept it together until it got to Lena."

"Where it became an angel." Claire sighed. "Well, it could have been worse. He probably returned to the light as soon as his head cleared from that punch."

"You think?"

"All the background information we have suggests angels can come and go through the barrier as they please. If you were him and you'd had the welcome he'd had, wouldn't you go back where you came from? Now, as nice as it is to have those questions answered," she continued when Diana nodded, "the hole created by reaction to the angel's appearance has been sealed, and I've got other work to do."

"But . . ."

"Merry Christmas, and I'll try to stay in touch."

"We really made an angel, then?" Dean asked as he turned out onto the road.

"In a manner of speaking, yes."

"Seems a little . . ."

"Light on the sausage stuffing." Austin lifted his head out of the box, his eye gleaming indignantly. "there's barely enough here for two people, let alone three."

"First of all, you're not a people, you're a cat." Sliding one hand under his chest, Claire lifted him onto her lap. "Second, if you've stuck your litter-poo paw in the sweet potatoes, I *will* hurt you. Third . . ." She stroked a finger down the back of Dean's thigh. ". . . I think we could've made an angel without Diana's or Lena's help."

It took him a moment, then he grinned, caught up her hand, and brought it to his lips. "Really?"

"Really."

"Are you two planning on continuing this sort of behavior?" Austin demanded from Claire's lap. "Because I'm old, you know, and I don't think my insulin levels are up to it."

Claire pulled her hand away from Dean's mouth

and smoothed down a lifted line of fur. "Someone's jealous."

"Of him?" The cat snorted and dropped his head down on his paws. "Oh, please."

"You sure?"

"Cats don't get jealous."

"Really?"

"They get even."

"Austin."

"I'm kidding."

Diana stood in the driveway until Dean's truck disappeared from view, and then walked back to the house kicking at clumps of snow.

. . . as nice as it is to have those questions answered . . .

Nice.

There were times when she just wanted to take Claire by the ears and shake loose that more-Keeper-than-thou attitude of hers.

She's always thought the sun shines out of her butt . . .

Having carefully negotiated a tight curve, Dean glanced over at Claire and smiled. He loved the way the light shone up and through the chestnut highlights in her hair, how it made her eyes seem dark and mysterious, how it. . . . *Hang on.* "Where's that light coming from?"

Claire sighed. "Just drive."

SIX

A little over an hour after leaving the Hansen house, Dean turned off York Street and stopped the truck in the parking lot of the London bus terminal. "Here, then?"

"Here."

"Inside?"

"No, over there." She pointed to a bus parked at the back of the lot, barely visible between the blowing snow and the fading daylight.

Dean put the truck in gear and moved slowly forward. Given the holiday, the terminal hadn't seen a lot of traffic, so the parking lot, unplowed since morning, lay under a mostly unbroken blanket of snow. About three meters from the bus, he felt the steering wheel jerk in his hand and then begin to spin with that horrible, loose feeling that could only mean all four tires had no traction at all. He fought the skid, thought he had it, lost it again, and shouted, "Brace for impact!" just as the truck stopped with its passenger door a mere two inches from the front fender of the bus.

"Brace for impact?" Austin asked, removing his claws from Claire's jeans. "Do you even know *how* to swear?"

Heart pounding, Dean shut off the engine. "What good would swearing do?"

"Since you have to ask, probably none at . . . hey! What did I say earlier about dangling?" he demanded as Claire lifted him off her lap.

"Sorry." Brow furrowed, she rolled down her window and peered at the bus fender.

"Excuse me! Old cat in a draft!"

"Austin, be quiet. Dean, I'm going to have to get out your side." She rolled up the window and reached under the cat to undo her seat belt. "We're so close to the hole, I'm not sure you can safely move the truck. We've got a cascade going on here," she added, sliding across, under the steering wheel, and out into the parking lot. As Dean struggled to hold the door against the wind, she leaned back into the cab. "Are you coming?"

"Is it summer yet?"

An icy wind blew pellets of snow down under her collar. "Not exactly."

Austin settled down, folding his front paws under his ruff. "Then I'm staying inside."

"All right. I'll reset the possibilities to keep you warm."

"Thank you. Although if you don't close that door," he added pointedly, "it won't make much difference."

Claire stepped back and nodded to Dean who, in spite of the wind, managed to close the door without slamming it. "You know anyone else would've just let it go."

"I'm not anyone else."

He had an arm on either side of her, gloved hands braced against the truck, and his smile was, if not suggestive, open to suggestion. Since they'd blocked the hole, effectively rendering it harmless, Claire figured it couldn't hurt to take a short break. Besides, Austin was locked away behind glass and steel, making it too good an opportunity to miss.

When they pulled apart a moment later, an eight-meter circle of parking lot had been cleared of snow. The asphalt directly underfoot steamed gently.

"Is that going to happen every time?" Dean asked a little shakily, following Claire around to the bus.

"I honestly don't know." Her lips felt bruised and all her clothing felt way too tight. "How about we stop for the night once I get this hole closed?"

Dean glanced at his watch. "It's ten after four."

"It's getting dark."

He looked up at the sky and down at Claire. "I saw a hotel just up the road."

"So did I." Dropping to her knees by the bus fender, she pulled off her glove and, holding a finger an inch or so off the chrome, traced a triple gouge in the metal

"That's it, then?" Dean asked behind her. "It's some small."

"A cascade doesn't have to be very big. The driver probably clipped a car on the way out of the parking lot—because clipping a moving car would have caused an actual accident—didn't stop, opened a hole, and flashed nasty possibilities all hither and yon on the bus route, probably causing a number of minor fender benders all day, which kept the hole from closing. Hence, cascade. It's kind of like if every one of those minor fender benders had picked off the scab."

Dean winced. "I wasn't after asking. But how do you know the driver didn't stop?"

"Driver stops, no hole." Reaching into the possibilities, she pressed her thumb hard against one end of the first gouge. The metal rippled. The gouge disappeared. Twice more and the hole was closed. "I expect I'll be closing a few holes this thing inspired," she said as Dean helped her straighten up. "Sign says London-Toronto but since we're still in London, it was clearly London-Toronto and back." Pulling her glove on, she noticed a new glow of adoration in his expression. "What?"

"You've never mentioned you do bodywork."

"I can rustproof, too."

"You can?"

She grinned up at him. "No, sorry. I just wanted to see your eyes light . . . Oh!"

"New Summons?"

"No . . ."

"No?"

"No. It's something else. Something close."

"So much for quitting early." He was disappointed, of course, but the cold had pretty much taken care of the actual incentive.

"No." Claire started across the parking lot. "*Really* close."

When she reached the sidewalk, she paused and turned right. "Whatever it is, it's inside the bus terminal."

The door was locked. The sign said, "TERMINAL CLOSES 4PM CHRISTMAS DAY."

"I guess that's it until tomorrow, then." Dean polished a few fingerprints off the glass and turned away. "Look, there's the hotel." A little confused, he watched Claire pull off her glove—not the reaction he'd been expecting. "What?"

"I guess this has never come up . . ." Reaching into the possibilities, she opened the door.

"Claire! That's breaking and entering!"

"I didn't break, so it's just entering." She grabbed two handfuls of his coat and shoved him inside. "Move. Life is so much easier if we don't have to explain to Bystanders."

"But this is illegal!" he protested as the door closed

behind them. When she stepped forward without answering, he grabbed her arm. "The mat!"

She jerked back and looked down. "What?"

"Wipe your feet."

Claire considered a couple of possible responses. Then she wiped her feet.

Half a dozen paces inside the terminal, she dropped down to one knee and pressed the spread fingers of her right hand against the tiles. "This isn't good."

"I'd say it's some disgusting," Dean growled, kneeling beside her. "How can anyone leave their floors in this condition."

"Dean . . ."

"Sorry. I expect you found something else that isn't good?"

Claire lifted her hand. The pads of her fingers sparkled. "Angel residue."

"Merry Christmas. You've reached the Hansen residence. No one feels like taking your call, so at the beep . . ."

"Not now, Diana, we've got a problem. I'm at a pay phone in the London bus terminal, and you'll never guess what I've found."

Phone jammed between ear and shoulder, Diana slid a platter of leftover turkey into the fridge. "Buses?"

"Angel residue."

"That would've been my next guess."

"Right. It seems like Lena's visitor hasn't gone home."

"Unless he's taking the bus." She reached into the possibilities, opened a pocket on the second shelf, and shoved in the cranberry sauce, half a bowl of sweet potatoes, and an old margarine container now full of gravy. "You know, kind of a 'this bus is bound for glory' thing. Say, how come you're not using the cell phone you got for Christmas? No long distance charges and the battery's good until the end of days. When you're standing at the start of the Apocalypse, you'll still have enough juice to call 911."

"And tell them what?"

"I dunno. Run?"

"I'm not using the cell phone because I left it in the truck. And I need you to go talk to Father Harris at St. Pat's. He's the last person who we know saw the angel. Maybe he knows where it's—he's—headed. I've got another Summons on the way out of town, and since I just closed a cascade, I expect to have a whole string of them all the way to Toronto, so I'll call you once we're settled for the night."

"No need. I'll e-mail anything I find out." As her sister started to protect, Diana rolled her eyes. "Claire, let's make an effort to join the twentieth century before we're too far into the twenty-first, okay? Later."

Hanging up and heading for her coat and boots,

she wondered what it was that made Keepers—herself excluded, of course—so resistant to technology. "Only took them a hundred years to get the hang of the telephone," she muttered, digging for mittens. "And Austin's probably more comfortable with it than Claire is. . . ."

"Austin, what are you doing with that phone?"

"Nothing."

"What do you mean, nothing?" Claire demanded as she slid back into the truck.

"I mean that there isn't a Chinese food place in the city that'll deliver to a parking lot."

After a last-minute discussion concerning the dishes and how they weren't being done, Diana walked out to the road, flagged down a conveniently passing neighbor, and got a ride into Lucan. Fifteen minutes later, still vehemently apologizing for the results of the sudden stop, she got out at St. Patrick's and hurried up the shoveled walk to the priest's house, staying as far from the yellow brick church as possible. Strange things happened when Keepers went into churches and, in an age when Broadway show tunes coming from the mouths of stained-glass apostles weren't considered so much miraculous as irritating, Diana felt it was safest not to tempt fate—again.

Strangely, Protestant Churches were safer, although locals still talked about the Friendship United bake sale when four-and-twenty blackbirds were found baked into three different pies. Claire, who'd been fifteen and already an adult to Diana's five-year-old eyes, had been both horrified and embarrassed, but Diana remembered their mother as being rather philosophical about the whole thing. There were, after all, any number of nursery rhymes that would've been worse. *Although not for the blackbirds,* she reflected, carefully stepping over a large crack in the sidewalk.

There were no synagogues or mosques in the immediate area and by the time she started being Summoned away, she was old enough to understand why she had to keep her distance. The incident at that Shinto shrine had been an unfortunate accident.

Okay, two unfortunate accidents, she amended climbing the steps to the front door. *Although I still say if you don't actually want your prayers answered, you shouldn't . . .* "Merry Christmas, Mrs. Verner. Is Father Harris in?"

The priest's housekeeper frowned, as though recognition would be assisted by the knitting of her prominent brows. "Is it important? His Christmas dinner is almost ready."

"We ate earlier."

"He didn't."

"I only need a few minutes."

"I don't think . . ."

A tweak of the possibilities.

". . . that vill be a problem." The heels of her sensible shoes clicked together. "Come in. Vait in his office, I vill go get him. You haf an emergency. You need his help. How can he sit and do nothing vhen he is needed? I vill pull him from his chair if I must. Pull him from his chair and drag him back here to you." She didn't quite salute.

A little too much tweak, Diana reflected as the housekeeper turned on one heel and marched away. She made a slight adjustment before Mrs. Verner decided to invade Poland.

The small, dark-paneled, book-lined office came with a claustrophobic feeling that was equally the fault of its size, the faux gothic decorating, and the number of faded leather-bound books. Diana couldn't decide if the painting over the desk—a three-legged figure standing on multicolored waves against an almost painfully green background—made the room seem smaller or let in the only light. Or both.

"It's Saint Patrick banishing the snakes from Ireland," announced a quiet voice behind her. "It was painted by one of my parishioners."

"Probably one who donated beacoup de cash to the rebuilding fund," Diana observed as she turned.

Father Harris took an involuntary step back, the sudden memory of St. Jerome belting out "Everything's Coming up Roses" propelling his feet. He didn't know why he was thinking about stained-glass and show tunes, but for a great many reasons he couldn't maintain a grip on, he was quite certain he needed a drink.

Diana smiled at him reassuringly. "Lena Giorno tells me her father brought an angel to you last night."

"A young man who *thought* he was an angel," the priest corrected. He was fairly certain the girl's smile was supposed to be reassuring, but it was making him a little nervous.

"*You* don't think he's an angel?"

"I very much doubt an angel would appear in such a way in the bedroom of a teenager girl."

"You mean naked?"

"That's hardly a suitable topic for you and me to discuss." Taking a deep breath, he folded his arms and gave her the best "stern authority figure" glare he could manage under the circumstances. "And now, young lady, if you don't mind my asking, what is your name and what is your connection to young Samuel?"

Diana's smile broadened. "Samuel," she repeated under her breath. "Should've known better than to give out his name." Refocusing on Father Harris—whose expression had slipped closer to "confused elder trying to make sense of the young and failing miserably"—she asked, "Did he stay here last night?"

"Yes, but he was gone this morning. Now, see here young lady . . ."

"May I *please* see where he slept?"

About to demand that she answer his earlier question concerning who she was and what she wanted, Father Harris found himself stepping back into the foyer and leading the way up the stairs.

The alleged angel had slept in a small room at the end of the hall. It held a single bed, a bedside table, a dresser, and what was probably another picture of Saint Patrick. This one was a poster, stuck to the wall with those little balls of blue sticky stuff that invariably soaked oil through the paper. The elderly saint had only two legs in this picture, was wearing church vestments, and was, once again, banishing snakes.

"I don't know what you thought you'd find." The priest folded his arms, determined to make a stand. This was his house and . . .

A phone rang.

Downstairs.

It continued to ring. And ring.

"*Please*, don't mind me," Diana told him. "I'll just stay up here a moment longer."

He was halfway back to his office before he wondered why Mrs. Verner hadn't answered the phone.

Diana reached into the possibilities as she stepped up to the poster.

The saint blinked twice and focused on her face. "And what'll it be, then, Keeper?"

"I need some information about the guy who stayed here last night."

The lines across the saint's forehead deepened. "Oh, and you haven't noticed that I'm up to my ankles in snakes here; what is it that makes you think I was paying any attention?"

"Well, I . . ."

"You wouldn't be having a beer on you, would you?" A short but powerful kick knocked a snake right out of the picture.

"Why would a saint want a beer?"

"I'm an Irish saint, and you can pardon me for being a stereotype, but I was originally painted five hundred years ago and I'm a wee bit dry. Now, what was your question again?"

"Do you know where the guy who stayed here last night went when he left this morning?"

"The angel?"

"Yes."

"I have no idea. But I'm telling you, Keeper, there was something funny about that boy." He shook his head in disgust, halo wobbling a bit with the motion. "Who ever heard of a confused angel, eh? In my day, angels had no emotions, they did what they were sent down to do and then they went home. Is this like to be some New Age thing?"

"I don't know."

Another snake ventured too close and was punted off to the left. "There's going to be trouble, you mark my words. An angel without a purpose is like a . . . a . . ."

"A religion with no connection to the real world?"

"Who asked you?"

"Did he use the bed?"

"Aye, he laid himself down although I can't say I know why since he doesn't have to sleep. Good old-fashioned angels, they didn't lay down. Have you heard he's got himself a . . ." His hand pumped the air by his crotch. . . .

. . . which wasn't a gesture Diana thought she'd ever see a saint make. "I heard."

"And what's the idea behind that, I ask you? You listen to me, Keeper; angels today, they have no . . ."

Figuring she couldn't really be rude to a metaphysical construct, Diana cut him off in mid rant. It looked like he was winding up for another kick, and she was starting to feel a little sorry for the snakes.

The hand of Mrs. Verner was apparent in the precision of the bed making—sheets and blankets tucked so tightly in they disdained a mere bouncing of quarters and were ready instead to host a touring company of *Riverdance*. Not expecting much, Diana checked for anything that might have been left behind—it was, after all, a day when miracles had already happened. Skimming the surface with her palm, she drew a two-toned hair from under the edge of the pillow but nothing else.

"Have you finished?"

The hair went into her pocket as she turned toward the priest. "Yes. Thank you. He didn't tell you where he was heading?"

"He didn't tell me he was going to leave," Father Harris answered shortly. At the bottom of the stairs he turned to face her. "I want you to know that if you kids are mixed up in drugs . . ."

"Drugs?"

"Yes, drugs. Nothing that boy said last night made any sense."

"Unless everything he said was the truth." Widening her eyes and cocking her head to one side, Diana gazed up at the priest. "Don't you believe in angels, Father Harris?"

"Angels?"

"Yes."

"His Holiness the Pope has argued for the existence of angelic spirits, and therefore the official position of the Catholic Church is that they are insubstantial."

"Okay. And you personally?"

"I, personally, remain uncertain. However," he continued, cutting off her incipient protest with an upraised finger, "I am sure that young Samuel was, and is, no angel."

"Why?"

"He had . . ." The priest's gesture was considerably less explicit than the saint's.

"An upset stomach? A basketball?"

"GENITALIA!"

Which pretty much ended the conversation.

Standing on the porch, Diana watched her breath plume out and came to a decision.

In the church, St. Margaret began singing "Climb Every Mountain."

"Uh, Claire, your head's kind of . . ."

"Pointy and striped? Don't worry, it's just hat head." She tossed the toque behind the seat and ran her fingers up through her hair, dislodging most of the red and white. "When Diana was ten, she decided to make everyone's Christmas present and this was mine. I know it looks dorky, but it's really warm and it's getting cold out there."

"Getting cold?" Austin pressed against Dean's thigh and glared up at her. "Getting? I'm warning you, don't touch me again with any part of your body or any one of your garments."

"Look, I'm very sorry that the edge of my jacket brushed against your ear."

"The frozen edge of your jacket." He flicked the ear in question. "And I accept your apology only because I seem to be getting some feeling back."

"Did you get the hole closed okay?" Dean asked as Claire fastened her seat belt. He told himself he watched only to be sure she was secured before he began driving, that it had nothing to do with the way the belt pressed the fabric down between her breasts. Unfortunately, he was a terrible liar and he didn't believe himself for a moment.

"No problems. It looked like one of those big off-road vehicles actually went off the road, and the driver had no idea of how to use the four-wheel drive because he'd only bought the car to prove his was bigger."

"And you could tell *that* from the hole?"

She flashed him a grin. "I extrapolated a little, there really wasn't much there. I probably only got Summoned because it was on the shoulder of a major highway and could have caused accidents. And, of course, the more accidents it caused, the bigger it'd get. You know."

He didn't, but he was beginning to get the idea. Shifting into first, he pulled carefully back out onto the 401. "Can I ask you something?"

"Seven. But none of them meant anything to her."

"Austin!"

"And Jacques was dead, so maybe he shouldn't . . ."

Claire grabbed a piece of turkey out of the box behind the seat and stuffed it in the cat's mouth.

"That wasn't actually the question," Dean admitted.

"And it certainly wasn't the answer." It was almost dark, and the dashboard lights left Dean's face in shadow. She wished she knew what he was thinking. She could know what he was thinking, if she asked in the right way. She only had to say, "*Please* tell me what you're thinking, Dean."

It slipped out before she could stop it.

"The headlights look a little dim; I'd better clean them next time we stop."

That was it?

"And, Claire? Don't do that."

"That? Oh. Right. Sorry. It's just . . ."

"You're used to having your own way with Bystanders."

"Sort of."

"Sort of?"

"Okay, yes." She slumped down in the seat. "So what was your question?"

"How could Lena create an angel? I thought angels just were."

"The light just is, but where angels are concerned, you can't separate the observer from the observed. Every angel ever reported has been shaped by the person doing the reporting—by what they believe, by what they need. If you need an angel to be grand and glorious, it is. Or warm and comforting. Or any other combination of adjectives. Wise and wonderful. Bright and beautiful. Great and small . . ."

"At the same time?"

"Probably not. Thing is, they usually deliver the message they were sent with and disappear."

"Message?"

"Oh, you know: Be nice to each other. Fear not, there is a supreme good and it hasn't forgotten you. Don't cross that bridge. Stop the train."

"Feed the cat." He looked up to see both Claire and Dean staring down at him. "Hey, it could happen."

"Anyway," Claire continued as Dean turned his attention back to the road, "message delivered, the angel goes home. This one seems to be hanging around."

"Why?"

"No message," Austin told them, climbing onto Claire's lap. "You two opened wide the possibilities, Diana made possible probable, and her little friend defined it—but it has no actual reason for being here. It's going to be looking for a reason." He pushed Claire's thigh muscles into a more comfortable shape. "But let's look at the bright side. At least she isn't Jewish, and it isn't Hanukkah. Old Testament angels were usually armed with flaming swords."

"I'd rather have flaming swords," Claire sighed. "It'd be easier to find. Given the stuff Lena had in her bedroom, we're probably talking a New Age kind of angel; human appearing, frighteningly powerful, smug and sweetly sanctimonious busybody."

"Kind of like a jed . . ."

Her palm covered the cat's mouth. "We don't have enough problems?" she demanded. "You want to add trademark infringement?"

"What I don't understand," Dean interjected before someone lost a finger, "is how an angel can be a bad thing."

"This kind of angel isn't, not in and of itself— ignoring for the moment the way they always think they know what's best for perfect strangers." She paused, and when it became apparent Austin was not going to add a comment, went on. "But I can't help thinking that much good walking around in one solid clump is well, bad."

"Good is bad?"

"Metaphorically speaking."

"And a remarkably inept metaphor it is, too," Austin sighed.

They drove in silence for a few minutes, then Dean said, "So what do we do?"

"We hope Father Harris tells Diana where the angel went and that he went with a purpose so that, purpose fulfilled, he'll go home. If not, we hope someone convinces him to go home before . . ."

"Before what?"

"I don't know." She stroked Austin's back and stared out at a set of headlights approaching on the other side of the median. "But I can't shake the feeling that something's about to go very, very wrong."

* * *

The darkness that had been seeping through the tiny hole in the woods behind J. Henry and Sons

Auto Repair since just before midnight Christmas
Eve struggled to keep itself together. While adding
a constant stream of low-grade evil to the world
might have been an admirable end result in times
past, this time, it had a plan. It didn't know patience,
patience being a virtue, but it did know that rushing
things now would only bring disaster—which it
wasn't actually against as long as it was the stimulant
rather than the recipient. Had anyone suggested it
was being subtle, it would have been appalled.
Sneaky, however, it would cop to.

It had been maintaining this isolated little hole for
some time, carefully, without changing anything
about it, unable to use it but keeping it open when
it might have sealed on its own—just in case. The
hole was too small to Summon a Keeper, and because
it was in the woods behind a closed garage outside
a small town no one ever came to on a road that
didn't actually go anywhere, it was unlikely that either Keeper or Cousin would ever stumble over it
by accident.

When the other end of the possibilities had opened
and shifted the balance so dramatically, it saw its
chance. It allowed the change in pressure to squirt it
up through the hole and the concentration of the
light to help keep it together.

Every action has an equal and opposite reaction.

Physics as metaphysics.

It grew steadily, secure in the knowledge that the nearest Keeper was too far away to stop it.

But, because inactivity would make them suspicious, it indulged itself with a little misdirection.

In the parts of the world that had just celebrated Christmas, holes created by family expectations widened and the first strike capabilities of parents against unmarried adult children became apparent.

In other parts of the world, low levels of annoyance at the attention paid to exuberant consumerism cranked up a notch, and several places burned Santa in effigy. The people of Effigy, a small village in the interior of Turkey, took the day off.

Somewhere else, a man picked up a pen, stared at it blankly for a moment and, shuddering slightly, signed his name, renewing "Barney" for another season. But that *might* have been a completely unrelated incident.

SEVEN

Anxious to get at whatever it was he was supposed to be doing, Samuel had slipped out before dawn.

Dawn. The first light of day. The rising of the sun. The sun. A relatively stable ball of burning hydrogen approximately 150 million kilometers away. Higher knowledge hadn't mentioned anything about how early it happened.

He yawned and scratched, then walked to the road, stepped over a snowbank, and stood looking around at the world—or as much of it as he could see from the sidewalk in front of St. Patrick's. It wasn't what he'd expected. It was quieter for one thing, with no evidence of the constant battle between good and evil supposedly going on in every heart. He'd expected turmoil, people crying out for any help he could give. He hadn't expected his nose hair to freeze.

Actually, until he'd traced the tight, icy feeling to its source, he hadn't known he *had* nose hair.

Wondering why anyone would voluntarily live in such temperatures, he started walking down the road.

Lena Giorno had called him because she wanted to see an angel. She'd seen him. Over. Done. Ta dah. Frank Giorno had wanted him out of his daughter's bedroom and in clothing. Both taken care of—with some unnecessary violence in Samuel's opinion, but no one had asked him. Father Harris, a fellow servant of the light, didn't need him, and, although he hadn't said it out loud, had practically been screaming at him to go away.

He hadn't gone far, but he'd gone.

So what now? He had to be here for a reason.

His sense of self had grown overnight, but he was still having a little trouble with the vague components of Lena's initial parameters. The whole higher knowledge thing seemed a bit spotty and, so far, not very useful. He understood mobility; he only had to want to go somewhere to be there except that he didn't know where he wanted to go. His hair *was* great. No argument.

And apparently, he was supposed to have come with a message. If he had, he'd misplaced it. Oh sure, he could come up with a few off the top of his head—*Love thy Neighbor, Cherish the Children, Reduce, Reuse, Recycle, Check Your Tire Pressure*—but they were so commonplace—not to mention common sense—they seemed almost trite.

I don't know what I'm doing here.

I don't know how to rejoin the light.

And while I know where I am, I don't know where I'm supposed to go.

If higher knowledge hadn't informed him that he was wiser and more evolved, he'd have to say the whole situation sucked. Big time.

Okay. I deliver messages. I'm some kind of nonunion, spiritual postal guy. Samuel looked around at a village of empty streets and dark houses. *So everything'll be cool as soon as I can tell someone something.*

Although why anyone would want things cooler, he had no idea, and he didn't even want to guess how a situation could draw something in by creating a partial vacuum.

Unfortunately, the only people currently awake behind the barricades of drawn curtains were young children and the parents of young children. The kids were—well, he supposed hysterical was as accurate a description as any. As for their parents, they didn't so much need him to pass on a spiritual message as they needed another three hours of sleep and the batteries that hadn't been included.

He was giving some serious thought to returning to Lena's room and having her fill in a few details when he heard a vehicle approaching. Turning, he watched the 5.2 liter, 230-horsepower, V-8 SUV come closer with no clear idea of why he suddenly found engine statistics so fascinating. He was wondering how it handled on curves when the surrounding cloud of desperation captured his attention. Someone in that vehicle was about to crack.

Was he supposed to fix cracks?

So now I'm doing spiritual plastering? Which wasn't as funny as he'd hoped it would be. He took a deep breath and dried suddenly damp palms against his thighs, wondering why he seemed to be leaking. *Still, a guy's got to start somewhere . . .*

And so far, this seemed to be the only game in town.

The vehicle was exactly twenty feet, seven and three-eighths inches away when he stepped in front of it. When it stopped, it was exactly three-eighths of an inch away. An exhausted looking man and an equally exhausted looking woman were sitting open-mouthed in the front seats. Brian and Linda Pearson. He flashed them both an enthusiastic thumbs up figuring that, hey, it couldn't hurt.

"Are you out of your mind?" Face flushed, Brian leaned out the driver's window. "I could have killed you!"

He seemed a bit upset. Samuel smiled reassuringly. Never let the mortals sense insecurity. He wasn't sure if that was higher knowledge, common sense, or some kind of basic survival instinct but he figured he'd go with it regardless. "I have a message for you."

"Get the fuck out of my way!"

"No."

"No?" His volume rose impressively.

"No. I need to tell you that no matter how it seems, your kids aren't deliberately trying to drive you crazy. You just need more patience." Smile slipping slightly, he added, "And a breath mint."

"You're insane!"

"Am not!" He felt his jaw jut out and his weight shift forward onto the balls of his feet. Where was that coming from? Lowering his voice, he fought the urge to challenge Brian Pearson to a fight, saying only a little belligerently, "I'm an angel."

Exhaustion warring with denial, Brian's bloodshot eyes widened as they were met and held. "Oh my G . . ."

Samuel raised a hand and cut him off, glancing around to be sure no one had overheard. "Don't even suggest that. Didn't you hear what happened to the last guy who tried to move up?" Whistling a descending scale, he pantomimed a fall from grace. The sound of an explosion at the end was purely extemporary but impossible to resist.

Dragging Brian back into the van, her gaze never leaving Samuel's face, Linda whispered something in her husband's ear.

He shook his head and glanced back over his shoulder. "We can't."

She whispered something else.

Unfortunately, higher knowledge didn't seem to extend to eavesdropping.

Leaning back out the window, Brian tried a wobbly smile. "Would you like a ride into London?"

Would he? London, England, seemed a bit far and he was fairly certain the Atlantic Ocean was in the way, so they probably meant London, Ontario, about an hour's drive down highway four.

"Sure."

"Good. Get in."

By the time he'd walked around to the passenger side, Linda had opened the back door. Her expression a curious mix of hope and guilt, she wished him a Merry Christmas and indicated he should climb inside. The second set of seats had been removed and an identical pair of seven-year-old twins, Celeste and Selinka, had been belted into opposite corners of the three seats running across the back of the SUV. If there'd been any more room between them and their parents, they'd have been outside the vehicle completely.

"Hey," he said as he folded himself into the middle seat and fumbled for the seat belt. "My name's Samuel, and I'm an angel. I'm here . . ."

" 'Cause Mommy said to Daddy you can distract us," announced Selinka.

"So Daddy can drive more safely," added Celeste.

"Mommy doesn't really believe you're an angel. She's desperate."

"She said she's ready to 'cept help from the devil himself."

"Really?"

179

Up front, Linda's shoulders stiffened, lending credence to the comment.

Samuel found his own shoulders stiffening in response. "You shouldn't, you know, repeat that."

"Why?" Celeste demanded, eyes narrowing.

"Because if an angel can be here, then so can a devil."

"You're stupid," sniffed Selinka. "And your hair looks dumb. Why do you smell like cotton candy?"

"He smells like strawberry ice cream."

"Does not!"

"Does too!"

"Why can't I smell like both?"

Celeste leaned around him. "You're right," she told her sister. "He is stupid."

Then they started singing.

"There was a farmer had a dog . . ."

At first it was cute.

"Let's all sing," Samuel suggested, leaning forward as far as the seat belt allowed. Singing was a good thing; he had a vague idea that angels did a lot of it. "The family that sings together . . . uh . . ." Wings together? Pings together? Then he realized that no once could hear him over the high-pitched little voices filling the enclosed vehicle with sound.

"B I N G O, B I N G O, B I N G O . . ."

It went on and on and on, just below the threshold of pain.

"Make it stop," moaned their father, beating his

forehead against the steering wheel as the SUV began to pick up speed.

Short of gagging them, Samuel couldn't figure out how to stop them. Nothing he said from well reasoned argument to childish pleas made any impression. After the fourth verse, gagging them was beginning to seem like a valid option. Finally, ears ringing in the sudden silence, he forced the corners of his mouth up into a smile and swept it over both girls. "Hey, I've got an idea. Why don't we do something that doesn't make any noise?"

They exchanged a suspicious glance.

"Like what?" asked Selinka.

"It had better be fun," added Celeste.

He opened his mouth, then closed it again. He could number the hairs on both girls' heads (three billion two hundred and twelve and three billion two hundred and fourteen) but when it came down to it, that wasn't even remotely useful. Unless . . . "I don't suppose you'd want to count each other's hair?"

Which was about when he discovered that a non-violent, geared to age level, designed to promote social development electronic game could raise one heck of a bump when thrown at close range.

"I'm feeling guilty about this," Brian Pearson murmured to his wife. "Are you sure he's going to be all right?"

"He offered to help."

"Actually, hon, he said he had a message for us."

"Same thing."

"Not quite."

"Well, it's a moving car," she pointed out philosophically, gnawing on her last fingernail. "He can't get out."

"We're going to London to see our Granny," announced Selinka.

"Do you have a Granny?" asked Celeste.

Good question. He ran through the order of angels above him; archangels, principalities, powers, dominions, thrones, cherubim, seraphim . . . "No, I don't."

"Why not?"

"I guess it's because I'm an angel."

The twin on the right narrowed her eyes and stared up at him. "Lemme see your wings."

"What?"

"If you're supposed to be an angel, lemme see your wings."

Samuel spread his hands and tried an ingratiating smile. "I don't have wings."

"Why?"

"I'm not that kind of an angel."

"Why?"

"Because I'm the kind of angel that doesn't have wings."

"Why?"

"If you're an angel, you're supposed to have

wings." Her voice began to rise in both volume and pitch. "Big, white, fluffy wings!"

The smile slipped. "Well, I don't."

"Why?"

Why? He had no idea. But going back for that long talk with Lena was beginning to seem like a plan. "I have running shoes," he offered.

Small heads bent forward to have a look.

"They're not brand name," said the twin who seemed to be running this part of the interrogation. "No swatches."

"Does that matter?" Was he wearing the wrong stuff? "What's a swatch?"

She folded her arms. "Dork."

"Wouldn't you girls like to have a nap?" Over the sound of their laughter, he thought he heard their mother whimper. "You know, if you were quiet, your parents would be really happy."

"They would?"

"Yes."

"Why?"

The twin on the left, taking her turn, poked him imperiously in the side. "Light up your head."

"What?"

"Light up your head! Like on TV."

"I don't . . ."

"Then you're not an angel."

"Yes, I am."

"No, you're not."

"Yes, I am." Just barely resisting the urge to grab her and shake her, he let a little of the light show.

"Ha, ha, made you light!"

An ethnically diverse, anatomically correct baby doll swung in from the other side by one foot, the molded plastic head completing its downswing in just the wrong spot.

The light went out.

His eyes were still watering when the SUV stopped at the corner of York and Talbot Streets and he stumbled out into a snowbank. Maybe Brian Pearson *did* need to know his kids weren't deliberately driving him crazy, but as the twins had survived for seven whole years, he could only conclude that both parents already had the patience of a saint. Each. He'd been with the twins for just over an hour and against all predisposition, he wanted to strangle them. He couldn't imagine what seven years would be like. And he was no longer entirely certain that Brian Pearson wasn't right.

The girls, not at all upset by the yelling he'd done, crowded to the window, and blew him kisses.

"Aren't they angelic," sighed their mother without much conviction.

"Not exactly," Samuel told her, clinging to the door until he could get his balance. "But if it helps, I don't think they're actually demonic."

She turned her head enough to meet his gaze. "You're not sure?"

"Uh." He took another look and heard the voice of memory say, *Because if an angel can be here, then so can a devil.* Or two. "No. Sorry."

"Well, you've been a lot of help."

He'd have been more reassured if she hadn't sounded so sarcastic. Shoving his hands in his pockets as the SUV drove away, he sighed and muttered, "That could've gone better."

Pushing through the narrow break in the knee-high snowbank that bracketed the street, he stumbled onto the sidewalk and took a moment to try and dig snow out of his shoes with his finger. Apparently, it was a well-known fact that angels left no footprints. Twisting around, he checked and, sure enough, he'd left no mark in the snow. Although there had to be a reason for it, he'd have happily traded footprints for dry feet. Were angels even supposed to have wet feet? At least he wasn't cold. At least *that* was working.

Nothing else seemed to be.

Maybe he just needed practice.

Straightening, he looked around. So this was London. Fotown. The Forest City. The Jungle City. Georgiana on the Ditch. Apparently, the 340,000 people who lived here had the most cars per capita in Canada. So? Where was everybody? All he could see were snow-covered, empty streets.

Looking east, a sign outside the deserted Convention Center wished everyone a Merry Christmas. A gust of wind whistling down the tracks blew a fan of snow off the top of the bank that nearly hid the train station.

Behind him, a car door slammed.

He turned in time to see a taxi drive away and an elderly woman struggling to drag a brown vinyl suitcase toward the bus station. Her name was Edna Grey, she had a weak heart, and she was on her way to Windsor to spend Christmas Day with her daughter. Maybe he didn't have a message because he *was* the message. Maybe he was supposed to show, not tell. Hurrying over, he lifted the suitcase easily out of the elderly woman's grasp.

"Stop! Thief! Stop!"

"Hey! Ow! I'm just trying to help!"

Edna Grey glared out at him from under the edge of a red knit hat, the strap of her purse clutched in both mittened hands. "Help yourself to my stuff!"

"No, help you carry your stuff." As she lifted the purse again, he dropped the suitcase and backed out of range, rubbing his elbow. "What've you got in that thing, bricks?"

Her eyes narrowed. "Maybe."

"Could you chill, Mrs. Grey. I'm just trying to do something nice for you." He knew he sounded defensive, but he couldn't seem to stop himself. And he had no idea why he wanted her to lower her body temperature.

"How did you know my name? You've been stalking me, haven't you?"

Stalking. The following and observing of another person, usually with the intent to do harm.

"No!" He stepped forward then retreated again as the purse came up. "I can't do harm. I'm an angel."

"You look like a punk." A vehement exhalation through her nose, sprayed the immediate area with a fine patina of moisture.

"I do?"

"Well, you sure don't look like no angel."

He didn't? "I don't?"

"You look," she repeated, "like a punk."

Frank Giorno had called him a punk as well. He couldn't understand why since punk had pretty much ended with the '80s. A quick check found nose and ears still free of safety pins. "I could light up my head." That seemed to be what angels did.

"You could set your shorts on fire for all I care. Now get out of my way, I gotta catch a bus."

"But . . ."

"Move!"

His feet moved before the barked command actually made it to his brain. He stood and watched as she dragged her suitcase the remaining twenty-two feet, six and three-quarter inches to the bus station door. Nothing else moved for as far as he could see and the only sound he could hear was the rasp of cheap vinyl against concrete.

At the door, she paused, and turned. "Well?" she demanded.

Higher knowledge seemed at a loss.

"Get over here and open the door."

"But I thought . . ."

"And while you were thinking, did you think about how a woman of my age could manage a big heavy suitcase and a door?"

"Uh . . ."

"No. You didn't. The world has gone to hell in a handcart since they canceled *Bowling for Dollars*."

Propelled by her glare, he ran for the door and hauled it open. Then, a bit at a loss, he followed her inside.

She shifted her grip on her purse. "Now where are you going?"

He didn't know. "With you?"

"Try again." She squinted up at the board. "Only other bus leaving this morning's going to Toronto."

"I should go to Toronto?"

"Why should I care where you go?" Grabbing her suitcase, she began backing across the room, keeping him locked in a suspicious glare.

"Fine." Edna Grey might not need his help, but in a city of three million, someone would. He'd go there and he'd help people and he'd finally figure out just what he was supposed to be doing, and when he'd done it he'd go back to the light and demand to know just what they thought they were doing sending him into the world without instructions. Well, maybe not demand. Ask.

Politely.

But for now . . .

The bus station flickered twice, then came back into focus.

Why wasn't he in Toronto? Wanting to be in Toronto should have put him there, but something seemed to be holding him in place. It felt as though he was trying to drag an enormous weight . . .

And then he realized.

"Oh, come on, that's a couple of ounces, tops!" A little embarrassed by the way his voice echoed against six different types of tile, Samuel looked up to see Edna Grey staring at him, wide-eyed, one mittened hand clutching her chest. While he watched, she toppled slowly to the ground.

"Mrs. Grey?" He landed on his knees beside her. "Mrs. Grey, what's wrong?"

"Heart . . ." Her voice sounded like crinkling tissue paper.

"Hey, don't do this, you're not supposed to die now!" Reaching out, he spread the fingers of his right hand an inch above the apex of her bosom, spent a moment stopping his mind from repeating the word bosom over and over for no good reason, then asked himself just what exactly he thought he was doing.

I'm helping. It's her heart.

Were hearts supposed to flutter like a gas pump straining at an empty tank?

He laid his left hand against his own chest.

Apparently not.

So?

Was this the message he was here to deliver?

A pulse of light moved from his hand to her heart and he felt an inexplicable urge to yell, "Clear!" Somehow, he resisted. Her heart stopped fluttering, paused, found a new rhythm, and began beating strongly once again.

"Mrs. Grey?" Feeling a little dizzy, Samuel leaned forward and peered into her face. "Can you hear me?"

"What? I'm old, so I'm deaf?"

"Uh, no." Maybe he should loosen her clothing.

She smacked his hand away. "What happened?"

"You had a heart attack."

Planting both palms against the floor, she pushed herself into a sitting position. "Well, are you surprised? You were there, then you weren't there, then you were there again."

"You saw that?"

"What? I'm old, so I'm blind?"

"Uh, no."

"And why does the whole room smell of pine?"

"I think that's the stuff they use on the floor."

"Or some cat's been pissing in the corner." Spotting the startled face of the bus station attendant peering over the ticket counter, her eyes narrowed. "And just what are you looking at, Missy? Good thing I didn't have to wait for her help," she muttered, "I'd be lying here until New Year's."

"Mrs. Grey? Do you want to stand up?"

"No. I'd rather sit here in a puddle of slush."

About to take her hand, Samuel sat back on his heels. "Uh, okay."

Muttering under her breath, she grabbed his shoulder and hauled herself to her feet. "So, what were you doing?" she demanded as he stood. "Here you are, here you aren't—I have a weak heart, you know."

"Had," he corrected helpfully. "I fixed it."

"You fixed it all right. Now answer the question: What were you doing?"

"I was trying to go to Toronto. But nothing happened." His shoulders slumped.

"You really are an angel?"

"Yes, ma'am."

"So, what's the message?"

"Well, uh, you see, it's like this, I uh . . ."

One foot tapped impatiently. "Angels are the messengers of God. So, what's the message? Is it Armageddon?"

He checked his pockets. Still no messages. "I'm pretty sure it's not Armageddon."

"Pretty sure?" She seemed disappointed.

"Actually, I'm beginning to think I'm, you know, not that kind of an angel."

"Oh. Then what kind of an angel are you?"

"Just, uh, the kind that . . ."

"The kind that pops in and out any where they want? Giving poor, helpless grandmothers heart attacks?"

"I didn't do it on purpose."

"Don't take that tone with me, young man. You can show a little respect for my age."

"What? You're old, so I should respect you?" It slipped out before he could stop it. For some weird reason his mouth seemed to have functioned without his brain being involved.

But Edna Grey only straightened her hat. "Yes," she said, "that's it exactly. So why couldn't you pop?"

"It's this form. It has . . ." Mouth open to explain about the genitalia, Samuel met a rheumy gaze, looked deep, and decided he didn't want to go there. Or anywhere near there actually. "It's not . . . I mean, it doesn't . . . It's sort of defining me. It's keeping me from doing things, and I can't get rid of it."

"Tell me about it."

His constant low level of confusion geared up a notch. "About what?"

"Be old, boy, if you want to be defined by your form." She sighed, a short, sharp, angry sound. "Old bones, old blood, old body, they keep you from doing most things, and you sure as hell can't get rid of them. But you know what's worse?" A mittened finger poked his chest. "The way other people think you can't do what you've always done 'cause you're old—whether you can or not." Her hand dropped back to her side. "Don't get old, boy. And don't let other people tell you what you can or cannot do."

"I can't get old," he told her. "And I can't get to Toronto either."

"Oh, yeah, can't get old, can't get to Toronto; that's a real similar comparison, that is." Bending, she scooped her purse up off the floor. "Apples and oranges as my sainted mother used to say."

"Actually she wasn't."

Edna Grey shot him an irritated glare as she straightened. "Wasn't what?"

"Sainted."

"I certainly hope not."

"But you said . . ."

"Never mind what I said. And if you want to get to Toronto so badly, buy a bus ticket."

"I need a bus ticket to go to Toronto?"

"If you're going by bus, you do."

A quick rummage through his pockets produced a cardboard square. "One of these?"

Her brows drew in. "Where did you get that?"

He shrugged. "Need provides."

"Because you're an angel?"

"I guess."

The intercom sputtered to life and spat incomprehensible wordage into the station.

"Your bus is boarding on platform 3." Samuel pushed her suitcase toward her, carefully, making no sudden moves. His elbow still hurt from the first assault.

"You understand that?"

He nodded again.

"Well, if I didn't believe you were an angel before, I sure would now. Understanding the gooblety goop that comes out of those speakers would take nothing less than direct intervention from God. Just wait until I tell that Elsa I met a real angel. Her and the way she's always talking about how she once met Don Ho."

"Mrs. Grey, your bus!"

"Right." Lifting the suitcase easily, she stomped off toward the buses, muttering. "Just wait till I tell my daughter I met a real angel. She's never even met Don Ho."

He waited until he saw her make her laborious way up the bus steps, refusing to let go of her suitcase, and sighed. "You're welcome."

"Look, kid, I don't care what you think you are and how little sleep you think I've had and how much you think I need to drive safely, but if you don't sit down, I'm going to kick your ass off this bus."

"But I have a ticket."

Barry Bryant sighed and rotated the heel of his left hand around his temple. "I don't care. The harpy behind the ticket counter has already told me I look like hell, so I don't need your two cents' worth."

Samuel leaned forward. "You don't, you know."

"I don't what?"

"Look like Hell."

"Sit. Down."

A soldier of the light knew when to obey a direct order. Samuel sat down beside the only person on the bus. "Hi, Nedra."

"Do I know you?"

"I'm an angel. I'm here to help."

She stared deep into his eyes, watched the gold flecks overwhelm the brown, lighting up the immediate area in a soft luminescence, and said, "Get lost."

"Get lost?"

"Yes." For some strange reason, after a perfectly equitable Christmas Eve, her parents had sent her on her way feeling guilty about their lack of grandchildren. She was facing a twelve-hour shift in a hospital that could pay millions for one piece of high-tech equipment but couldn't afford to order new bedpans, and she was in no mood to deal with someone who smelled like canned ravioli, a food her rising cholesterol level no longer allowed her to eat. "Get lost."

"I can't," he admitted, glancing around at the confined space.

"Try."

"But . . ."

"Now."

He'd just settled himself as far from Nedra as possible when the driver climbed on board and glared in his direction. "What?"

Lip curled, Barry dropped into the driver's seat. He'd got to bed at about three, got up again at six, and knew damned well he shouldn't be driving. The last thing he needed at the beginning of a run to Toronto and back on a snow-slicked highway was some smart-ass teenager pointing that out. Of course it wasn't safe. He knew it wasn't safe. What did he look like, an idiot? But what was he supposed to do? Cancel the run? Call another driver in on Christmas Day? Fat chance. He had to do it, so he was going to do it, and there was nothing more to be said. Besides, it was double time and a half, and he wasn't giving up that kind of cash.

Head pounding, he rammed the bus into gear. "And I don't feel guilty about it either," he growled.

"Yeah, you do."

Barry whirled around. There was no way he could have heard the protest or been heard in turn from the back of the bus. *I am not hearing things.* Shoulders hunched, he eased off the brake and headed for the road. *I'm fine.*

The only other vehicle in the parking lot belonged to the cow behind the counter who'd probably report him and then he'd get suspended and lose as much as he was making today—so why was he even bothering?

He swung out just a little wide and the bus brushed against the fender of her car like an elephant brushing against a paper screen.

As they pulled out onto York Street, Samuel twisted in his seat and stared back at the crumpled chrome, wondering if he should do something. *He knew he shouldn't have done that, but he did it anyway. What gives?* It was like nothing Samuel'd ever come in contact with before. It was . . .

Free will. His eyes widened, and he squirmed around to stare at the back of the driver's head. When given a choice between good and evil, humans could freely choose to do evil, and sometimes they did. Okay, admittedly on a scale of one to ten where one was deliberately hitting a parked car and ten was committing genocide, this was closer to, well, one, but still. Free will. In action.

After that, the trip to Toronto was uneventful.

Although there did seem to be a number of off-road vehicles suddenly driving off the road.

Samuel would have enjoyed the ride had he not continued to slide down the angle forced into ancient seats by thousands of previous passengers, catching himself on his inseam. He had no idea why anyone would put such a torture device right over so much soft tissue, but by the time the bus reached Hamilton he was certain the Prince of Darkness himself had been involved.

Toronto had the turmoil he'd been expecting earlier. Samuel stepped out of the Elizabeth Street Bus Terminal and stared. Everything seemed overdone. There were just too many buildings, too much concrete, too much dirt—but not too many people given that it was nearly noon on Christmas Day.

"Hey man, you look lost."

Samuel glanced down at his feet—he hadn't known snow came in that color—then up at the twenty-something blond man, with the inch of dark roots, now standing beside him. "No. I'm right here."

"Hey, that's funny." The smile and accompanying laugh was a lie. He wore a black trench coat, open over black jeans, black boots and a black turtleneck. It was supposed to look cool, or possibly kewl, but Samuel got the impression kewl had moved on. This guy hadn't. "You just get to the city?"

"Yeah."

"You got a place to stay?"

"Do I need a place to stay?" Was he staying?

"You going to try and make it on the streets?"

"I was going to stay on the sidewalks."

"Like I said, a funny guy." The outstretched hand ended in black fingernails. Definitely left behind by kewl. "I'm Deter."

"Deter?" Higher knowledge finally provided information that wasn't a fashion tip. "Isn't your name Leslie?"

The hazel eyes widened, the hand dropped, and Leslie/Deter shot a glance back over his shoulder at two snickering men about his own age. "No, you're wrong, man. It's Deter."

"Hey, it's okay. I understand why you changed it."

"I didn't change it."

"Yeah, you did."

"No, I didn't!"

"Yeah, you did. It was Leslie Frances Calhoon. Now it's Deter Calhoon."

"Leslie Frances?" howled one of the two laughing men.

"Shut up!" He whirled back around to shake a finger under Samuel's nose. "And you shut up, too!"

"Okay."

"Do I know you?"

In his existence to this point, Samuel had met eight people, not counting Nedra who he didn't think he should count because she'd made it fairly clear she hadn't wanted to meet him. "No."

"So stop calling me Leslie!"

"Okay."

"You don't have a place to stay?"

Was he staying? "No."

"Fine. So you're coming with us."

"No."

"So you're going to stay on the street, on the sidewalk, whatever. Fine. Here." Breathing heavily through his nose, Leslie/Deter thrust a pamphlet into Samuel's hand. "Greenstreet Mission. We're doing a Christmas dinner. You can get a meal and hear the word of God."

Samuel smiled in relief. This, finally, he understood. "Which word?"

"What?"

"Well, God's said a lot of words, you know, and a word like *it* or *the* wouldn't be worth hearing again but it's always fun listening to Him try to say aluminum."

"What are you talking about?"

"What you were talking about."

Leslie/Deter glared over flaring nostrils. "I was talking about the word of God."

"Which word?"

He snatched the pamphlet out of Samuel's hand. "Forget it."

"But . . ."

"No. Just stay away!" The black trench coat swirled impressively as he stomped back to his snickering friends and shoved them both into motion.

Wondering what he'd said, Samuel lifted a hand in farewell. There didn't seem to be much point in offering to help with the pamphlets. " 'Bye, Leslie."

If Leslie/Deter had a response, it was probably just as well that the renewed howls of laughter from his companions drowned it out.

*   *   *

Because the hole was so small, it had taken over twelve hours to push enough substance through. Toward the end, as the light and dark in the world moved closer to balance, it should have gotten more difficult, but there was now such a vast amount of enthusiastic darkness pushing from below that care had to be taken. Tipping the balance the other way would do no good at all. Since, technically, doing no good at all was its *raison d'être*, the contradiction was making it feel more than a little twitchy.

It didn't even want to get into the problem of keeping it all together without actually achieving consciousness too early. Without a physical body it was both disoriented and exhausted. It had never had such a bad day. Which was sort of a good thing. Except that good things were bad. If it'd had a head, it would've had one hell of a headache.

Literally.

It could feel good and evil leveling out. Balance being restored. It pulled itself together, the shadow that had lain over the frozen hollow since midnight growing darker, acquiring form.

Then, as all things were equal—or all the things it was concerned with at any rate—it closed the hole and looked around.

"I'M BAck."

It coughed and tried again.

"I'M back. I'm back." It just kept getting worse. "What the Hell is going on here?"

Attempting a perfect balance, it had allowed the weight on the other side of the scale to define the shape it would wear. Becoming its perfect opposite. Impossible for one to be found as long as the other existed. It would cheerfully use the light to further its own ends. Well, maybe not cheerfully. Cynically.

It seemed to be a young female. Late teens. Long dark hair. Fairly large breasts. She looked down. Everything seemed to be there.

Three things were immediately clear.

One. She appeared to be a natural blonde, which explained the uniform black of the hair. Bad dye job.

Two. Demons, like angels, were sexless. The actions of incubi and succubi were more in the order of a mind-fuck than anything sweaty. But . . .

. . . since she had a set, he had a set.

Three. Given gender, and she certainly seemed to have been given that, something had gotten significantly screwed up somewhere.

She'd have been happier about that were it not for the sudden rush of emotions. Every possible emotion. She was up, she was down, she was happy, she was sad, she was royally pissed off . . .

Which was the one she decided to go with.

EIGHT

From the bus terminal, Samuel walked over to Yonge Street and up two blocks to Gerrard, staring in amazement at the amount of stuff on display in the windows of the closed stores. The stereo system dominating a small electronics shop drew him close to the glass—five disk CD changer, digital tuner with forty presets, six-mode preset equalizer, dual full-logic cassette decks, extra bass—and he found himself wondering covetously about sub-woofers and wattage. From deep within came the knowledge that if it came to it, he'd buy that stereo before he bought groceries.

Then he noticed the leather shop next door. Stereo forgotten, he took two long side steps and stared wide-eyed at the mannequin barely dressed in a red leather corset, black leather panties, and stiletto-heeled thigh boots.

Which was when the unexpected happened.

He backed up so quickly he slammed into a newspaper box.

His genitalia were functioning without him!

It was like, like they had a mind of their own.

Well, not *they* exactly . . .

Beginning to panic, he stared down at the tent in his pants and wondered what he was supposed to do.

Fortunately, the panic seemed to be taking care of the problem.

A few minutes later, heart pounding, gaze directed carefully at the sidewalk, he started walking again, faith in his physical integrity shaken. What would have happened had it not been a holiday? Had he actually been able to go into the store and . . .

It didn't bear thinking about.

Brakes squealed. A door panel brushed his knee. The deep red 1986 Horizon stopped. Backed up. The window opened.

"You've got the red, asshole!" the driver screamed, then gunned the motor and roared away.

Samuel had no idea they came in other colors. Or, for that matter, what color they usually were. And how had the driver known? Were any other bits of his body likely to surprise him?

Eleven seconds later, the first pigeon settled on his head, claws digging through his hair and into his scalp. When it finally lost the fight to keep its perch, it slid off to land with a thud on his right shoulder. It was mostly white with a few gray markings and the distinct attitude that it had arrived where it was supposed to be.

The second pigeon went directly to his other shoulder.

The rest fought for less prime locations and, for the most part, had to content themselves with huddling close around his feet.

He spoke fluent pigeon—which wasn't really difficult as the entire pigeon vocabulary pretty much consisted of: "Food!" "Danger!" and "Betcha I can hit that guy in the Armani suit."—but nothing he said made any difference. They were where they felt they ought to be. Case closed. When he started walking again, they lifted off with an indignant flapping of wings. When he stopped, they landed. He kept walking.

At College Street, he flipped a mental coin and turned right.

The sedan traveling southbound missed him by seven centimeters. The pickup traveling north missed him by three. The driver of the pickup taught him a number of new words. The pigeons knew them already.

The east side of Yonge—where College Street became Carlton Street—seemed to lead into a more residential area. That had to be good. People equaled problems and sooner or later, if he was right about being the message not merely the medium, he'd *have* to fix the problem that would let him go home.

By the time he reached the park across from Homewood Avenue, he was traveling in a shifting cloud of fat bodies and feathers. Visibility was bad, the footing was getting a little tricky, and the surrounding air had begun to smell strongly of motor oil and old French fries. He clearly had to get rid of his escort.

He flailed his arms.

He used the new words, rearranging them into a number of different patterns.

Nothing worked.

Climbing up and over a snowbank, he brushed off the end of a bench and flopped down onto the cleared spot.

The pigeons settled happily.

His vision slightly impaired by a fan of tail feathers, Samuel watched a police car make a tight U-turn across Carlton Street and pull up more or less in front of him. The driver's name was Police Constable Jack Brooks, his partner, Police Constable Marri Margaret Patton. They sat and stared for a full minute. He could feel their mood lightening as they studied him, and he knew he should be glad he'd added a little joy to their day but, preoccupied by the sudden warmth dribbling down behind his left ear, he found he didn't much care.

Finally, they got out of the car and waded through

the snow toward him, valiantly but unsuccessfully attempting to suppress snickers.

"Are you, uh, all right under there?"

Samuel sighed and spat out a feather. "Sure," he answered shortly.

"Have you tried standing up?"

He stood. Wings flapped. He could see PC Patton's lips move, but he couldn't hear what she was saying above the noise. He sat down again. The pigeons settled.

After a moment of near hysterical laughter, the police settled as well.

Fighting to catch his breath, PC Brooks managed to gasp, "Are you feeding them?"

"As if." If he was feeding them, he could stop. And they'd leave. "They want to be with me 'cause I'm an angel."

"An angel?"

"Yeah; I guess it's that dove thing."

"These are pigeons."

"Same old."

As three birds squabbled over position, PC Brooks got his first unobstructed look at facial features and knocked five years off his original estimate of the young man's age. "What's your name, son?"

"Samuel."

"Samuel what?"

"Just Samuel."

"And you're an angel?"

"Yes."

"If you're an angel, where are your wings?" Beside him, he heard his partner smother a snort.

Samuel sighed and spit out another feather. "I'm not that kind of angel." Without much enthusiasm, he added, "But I *can* make my head light up."

"Maybe next time." Frowning slightly, PC Brooks took a closer look, found his gaze met and held, found himself watching the gold flecks in the brown eyes swirl into soft luminescence. He blinked and forced himself to look away. "What are you on, Samuel?"

"Concrete and fiberglass."

"Uh-huh. Look, son, it's Christmas Day, why don't you go home."

"I can't!"

The pigeons took flight, circled once, and settled again.

PC Patton took her partner by the sleeve and dragged him a few steps away. "It's not against the law to be covered in pigeons," she reminded him, grinning broadly.

"I know."

"Neither is it against the law to impersonate an angel." She glanced back over her shoulder. "Whatever he's on . . ."

"Concrete and fiberglass."

". . . he's not a danger to himself or society, and he's probably fairly warm under there."

"But it's Christmas."

So it was. She sighed, watched her breath blossom in the frosty air, and turned back toward the bench. "Why don't you get in the car and we'll take you somewhere you can get some Christmas dinner."

"Can the pigeons come?"

"No."

That was the best news he'd heard in a while.

The pigeons, who recognized the police as Nice Dark Targets, refused to cooperate.

Samuel finally backed up about twenty feet, raced forward, and flung himself into the back of the squad car, giving PC Patton about six seconds to slam the door before the birds caught up. When the first bird hit the window, she almost peed herself, she was laughing so hard.

*   *   *

Darkness had emerged just outside Waverton for a reason. The tiny town was not only far enough off the beaten track that a Keeper wouldn't stumble on it by accident, it was fairly close to the bloated population base along the Canada/U.S. border—there was a limited amount of trouble that could be caused without active human participation and darkness didn't like to waste time. Parts of central Russia, Africa, and Nevada also fit the geographic criteria, but appearing in any of those areas would have been redundant at best.

She found a pair of denim overalls, black canvas sneakers, and a nylon jacket in what had been the office of J. Henry and Sons Auto Repair. While appreciative of the chaos she could cause walking around naked, keeping a lower profile seemed the smarter move. The outfit wasn't stylish, but it was serviceable.

Although to her surprise, she *was* a little concerned that the overalls made her look fat.

Which soon became a minor problem.

Once in the world, she should have been able to move instantaneously from place to place, but something seemed to be stopping her. It didn't take long to figure out what. While walking the four and half kilometers into town, she decided that staying as far away from the light as possible was no longer an option; her new plan involved finding him and kicking his holier than thou butt around the block a few times. *What had he been thinking?*

Actually, given which set he'd gotten, she had a pretty good idea of what he'd been thinking.

"Men," she'd snarled at a hydro pole, left forearm tucked under her breasts to stop the painful bouncing. "They're all alike."

The power went off in half the county.

Which made her feel only half better.

She'd planned on finding a ride south as soon as

she got to Waverton, twisting the weak and pitiful will of some poor mortal to her bidding. Unfortunately, there was no one around; the only thing moving on Main Street was the random blinking of a string of Christmas lights hung in the window of one of the closed businesses. She could have shot a cannon off in any direction and not hit a soul. And *if* she'd had a cannon, she *would* have shot it off.

As she didn't . . .

The bank on the corner burst into black-tipped flame.

Rummaging about in her pocket, she pulled out a marshmallow.

Need provides.

Twenty minutes later, the scene seethed with people—volunteer firefighters, both constables from the local OPP detachment, and most of the remaining population.

Now that's more like it. Bonus points for pulling a Keeper up into the middle of nowhere to close this hole opened by arson, leaving more populated areas unprotected. Jostled by the crowd, she snarled and drove her heel as hard as she could down on the nearest toe.

"Ouch. Excuse me."

Confused, she turned and glared into soft brown eyes bracketed between a dark pink hat and a pale pink scarf. "Why are you apologizing? You're the victim."

"No one has to be a victim, dear." The older woman frowned slightly, her gaze sliding from dyed hair to running shoes and back up again. "You're not from around here, are you?"

Strangers were universally suspect when something went wrong. Settling her weight on one hip, she folded her arms. "No, I'm not."

"Are you alone?"

She glanced over her shoulder at the tendril of darkness seeping out of the hole, watched one of the firefighters "accidentally" turn the hose on another, and she smiled. "Mostly." Once accused of setting the fire, she'd be able to cause all sorts of havoc. She'd be able to turn their anger at her onto other targets, counter-accusing once she had the attention of the crowd. Maybe the good townspeople would like to know about Mr. Tannison, the bank manager.

"A stranger," the woman repeated thoughtfully, the flames reflecting in both halves of her bifocals. "And all alone."

Here it comes, she thought.

"How did you get here? We're not exactly in the center of things." Her eyes widened. "You've run away, haven't you?"

"No, I . . ."

"All alone. In a strange place. And on Christmas, too." Pink-mittened hands clasped over a formidable bosom. "Where were you running away to?"

"The city . . ."

"Of course, the city." Her sigh plumed out silver-white. "But for right now, you have nowhere to go for Christmas dinner, do you?"

"I don't eat."

"That's what I thought."

And the strange thing was, that *was* what she thought. Which made less than no sense.

"My name is Eva Porter, and you're going to join my husband and I for turkey and all the trimmings. I won't take no for an answer." A pink wave toward the burning bank. "That's my husband by the tanker truck."

"You want me to join you for dinner?"

"That's right."

"You don't know me."

"You don't know *me*."

She couldn't argue with that. Eva Porter was way outside her experience. "Are you going to torture me?" That would at least explain the invitation.

"Goodness, no."

"You only want to feed me?"

"That's right."

"And it doesn't bother you that I'm a demon? Darkness given human form?"

Eva's smile slipped.

Before she could enjoy the expected reaction, wool-covered fingers gently lifted her chin and looked her right in the eye.

"I don't know who told you such a thing . . ."

"No one had to tell me."

". . . but you are a beautiful young woman."

"I am?" She caught herself feeling good about that and hurriedly squashed the feeling.

"Yes, you are. What's your name?"

"Uh . . ." She pulled one at random from the possibilities. "Byleth."

"That's a pretty name."

"It is?" It wasn't supposed to be. This had gone quite far enough. "Listen, lady, I don't know what you think I am, but I'm not."

"Not what?"

"That. What you think." The pale gray of her eyes began darkening like tarnished silver. "I set that fire! I desired flames—and there they were."

Eva frowned. "What are you on, Byleth?"

She glanced down, totally confused. "Packed snow and concrete."

"And those shoes are just canvas, aren't they? Your poor toes must be frozen."

They hadn't been. But now . . .

"And a nylon jacket isn't enough for this weather. It's below zero out here. Just look at the ice forming on those hoses."

She looked. Her teeth began to chatter. "Okay, but I'm just going with you to get warm."

"That's fine. You don't have to do anything you don't want to."

"That's right. I don't." Hugging herself in a valiant

214

effort to contain body heat, Byleth followed the confusing mortal down Main Street. Ignite the bank. Open a hole. Allow a little darkness into the world. All that had gone by the book. But reassured, warmed, and fed? Not to mention apologized to?

She wasn't supposed to like people being nice to her. Well, so far only *person* not *people*, but still . . .

It wasn't right.

Or more to the point, it wasn't wrong.

* * *

"No shit, man! I'm an angel, too!"

Samuel studied Doug's slightly furry, gap-toothed smile and bloodshot eyes and shook his head. "No, you're not."

"Yeah, I am." Carefully placing his fork beside his half empty plate, Doug leaned forward and lowered his voice. "I'm undercover. That's why, you know, no wings."

"Can you make your head light up?"

"Fuck, yeah." He glanced around, checking for eavesdroppers. Satisfied that no one else in the crowded room was paying any attention, he elaborated. "It's usually pretty lit by now, but they don't allow that stuff in here."

"But shouldn't I know it if you're an angel?"

"I didn't know till you told me. Why should you know till I told you?"

That made sense. Not a lot of sense but, under the circumstances, enough. And Doug wasn't lying. Samuel could tell when people were lying and Doug believed every breathy, fermentation-redolent thing he'd said. Feeling as though the weight of the world had been lifted off his shoulders, Samuel leaned forward as well. "Do you get covered in pigeons?"

"Nope. Butterflies. Hundreds of 'em, movin' their little feet all over my body." Eyes widening, he glanced down at this chest and began smacking himself with alternating palms. "All. Over. My. Body."

Samuel grabbed his wrists. "What are you doing?"

"Swattin' butterflies."

Ignoring for the moment the absence of butterflies to swat, Samuel looked sternly across the narrow table. "Angels can't enact violence on a living creature."

"What the fuck does that mean?"

"We don't swat!"

"You never wanted to swat them pigeons?"

"Well . . . yeah." Which wasn't something he wanted to discover about himself—even justifiable urges to commit violence on a flock of flying rats was just anti-angel. Releasing Doug's wrists, he buried his head in his hands. "I'm very confused."

Doug nodded sagely. "Happens."

"I don't know why I'm here."

"I do."

That was more than he'd dared to hope for. "You do?"

"You're here to eat."

And hope died.

About to point out that angels didn't eat, Samuel watched Doug lift a forkful of mashed potatoes and gravy. Doug was eating. Most of it was even going into his mouth. Wrapping his fist around his own fork, he mirrored the motions of the undercover angel sitting across from him. After a few moments, he got the hang of not chewing his tongue with the food. Then he swallowed.

All of a sudden, he was ravenous.

When a bit of stuffing came back up through his nose, he slowed down enough to breathe. He drank juice until it was gone, then he switched to water. He had seconds. And, although what food remained had become a little difficult to identify by then, he even had thirds.

This was the best thing that had happened to him in this body. He couldn't believe what he'd been missing. He wanted to thank Doug for the gift he'd been given, for new information shared, and all he could think to do was to share information in turn.

"I have genitalia."

"They're called giblets, kid."

*　　*　　*

She'd poison the gravy. Given who—or rather what—she was, it was the only logical thing to do under the circumstances. The box of rat poison tucked neatly onto the shelf of gardening supplies had called out to her as Eva Porter led her through the enclosed porch and into the house. At least she thought it was the rat poison, her teeth were chattering too loudly to be sure.

"Now, then, let's get you out of those wet shoes and socks, eh."

"I don't *have* socks."

"Then I'll get you some." Unwrapped, Eva wore a dove-gray sweat suit over a white turtleneck. Given her proportions . . .

"You look like a pigeon," Byleth muttered sullenly.

"I do, don't I." Her eyes widened as she took in the overalls. "Good heavens, child, you're hardly wearing anything at all. Well, I can do something about that, can't I?"

"Can you?" She'd intended the question to be sharp edged, mocking, but it emerged sounding rather pathetic. Holding the freezing length of the overalls' zipper away from her body, she followed Eva into the living room and watched wide-eyed as she pulled several brightly wrapped packages out from under the tree.

"These are for my granddaughter, Nancy; she'll be coming up to spend New Year's with us. Fortunately, you're about the same size."

"You're giving me your granddaughter's presents?" She'd have refused the kindness except she'd caught sight of her reflection in the living room window. The overalls were gross. And they *did* make her look fat. *Still: Granny gives Nancy's presents away. Nancy gets angry. Big family fight.* Byleth could live with that. Of course if Nancy was as whacked as Granny, she might not mind. *Don't ruin things,* she told herself sternly, following Eva upstairs. *Believe anything that'll get you out of these overalls.*

As instructed, she had a nice hot shower, staying in until she'd emptied the tank. She left the soap sitting in water in the soap dish and the towels in a crumpled heap on the floor. It wasn't much, but it felt good to be proactive again.

Black jeans. Black, ribbed turtleneck; tight enough to offer some support to the breasts which were rapidly becoming a colossal nuisance. Thick red sweater. Red fuzzy socks.

Pivoting in front of the mirror, toes working against the thick fleece, she realized she looked good. The black, the red, the hair—it was working. Back in the bathroom, she went through Eva's makeup bag, pulled out the reddest lipstick she could find and applied it liberally. She liked the effect so much, she completely forgot about her intention to infect the lipstick with a particularly virulent STD.

Harry Porter was standing in the living room when she came downstairs. He smiled and introduced himself. "Just between you and me," he added, leaning toward her slightly, "that outfit looks much better on you than it would have on Nancy."

Had there been anything remotely sexual in the comment, she'd have known how to react. But there wasn't.

Why were her ears so hot?

She tried a provocative smile anyway.

Harry deflected it with amused indulgence.

Her ears grew hotter. So did her cheeks. What the hell was going on?

"I'llgohelpwithdinner." The words came out weirdly strung together. Hurrying into the kitchen, she held on tightly to the thought of the rat poison and getting her world back on track.

It took only a little more momentum to bounce into Eva and spill cranberry juice all over her.

"Oops, sorry, dear."

Byleth closed her eyes and counted to three. "Why," she demanded when she opened them, "are you apologizing? I bumped you."

"True enough. I spoke to Harry and he says if you still want to go to the city in the morning, he'll drive you to the bus station in Huntsville."

The bus? There was just no way she was taking the bus. Smelly people took the bus. Poor people took the bus. People being environmentally aware and not driving their cars took the bus. Demons did *not* take the bus. Unless they took it somewhere really, really nasty and left it there. If Harry wanted to play taxi, he could drive her all the way to the city. He'd be easy enough to coerce.

"Byleth? Would you mind stirring the gravy?"

Since Harry had just become useful and she couldn't poison Eva without killing him, there could be only one answer. "Yes."

"Thanks, dear."

Staring at the spoon in her hand, the other end circling around in the pan of gravy, she wondered how that had gone wrong.

* * *

519 Church Street served food but couldn't provide shelter for the night. Unwilling to lose the company of the only other angel he'd ever met, Samuel followed Doug out the door and fell into step beside him.

They walked for a while in silence. Higher knowledge informed him that pigeons roosted after dark so, until sunrise, life was good. Or it would have been except . . .

"What's the matter, kid?"

He shook his head, he wasn't sure. "There's pressure." A quick glance down showed a small wet spot on the front of his trousers. "And I'm leaking! Again. First my hands and now this. Am I supposed to be leaking?"

"Must be time to take a piss." Grabbing for the front of his own trousers, Doug crossed the sidewalk and stood facing the wall of Harris' Auto Body.

"We can't take something that doesn't belong to us." In a world of uncertainties, this he remained sure of.

Doug rolled his eyes as a stream of liquid hit the bricks with enough force to knock off a few peeling paint chips and wash them down to float in the streaming puddle on the concrete. "Urinate, kid. Your. En. Eight."

Discharge urine. A pale-yellow fluid secreted as waste by the kidneys, stored in the bladder, discharged through the urethra.

"Oh." Opening the zipper turned out to be more difficult than it looked. Closing it when he finished . . .

"Don't worry about it, kid. Hardly anyone keeps their foreskin these days."

Still unable to completely straighten, Samuel found that of little actual comfort. Moving awkwardly, he followed Doug up a set of broad steps and was astonished to discover they were entering a cathedral. When he paused, Doug grabbed his arm and pulled him ahead.

"St. Mike's only got room for fifty, kid. He who hesitates sleeps outside. Merry Christmas, Father."

The priest nodded without glancing up from the clipboard. "Names?"

"I'm Doug. This here's Samuel. Samuel, not Sam. We're angels."

"You know the rules?"

"You betcha, Father."

"Go on, then. Clear the door."

"This is my favorite flop in the whole city," Doug confided as he dragged Samuel across the nave and in through the big double doors. "Whadda you think?"

The peace and beauty of the Sanctuary wrapped around the angel like a blanket. Like arms of light.

"Did you know your eyes was glowin', kid?"

"Sorry."

"Not a problem. Kind of pretty." Arms spread wide, Doug turned on the spot, thin gray ponytail streaming out behind him, dirty gray overcoat flapping like wings. Pigeon wings. But why ruin the image. "Can you think of a better place for two angels to sleep?"

Actually, he couldn't.

*　　*　　*

Byleth had merely picked at dinner, pushing the food in circles around her plate, unable to forget how huge her butt had looked in the overalls. Then Eva brought out the lemon meringue pie, a quivering

three inches deep with drops of liquid sugar glisten-
ing in the valleys of the meringue. Suddenly remem-
bering that gluttony was one of the big seven, she
had three pieces. An hour later, when the sugar high
suddenly wore off, she'd found herself blinking stupidly at *White Christmas*—a movie too woogie for
words—and had allowed Eva to steer her unpro-
testing up to bed.

She made an explicitly salacious invitation—more
because she felt she should than through any desire
to corrupt—which Eva didn't even begin to understand. Without the energy to explain the unfamiliar
terms, she merely took the offered nightgown and
staggered off to bed.

The sheets in the spare room smelled of fabric softener. The mattress was soft. The blankets warm. She
had nothing against comfort; a lot of very nasty
things had been done for comfort's sake.

"She's certainly rude."

"Yes, she is."

Rolling over on her stomach, she peered off the
edge of the bed at the hot air grate set into the old
linoleum floor.

"She left the bathroom in a mess and borrowed
my makeup without asking."

"I saw that."

Eva's and Harry's voices drifted up through the
grate from the living room below.

"Her table manners are atrocious. You'd think she'd never held a fork before."

"And the hysterics in the bathroom later . . ."

Well, how was she to know that was supposed to happen?

At least she seemed to be having a negative effect on the Porters. As long as they were complaining about her, the evening hadn't been a total waste.

"Did you see her go through that pie?"

"I know; isn't it nice to have a teenager in the house again?"

"I am not a teenager!" Both palms hit the floor as she threw herself off the bed toward the voices. "I am a *demon!*"

The house was silent for a moment.

Then . . .

"Did you put Byleth in the front bedroom?"

"Yes, I did."

Eva's voice grew suddenly louder, as though she now stood directly under the grate. "Sorry, dear. We forgot you could hear us."

Teenager.

That apology, she'd accept.

Claire closed her new laptop with a snap. The machine and the e-mail account had been another Christmas present from her parents. While she appreciated the difficulties the Apothecary'd overcome setting the system up, she couldn't help thinking that socks and underwear would have been more useful. "According to Diana, Father Harris has no idea where the angel went. Didn't even realize it—*he*— was an angel."

"So what are we after doing?"

"We keep answering the Summons . . ." She frowned, searching for a plural. ". . . s I get. Nothing else we can do."

Unconvinced, Dean sat beside her on the bed. "Shouldn't we tell someone, then?"

"Who?"

"Other Keepers?"

"Actually, they know."

"They know?"

"Not exactly about the angel, but they know we, uh, consummated our relationship. Apparently it echoed through the possibilities." He looked so appalled, she managed what she hoped was an encouraging smile in spite of her own pique. "Everyone was very impressed. Keepers who've never used anything more complicated than a ballpoint pen suddenly felt obliged to send me an e-mail about it. Isn't technology wonderful. But," she added emphatically, the smile slipping, "since the world's in no danger, I'm not telling them about the angel until we absolutely have to. There's no point giving them more to discuss, is there? They'll all start telling me we should have used precautions."

"We did."

"Metaphysical precautions."

"Oh." Cleaning already spotless glasses on the edge of his T-shirt gave him a moment to find the right words. "Claire, I'm not happy with our . . . with what we do, being discussed, you know, electronically."

"I'm not happy about it either," she admitted, tossing the laptop to one side. "But all they know that the Earth moved. Nothing specific. Without details, they won't discuss it for long."

"The Earth moved?"

"Well, only around the Pacific Rim . . ." Rising up onto her knees, she took the edge of his earlobe between her teeth. ". . . so you needn't get too impressed with yourself."

He twisted, caught her around the waist, and they fell back on the bed locked together.

"Hey! Watch the tail!"

"Oops, sorry, Austin." As Dean sat up, Claire rolled off the bed, grabbing a pillow in one hand, scooping Austin up with the other. "And thanks for reminding me that you'll be starting out in the bathroom tonight."

"Oh, please. I have no interest in watching the two of you do whatever it is the two of you are intending to do."

"I'm not so much concerned about the watching," she told him, adjusting her hold, "as I am about the commenting and the criticizing."

227

"Look, if you can't take a little criticism . . ."

"Good night, Austin."

He glared at her as she set the pillow down just inside the bathroom door and then set him on it. "This is cat abuse. You'll be hearing from my lawyer."

"Would a salmon treat forestall litigation?"

"No. But a salmon might."

"Dream on." Handing over the treat, she pulled the door closed. "Feel free to join us after we go to sleep."

"Uh, Claire . . ." Dean nodded toward the door. "How can he join us if that's closed?"

"A closed door has never stopped a determined cat."

"Uh-huh." His T-shirt stopped halfway up his torso. "So you're saying he can come out any time, then?"

"No." Smiling, she reached into the possibilities and laid them against the latch plate. "He can come out when that wears off."

Austin's indignant, "Cheater!" was muffled but distinct.

"I'm sorry, Claire. This has never happened before."

"You've only done it once before."

"And this didn't happen!"

Rising up on one elbow, she bent forward and kissed him softly. "Just relax." Kissed him a little harder. "Everything's going to be fine." Kissed him with more enthusiasm. Stopped kissing him. Leaned back. "Or maybe not. You're so tense I could bounce quarters off you . . . well, off most of you. . . . What's wrong?"

"Nothing."

"Is it me?"

"You?" Her question had been delivered with a total absence of emotion. Without his glasses, he couldn't tell for sure if she looked hurt or angry. "It's not you. It's nothing."

"And I know when you're lying, remember?"

Dean sighed and surrendered. "Okay." He stared up at the tiny red dot on the hotel room's smoke detector and thanked all the gods who might be listening that Austin was in the bathroom. "I can't stop thinking about what happened the last time, and it's got me some caudled up, I can tell you."

"Shouldn't those be happy thoughts?" Deep burgundy fingernails tapped against his skin in a way that should have been enough to raise a reaction all on its own. It wasn't.

His cheeks flamed. "Not those thoughts. I keep thinking about how we made an angel."

"And you're worried it'll happen again?"

"No . . ."

"You're worried it won't?" His silence was all the answer she needed. "But we don't want it to happen again."

"But you want it to be that good."

229

"Well . . ."

"Good enough to make an angel."

"Yes, but . . ."

"That's *some* good."

All at once, she understood. "You're afraid you won't be that good again!"

A faint "I heard that," sounded from the bathroom.

Dean closed his eyes. *That* was all he needed to finish the night off right.

Resting her chin on his sternum, Claire considered the situation. She supposed she could see how ripping a hole through the fabric of the universe big enough to slip an angel through the very first time he had sex might cause Dean some performance anxiety. She didn't know what to do about it though. "Dean, you can't expect to make an angel every time."

"I know."

Now she was really confused. "Well, then . . ."

"It's not about knowing. It's about *knowing*." He waved his outside arm for emphasis, hoping that its shadow movement through the dark would add clarity.

It didn't.

"It's me, isn't it?"

NINE

Vaguely aware he was being pulled from sleep, Dean sighed deeply and arched his back. He could feel the sheet sliding away, warm air currents brushing against him, and . . . His eyes snapped open. "Claire, what are you doing?"

She smiled up at him. "Solving the angel prob . . ." Glancing down, she sighed. "Okay, should have worded *that* differently."

"Claire!"

"I just thought that if you got going without thinking about things, momentum would keep you going. And it was working." In the dim winter light seeping around the edges of the hotel curtains, she looked distinctly miffed. "I should never have said the 'a' word."

He fumbled for his glasses. "Claire, I'm sorry."

"No, I'm sorry."

"You're both pathetic."

Ears burning, Dean dragged a blanket around his

waist and slid out of bed. "I've, uh . . . you know . . . bathroom."

"Try a verb," Austin snorted from a pile of Claire's clothes on the unused bed.

As the bathroom door closed behind Dean—and then opened again as he pulled the blanket inside—Austin leaped carefully to Claire's side. "Do you want me to talk to him, *mano a mano*?"

"Thanks for the offer, but no."

"Why not?"

"Well, to begin with, you had your mano removed."

"Not my idea."

"Still." She stroked the velvet fur between his ears with her thumb. "I think this is something Dean and I have to work out on our own."

"You mean something Dean has to work out on his own. It's not actually about you."

Claire shook her head. "You're wrong."

"Of course, I'm wrong." Austin sat down and curled his tail around his front toes. "This has nothing to do with a young man who desperately wants to make you happy and, because of an inadvertent angelic evocation, is afraid he'll never be able to make you that happy again. Oh, no, this has to do with you being older and more experienced so that he's intimidated. Or it has to do with you being a Keeper because he wouldn't have caused an angel if you weren't. Or it has to do with you being a Keeper and therefore responsible for everything under the sun.

"That was sarcasm, wasn't it?"

The cat sighed. "Duh."

"So what should I do? No, wait." A raised hand cut off his reply. "Don't tell me. I should feed the cat."

"Good choice." Jumping from the bed to the dresser, he sat down again by his food dish. "You see how much easier life becomes when you concentrate on the essentials?"

The hair Diana had found in Father Harris' house was very dark at the bottom and very blond at the tip. The style was popular with the male trendies at her school, but she'd never considered it an especially angelic look. Apparently, Lena did.

Technically, the angel—Samuel—was none of her business. Technically, he wasn't Keeper business at all.

"Mom? Do you have any clear packing tape?"

Attention on breakfast preparations, Martha pointed across the kitchen with the spatula. "It's in the junk drawer."

Junk accumulates. Even those with very little, those chased from their homes by war or natural disaster, those for whom home is no more than a rough shack or a circle of barely roofed thatch, even they find themselves accumulating odds and ends for

233

which they have no immediate need. In North American kitchens, the junk drawer can be found two drawers below the cutlery, just above the drawer holding the clean dish towels.

"It's jammed."

"Jiggle it."

Even in houses with no more metaphysical content than could be found in a frozen, microwavable dinner—which at that, has more metaphysical content than actual food content—these drawers contain far more than is physically possible.

"Dart of Abaris, elf shot, scissors, string, Philosopher's Stone, half a dozen ponytail elastics . . ." Diana's eyes widened as she dumped the cloth-covered elastics into a small golden chalice. "Do you even care we could get big bucks for this thing on eBay?" she demanded, brandishing a tiny beanbag polar bear with a maple leaf on his chest.

Her mother glanced up from the toaster. "E what?"

"Gack. Am I the only person in this family who pays attention to *this* century?"

"Yes."

"Explains a lot," she muttered, shoving three plastic forks and a discolored envelope of dried mugwort aside to finally pull out the packing tape. "I'll be heading into the closet later, so don't worry if you can't find me."

"Diana, we talked about this . . ."

She sighed and grabbed a piece of toast on her way out of the kitchen. "I'm not going to *consciously* impose my will on the Otherworld."

"Again."

Continuing down the hall, she raised her voice without turning. "It was an accident, Mother."

"It's always an accident, Diana, but no one likes replacing all their closet doors."

"It's not like I didn't apologize," she muttered, shoving the last of the toast in her mouth and grabbing her coat and boots from the front hall. "And, hey, not my bad the tabloids got involved; if you don't want people to know you have skeletons in your closet, don't keep skeletons in your closet." It had been sheer bad luck for that British Keeper that the force of the explosion had blown the tibia out the window and onto the street.

Back in her bedroom with the door securely closed and warded behind her, Diana threw her coat on the bed, pulled off a piece of tape about twenty centimeters long, picked up the angel hair with it, and wrapped it around her wrist. While she hadn't exactly lied to her mother—she *was* going into the closet—she'd neglected to mention that she planned on going out the other side, a maneuver generally considered too dangerous to attempt.

The only reason Keepers exited at the same place they entered was plain old lack of imagination as far as Diana was concerned. So what if there were no other geographical references to the real world—she had that covered.

And all she had to do was make a phone call.

"Isn'titabeautifulmorning!Lookatthewaythesnow sparkles!"

Doug sucked muffin out of his teeth. "First cup of coffee, kid?"

"Ican'tbelieveI'vebeenherefortwodaysandIonlyjust discoveredthis." Grinning broadly, Samuel raced down the front steps of St. Mike's and back up again.

"You have to remember to breathe, kid."

"I do?" Well, now he did. Sucking in a huge lungful of cold air, he started to cough.

"Cough into your cupped hands," Doug told him. "Then you breathe in the warmed air."

It took Samuel a minute to catch on, then another minutes for his lungs to get the idea. Finally, eyes watering, nose running, he looked up and gasped, "Ow."

Doug nodded agreeably. "Life's a bitch."

"A female dog?" Samuel asked, wiping various bodily fluids off his face before they froze.

"Oh, yeah."

And things were just starting to make sense. . . . Trying to work out this new worldview, Samuel turned, stiffened, and raced down to the sidewalk. "Are you crazy?" he demanded, yanking the cigarette out from between cracked lips and throwing it on the ground. "You're destroying your body! You only get *one*, you know."

Craig Russel, who'd been smoking since he was twelve and in better economic times had maintained a two-pack-a-day habit, peered out at Samuel from between the tattered ear flaps of his deerstalker, then down at his cigarette lying propped almost on end by a bit of dirty snow. Not entirely certain what had just happened, he squatted and extended fingers stained yellow-brown with nicotine.

"Didn't you hear me?" Samuel ground the cigarette into pieces and the pieces into the snow. "Those things are bad for you!"

Grizzled brows drew in. "You smashed my smoke."

"Well, yeah. It's poison."

"You smashed my smoke." Craig stood, slowly, and leaned forward to stare into Samuel's face. "My last smoke."

Eyes beginning to water again, Samuel leaned back. "Do you have any idea how bad those things made your breath sm . . ." His mouth opened and closed a few more times, but no sound emerged. Up on his toes, back arched, he pushed at the air with stiff fingers.

"Let him go, Craig."

"He smashed my smoke. My last smoke."

"Yeah, I know, but you keep hold of his balls any longer and people'll start to talk."

Craig stared down at his right hand as though he recognized neither it nor the crushed fabric and flesh it held. "He smashed my . . ."

"No shit. But I bet he's really, really sorry." Scratching at a scab buried deep in the stubble on his chin, Doug turned a bloodshot gaze on the younger man. "Ain't you, kid?"

Samuel nodded. Vigorously. The pigeon about to land on his head banked left and settled on his shoulder. A second pigeon, following close behind, touched down on the other side.

"Oh, man." Eyes wide, Craig opened his hand and backed away. "He's got pigeons!"

Three.

Four.

Craig turned and ran.

Bent nearly double, both hands cupping his crotch, Samuel whimpered. Five pigeons landed on his back, jostling for space.

"You shouldn't of smashed Craig's smoke, kid."

"But they're . . . bad for . . . him."

Finally freeing the scab, Doug flicked it away. "Worse for you."

That was hard to argue with. "He's stronger than . . . he looks."

"Yep."

Finally beginning to get his breath back, Samuel cautiously straightened, dumping the five pigeons into the feathered crowd gathered around his feet.

"Is there an up side to these things?" he demanded, cautiously pulling fabric away from his body. "They've been nothing but trouble since I got them."

"Them? Oh. Them. Well, there's girls."

"What do they have to do with girls?"

Doug frowned thoughtfully. "I forget."

Half a block away, a pay phone began to ring. The diaspora of street people fanning out from St. Mike's paused as one, then began moving again. Phones had nothing to do with them.

"Half a mo, kid. That's probably my bookie." A little more than half a minute later, he was back. "Not mine, kid. Yours."

"But I don't have a bookie."

"Que sera. She still wants to talk to you."

The pigeons reluctantly gave way before him and fell in behind.

Samuel picked up the phone—patented by Alexander Graham Bell in 1876, and he had no idea why he knew that but didn't know which end he was supposed to speak into. Finally, he figured it out. "Hello?"

"Samuel? My name is Diana, and I'm a Keeper. Do you know what a Keeper is?"

"The people who maintain the metaphysical balance of good on this world."

"Ta dah."

He thought about everything he'd seen and heard over the last two days, especially about the things he'd heard last night in the shelter. "You're not doing a very good job."

"Give me a break, I'm still in high school. I want to meet you, so I need you to do me a favor. Find a closet door, open it enough to get your arm through, and wave it around."

"Wave it?"

"Your arm. When I grab your hand, pull me through to your side."

"You'll fit through a space I can get my arm through?"

"Excuse me?"

"You said . . ."

"Yeah, I know what I said. You can open the door a little wider when you pull me through."

"Oh." He wondered if she was pretty. Then he wondered why it mattered. Then he found himself wondering about her breasts. He had a feeling he shouldn't be, but he couldn't seem to stop.

"Samuel?"

He pushed a pigeon out of the phone booth. "How do you know my name?"

"Father Harris told me. Are you all right?"

"My genitalia hurts."

"What have you been . . . never mind. I don't want to know. *Can* you find a closet door?"

Samuel sighed and shrugged even though he knew the Keeper couldn't see him. "Sure."

"Brillig. I'll be there as fast as I can."

*   *   *

St. Patrick was right. There *was* something funny about that boy. Lacing up her boots, Diana went over their conversation but couldn't put her finger on it. For an angel, he'd sounded pretty much like any of the guys she went to school with, right down to that last, irritating *"Sure."*

Minus the comment about the genitalia.

Or given a different choice of words at the very least.

She shoved her arms into her jacket, stuffed her hat and mittens into the outside pockets, checked her inside pocket for her wallet, and stepped into the closet, pulling the door closed but not latching it behind her. She'd have preferred to be traveling with her backpack, her computer, and her cell phone, but the possibilities reacted badly to electronics. Last time she tried to take her computer in with her, every window in the Otherworld had to be closed and reopened before things stabilized.

Tripping over a pile of shoes propelled her half a dozen staggering steps into the darkness. Arms flailing, she finally regained her balance after careening off a number of hard objects she couldn't identify through the bulk of her jacket.

"Stupid goose down . . . makes me look like the Michelin Man."

Stupid winter.

Stupid cold.

"Like it would've killed my parents to have settled outside of Disney World?" she asked the darkness. The darkness answered with the distant strains of a familiar theme song. Wincing, she redirected her concentration toward the angel, wondering just what made subconscious control of the Otherworld so different from conscious control.

Worse luck that Samuel wasn't in Florida. She could use a break from late December in Canada.

It grew lighter.

The ground compacted under her boots.

A jack pine dropped a load of snow down the back of her neck.

"Oh, man!"

By the time she finished dancing around, flapping the snow away, it was fully light. Or as light as it was going to get at any rate. Snow-covered hills rolled away into the distance. To her right, a jagged rock outcrop rose up only a little grayer than the sky. To her left, and pretty much directly above her, evergreens bowed under their burden of snow.

Blowing out a disgusted plume of air, Diana dug for hat and mitts thinking that Mrs. Green, her Can-Lit teacher, 'd be creaming herself at so much landscape and isolation. "Yeah, right," she muttered, dragging her hat over her ears. "Like Canada in late December doesn't include coffee shops and Boxing Day sales. Couldn't have landed in an Otherworld Starbucks or HMV, oh, no. *That* would be too easy."

What made subconscious control of the Other-world so different from conscious control? Well, that was obvious: conscious control created a place where people actually wanted to be.

She couldn't see the angel's arm.

Which wasn't surprising since there weren't any doors.

"You can't go back in there, kid."

Samuel paused, one hand on the small door leading into St. Mike's. "Why not? It's a House of Light, and I'm an angel."

"Well, yeah, but the priests get all bent out of shape if you hang out inside during the day. They got stuff to do, you know."

"I won't get in the way. I have to stick my arm into a closet."

"Why?"

"It's for a girl."

"Hey." Both Doug's hands went up. "Say no more re amore. You go put your arm in a closet, and I'll be waiting right here when they toss your ass back into the cold."

"Sure." Hurrying along the side of the sanctuary, he found himself really loving that word. It was a good, all-purpose sort of a word. "Sure," he told himself softly. It could mean anything. Passing a niche holding a statue of Mary cradling an infant Christ, he smiled up at her. "Sure," he said.

"And just what does that mean?" she demanded, shifting the baby to her other hip.

"You know . . ."

"If I knew, I wouldn't have asked. Stand up straight, Samuel, don't slouch. And what have you done to your hair?"

"Um . . ." He touched his head. He hadn't done anything to his hair. Had he? "I, uh, have to go put my arm in a closet."

"Fine. Just remember to clean up when you're done."

"Sure. I mean, okay."

"Teenagers," the statue sighed as he hurried away.

"I refuse to believe my subconscious had anything to do with this," Diana sighed.

"Beg pardon, Miss?"

"Never mind." She settled back in the furs, left arm held out, coat shoved up, mitt shoved down. As they came out from under the trees and started across a rolling expanse of snow, the glowing angel's hair taped around her wrist began to fade. When she pointed to the right, the driver, a pure white Alaskan Malamute, leaned out, barking, "Gee! Gee!"

The seven Mounties in the traces angled to the right, the sled came around, and the hair began to glow strongly again.

The Mounties were fresh and running well. They were making good time.

* * *

Standing in the basement of St. Mike's with his arm stuffed into a broom closet, Samuel wondered why his hand was getting cold.

"There's the trading post, Miss. Smells like we've found your exit."

Diana sniffed at the frigid air, then rubbed her nose with the back of her mitten. "All I can smell is aftershave."

"I had the Mounties groomed this morning."

"Let's just not go there, okay?"

The hair taped to her wrist blazed, and an answering light waved up and down at the trading post door. It disappeared for a moment then, just as Diana was beginning to worry, it reappeared again. A closet, wardrobe, armoire, or the like was necessary to enter the Otherworld but any door would do for a way out. Under normal circumstances, walking into the trading post with an intent to travel would put her back in her bedroom, but Samuel straddled both worlds as a metaphysical construct, and could, therefore, anchor an exit. Diana had thought out the theory very carefully.

Checking the ancient texts . . .

Consulting the mystic oracles . . .

Watching the *National Geographic* special on PBS . . .

Actually, the idea had come to her at two a.m. when a particularly loud whir/click from her clock radio had pulled her from a dream where she seemed to be either Sharon Stone or Barney Rubble. Which was in no way connected to anything much.

Since here she was and there was Samuel, the theory seemed sound and nothing more would have been accomplished even had she checked, consulted, and spent the evening with public television instead of Laura Croft.

By the time the sled pulled up in front of the trading post, Diana had untangled herself from the furs. Swinging both legs over the side, she sank up to her boot tops in the snow, staggered and would have fallen had the husky not stretched out a foreleg to help her. "Thank you." Balance regained, she moved away from the runners, just barely managing to resist a totally inappropriate urge to rub his tummy.

"Glad to be of service, Miss." He touched the edge of a pointed ear with one paw, whistled to his Mounties, and rode off into a convenient and localized sunset.

Diana watched them disappear, then climbed the thick plank stairs toward the light. Which disappeared.

Samuel rubbed his arm where the door kept closing on it and wished the Keeper would hurry.

The light reappeared, and from beyond it, Diana heard a voice say: "Why the hell does that damned door keep opening?"

Then the light disappeared again.

* * *

"Ow!"

Appeared.

"There's nothing wrong with the damned latch."
Disappeared.

"OW!"

Appeared.

This time, Diana had her mitten off. She reached into the light, felt fingers close around hers, and kicked the door open.

She heard the unmistakable hollow impact of wood hitting forehead, half an expletive, and then she was standing in a dim basement staring into the gold-flecked eyes of the angel. She could see the light he was made of, and that was good, but that wasn't all she could see, and that was bad. Standing almost nose to nose, she realized he wasn't much taller than she was and unthreateningly attractive in a boy band sort of way.

"Thanks for hurrying," he muttered, releasing her hand and cradling his arm against his chest.

Diana blinked. "Are angels allowed to be that sarcastic?"

"Apparently."

"Hey! What are you kids doing down there?"

They turned together to face the middle-aged nun stomping toward them.

"*Please*, excuse us, Sister. We were just leaving."

She stopped in mid-stomp. "Right. Fine. Get going, then!"

"You can't do that to a servant of the light," Samuel protested as they hurried up the stairs.

"Yeah, I can. Just did."

"But you're not supposed to."

"Did you want to explain what we were doing down there to Sister Mary I've-spent-more-years-teaching-teenagers-than-you've-been-alive-so-don't-give-me-any-lip?"

"Her name is Sister Mary Francis."

"So what? Look, Samuel, some things you can explain to Bystanders, some things you can't. Pulling a Keeper out of a closet is totally can't."

They retraced Samuel's path along the Sanctuary. He carefully avoided eye contact with the statue of the Holy Mother.

Half a dozen pigeons waited with Doug on the front steps. As Samuel stepped outside, they started toward him, noticed Diana, and came to a sudden, feather ruffling stop.

"The flying rats with you?" she sighed.

"Sort of. I can't get rid of them."

"Not a problem." She raked a disdainful gaze over the birds and without raising her voice said, "Scram."

A moment later, the steps were clear, a lone feather lost in the panic the only indication the pigeons had ever been there at all.

"Why didn't it work when I did that?" Samuel muttered, hands shoved into his pockets.

"You wouldn't hurt them, and they knew that. I, on the other hand, am perfectly capable of roasting them with a few chestnuts over an open fire and they knew that, too."

"But you wouldn't."

"You don't know that."

The gold flecks swirled into the brown. "Yes, I do."

"Stop it!"

"Kids, kids, kids." Doug heaved himself up onto his feet and walked over. "Not the place to be spatting."

"Spatting?" Diana wrinkled her nose at the smell. "Who are you?"

"This is Doug, he's an angel, too. He taught me how to eat, how to urinate . . ."

"Eww, gross."

". . . where to sleep. I wouldn't have gotten through last night without him."

"You'd have managed, kid."

Diana snorted. "*You're* an angel?"

He spread his arms. The smell intensified. "Fuckin' A. But my work here is done." Sliding sideways a step, he elbowed Samuel in the ribs. "You've got your girlie to take care of you now, kid. Me, I hear a bottle of . . ." His brows drew in. "Doesn't really matter what's in the bottle, come to think of it." A grayish tongue swept over dry lips. "But something's callin' me, that's for shittin' sure. See ya, kid."

"See you, Doug."

Watching Doug descend to the sidewalk and head north, Diana couldn't think of a less likely angel— although she supposed it was a harmless enough delusion. "Come on, I'm freezing, let's walk."

Samuel shrugged. "Sure."

At the sidewalk, she glanced back up at the impressive front of the cathedral. And frowned. It had been snowing lightly, enough to obliterate all but the most recent footprints. A single line matching her boots led up to the wide double doors. She looked down at Samuel's feet, then she looked north. The snow lay like an ivory carpet, surface unbroken to the corner.

"Son of a . . ."

A small dog trotting by on the other side of the street paused expectantly.

Diana waved him on. "Never mind."

"Claire!"

Down on one knee by the side of the road, Claire waved at Dean to be quiet. She almost had the stupid hole closed and . . .

Grabbing her under both arms, Dean threw her back toward the truck just as the SUV fishtailed across the highway, slid right over the hole, and came to an abrupt halt at the edge of the ditch.

Claire stared at the skid marks, noted that the heavy vehicle would have gone right through her, then squirmed around in Dean's arms. "Thank you," she said, and pulled his mouth down to hers. After a moment, in spite of heavy clothes and subzero temperatures, she got the distinct impression that they could solve the angel problem right there.

"I should see if the buddy in the car's all right, then," he murmured, separating their mouths only far enough to speak.

"You should." She flicked her tongue against his lips and slid her hand up under his coat.

Dean jerked back and slammed his head into the truck. "Lord t'undering Jesus, Claire! Your fingers are like ice!"

"Sorry."

He touched a hand to the back of his head and winced. "It's okay."

"No, it's not okay. That sounded like it really hurt."

"Hey, Florence Nightingale." Austin's head appeared over the tailgate. "The man knows if he's okay. Get back to work. I'm freezing my furry little butt off out here!"

"You could have stayed in the truck," Claire reminded him as she stood and wondered if it was against some sort of guy code to help Dean to his feet.

Austin flicked his ear to dislodge a snowflake. "I had to use the little cat room. Now, you," he fixed Dean with a baleful glare, "check the yuppie mobile. You . . ." The single eye switched targets. ". . . close the hole. And you . . ." Lifting his head, he scowled at the sky. ". . . stop snowing on me. I'm old."

"Austin, that's not . . ."

A sudden gust of wind blew the last flakes sideways. No more fell.

Only the front wheels of the SUV had gone into the ditch; a good two thirds remained firmly on the wide shoulder. The engine purred quietly to itself, the sound barely audible and nothing came out of the exhaust in spite of the cold. It was a deep maroon with a high gloss finish that looked like it could withstand a meteor strike and, in spite of four-wheel drive and heavy duty suspension, this was likely as far off road as it had ever been.

Squinting through the tinted glass, Dean realized the thin, blonde woman behind the wheel was on the phone. When he tapped on the driver's door window, she opened it a finger's width but continued looking down at the laptop open on the leather upholstery of the passenger seat. "Ma'am, you don't need to call for a tow. You're barely off the road; you can just back up."

She ignored him and kept talking. ". . . telling you the bank beat by nine cents the average estimate of sixty cents a share."

"Ma'am?"

A slender hand in a burgundy leather glove waved vaguely in his direction. "But you're forgetting that volatile capital markets allowed a forty-five percent increase in fees, and that's where you can attribute most of the profit growth."

"I'm after heading back to my truck now."

"Look, Frank, it was loan volumes that brought the interest income up nine percent to three hundred and thirty-seven million dollars."

"Ma'am?"

"Three hundred and thirty-seven million dollars, Frank!"

"Never mind."

Claire and Austin were waiting inside the truck.

"I guess the driver's all right," Dean told them as Claire lifted Austin off the driver's seat and onto her lap, "but she wouldn't actually talk to me."

"She? Should I go?"

"Got three hundred and thirty-seven million dollars?" When Claire answered in the negative, he grinned. "Then I doubt she'll talk to you either." Putting his glasses back on after carefully wiping the condensation off the lenses, he frowned. "What's wrong?"

"A new Summons; stronger than these little roadside things." She rested her chin on the top of Austin's head. "It feels strange."

"Is it the angel, then? 'Cause if I wasn't scared abroad by Hell, an angel won't trouble me much."

"I don't think so."

"Only one way to find out." He pulled carefully onto the highway. "Which way?"

"North."

"So, dear, when you call yourself a demon—is that a club?"

"No." Byleth sagged farther down in the back seat, the shoulder belt preventing a really good slouch. "It's not a fu . . ."

"Language." Half turning, Eva raised a cautioning finger.

"It's not a club." Byleth had no idea how the mortal woman did it. Something about her tone of voice, her expression, evoked an instinctive obedience. If the Princes of Hell could figure it out, they'd be . . . well, since they were already ruling Hell, nothing much would change but the shouting. Hell could do with a little less shouting in Byleth's opinion.

"It's not a gang, is it?" Harry asked, trying to catch her gaze in the rearview mirror. "Because I know how seductive gangs can be. Black leather and motorcycles and . . ."

"Harry."

Under the edge of his tweed hat, Harry's ears pinked.

Eva half turned again. "Harry had a bit of a past before he met me."

"I'll bet he did," the demon muttered.

"What was that, dear?"

"It's *not* a gang."

"Oh, that's good."

The day was not going as planned. Coercing the old man into driving her to Toronto had somehow turned into a cheerful family outing. With snacks. She should have walked out right after that big homemade breakfast and found some punk kid who'd just got his license and who'd do anything she asked if she just bounced those really annoying breasts at him in a promising sort of a way. Not that she'd keep the promise, of course. Her kind excelled at broken promises.

"Shall we play license plate bingo, dear?"

Fortunately Harry answered before she could.

"Byleth's too old for that, Eva. Remember what our lot were like at her age?"

"The boys," Eva began, but Harry cut her off, one hand leaving the steering wheel just long enough to pat a rounded knee.

"The boys played to make you happy, but our Angela drew the line about the same time she started high school."

"I suppose," Eva sighed. Then she perked up and

half turned one more time. "Where do you go to high school, dear?"

"I don't."

"Oh, you have to get an education, dear. After all, knowledge is power."

"Power is power," Byleth snarled. She should have power. She should be able to reach into the dark heart of humanity and twist it to her purposes. Not only had some extra anatomy put an unexpected crimp in her plans—and she was so going to kick that angel's ass when she found him—but her current minions gave her very little to work with.

"Hey, Mr. Porter, that guy in the import flipped you the finger as he passed."

Which is not to say she didn't do what she could.

"Harry, that's no reason for you to drive faster," Eva warned.

He smiled at her briefly. "Of course not."

But the speed crept up.

It didn't take much to keep it rising.

The inevitable siren brought a smile and a frisson of anticipation.

Lips pressed into a disapproving line, Eva kept silent as Harry pulled over and turned off the engine.

Behind them, a car door slammed and footsteps approached along the gravel shoulder. When Harry rolled down his window, Byleth straightened to get a better look.

"License and registration, please."

The Ontario Provincial Police constable was tall and tanned, his hair gleaming gold in the winter sunlight. His eyes were blue, his voice was deep, and his chin had the cutest cleft. The breadth of his shoulders filled the window.

"Do you know how fast you were going, sir?"

In the back seat, Byleth sat up straighter, tugging at her jacket.

"I'm sorry, Officer. Some kid passed me in a sporty little import, and I guess I just rose to the challenge."

A quick swipe of her tongue across her lips. Did she still have any lipstick on? She *knew* she should have put more on at the last rest stop.

"You can't let other people do the driving in your car, sir."

That was clever. He wasn't only the cutest thing she'd seen since she arrived, he was *smart*, too.

"Now 113km in an 80 should be a three-hundred-dollar fine and six points off your license, but . . ."

Why didn't he look at her?

". . . I'm going to let you off with a warning. This time. If I pull you over again . . ." His voice trailed off.

And he was merciful.

Handing back Harry's paperwork, he finally glanced into the back seat, but his gaze slid over her like she was completely unworthy of being noticed.

Arms folded, brows in, she slid back into her

slouch, achieving new lows. What the hell did she care about merciful anyway?

"Thank you, Officer."

"Drive safely, sir. Have a good day, ma'am. Miss."

Her eyes narrowed. "Whatever."

He glanced into the back again, then he smiled at Harry. "Teenagers, eh?"

"Teenagers, eh?" Byleth mocked as the officer returned to his cruiser. "What a jerk."

"Good-looking man, though. Wasn't he, dear?"

"I never noticed. And what are you smiling about?" she demanded as the Porters exchanged an amused glance.

"Nothing."

"Good." Glaring straight ahead, she refused to acknowledge the police car as it passed, repeating, "Jerk. Jerk. Jerk. Jerk," vehemently under her breath.

"Careful, Austin." Scooping him back up onto the seat, Claire wore a worried expression. "Are you all right? You were sound asleep, and then . . ."

"And then I wasn't. Yeah, I know." He got his legs untangled and climbed over to her right thigh, where he could stand and look out the window. "Something we passed woke me up."

"Do you want me to pull over?" Dean asked.

"No." He put a paw on the glass and watched the traffic across the median speeding south. "It's gone now."

TEN

"You are *so* not like what I imagined an angel
to be. Your hair, your clothes . . ."

"My genitalia," Samuel added a little mournfully.

Diana made a disgusted face and shoved mittened
hands deeper into her pockets. "I wouldn't know,
and I'd really rather you quit mentioning it."

"Them."

"What*ever*."

"Why?" For no good reason, he jumped up and
smacked the No Parking sign, checking out of the
corner of one eye to see if the Keeper was impressed.
She didn't seem to be.

"They're just not something people talk about in
public."

"Should we go someplace private?"

"You wish."

"For what?"

"Pardon?"

"What do I wish for?"

"Well, if you don't know, I'm not going to tell you."

"But if I knew, you wouldn't have to tell me," he pointed out reasonably as they turned the corner onto Yonge Street. Across the road, a double line of people stood stamping their feet and blowing on their hands. "Those people are cold. Why are they standing there?"

"Best guess, they're waiting to get into the electronics store for the Boxing Day sale."

"Why?"

"What do you mean, why? Because it's a sale." She rolled her eyes. "I thought you had Higher Knowledge."

"I do. The 26th of December is called Boxing Day because in Victorian England that's when the rich boxed up their Christmas leftover for the poor."

"Really?"

"It's one theory. But it still doesn't explain that." He waved a hand at the crowd across the street. "Most of those people are anxious, over half are actually unhappy, and although they'll be saving money, they'd all be better off if they just didn't spend it. A new stereo won't give meaning to their empty, shallow lives."

Diana grabbed the back of his jacket as he stepped off the curb. "Where are you going?"

"To tell them that."

"I'm just guessing here, but I think they know."

He half-turned in her grip. "Really?"

"Uh-huh. It's a human thing; a new stereo will help them *forget* their empty shallow lives."

"Human memory is that bad?"

"Well, duh. Why do you think platform shoes and mini skirts have come back? Because people have forgotten how truly dorky they looked the first time." Diana shuddered. "Me, I've seen my mother's yearbook pictures." She hauled him back up onto the sidewalk. "You hungry?"

"Starving."

"You're not supposed to be." His situation had deteriorated farther than she'd feared. "Come on, I'll buy you . . ." She checked her watch. ". . . lunch and we'll talk."

". . . and that's why you're here." Diana peered over the pile of fast food wrappers in front of the angel. "Are you blushing?"

"You said your sister . . . you know," he mumbled.

"I really think you've got more to worry about than my sister's sex life." Elbows up on the table, she ticked the points off on her fingers. "One, angels are, by definition, messengers of the Lord, but because of the way you came into being, you have no message, thus leaving you with a distinct identity crisis."

"Thus?"

"Don't interrupt. Two, you can't return to the light,

so you're stuck here even though you have no reason to be here and no visible means of support. Three, from what I've seen so far, the boy bits seem to be doing all the defining."

"The what?"

She sighed. "Don't make me say it."

"Oh. Them. No, they're not."

"Yeah, they are."

"No."

"Yes. You shouldn't be perpetually hungry. You shouldn't know what a six-liter engine is." Her eyes narrowed. "And you shouldn't be looking at my breasts!"

Ears burning, he locked his gaze on her right eyebrow. "You're a Keeper. You could send me back."

"Only if you want to go." Pushing a desiccated French fry around with a fingertip, she sighed again. This was, after all, why she'd come to Toronto. It had only taken a small prod from St. Patrick for her to realize that an angel designed by committee would need a Keeper's help to go home—her help. "The problem is," she said slowly, "if I send you back, you won't be you anymore. You'd just be light."

"But that's what I am."

Diana shook her head. "That's not all you are. If I send you back, then the you that I'm talking to, the you that's experienced the world, he'll disappear. I'll have killed him."

"Killed me?" When she nodded, he frowned. "That sucks."

"Tell me about it."

"You already know about it."

"Figure of speech, Samuel. I was agreeing with you." She dropped her chin onto her hands. "I don't know what to do, and I really hate that feeling."

"Tell me about it," Samuel muttered, unwrapping a fourth . . . something that seemed to involve chicken ova, a slice of pig in nitrate, and melted orange stuff probably intended to represent a dairy product. He'd eaten the first three too fast to really taste them, which all things considered, had probably been smart. "So, what you do think of the idea that I am the message? That I'm here to help people?"

"How? And don't give me that look," Diana warned him. "I'm not being mean, I'm being realistic. You can't even help yourself."

"I've been managing."

"No. You haven't. Can I think of an example? Hmmm, let's see." She leaned forward. "How about: without me, you'd be covered in pigeons."

"Well, yeah, but . . ."

"And pigeon shit."

His brows drew in. He didn't know they could do that. It was an interesting feeling. "I'm still a superior being, I can figure stuff out."

"How do you know you're a superior being?"

"I just . . . know."

"So does every other male between twelve and twenty," she snorted, folding her arms. "But that doesn't solve their problems either."

Samuel stared at her for a long moment, then he smiled. "I could be insulted, but I know you're only saying that because of your own sexual ambiguity." He took a large bite and chewed slowly. "I mean, you say you're a lesbian, but you've never actually made it with a woman although you did make it with a guy and it wasn't entirely his fault it was such a disaster."

Her lip curled. "If you were to choke right now, I wouldn't save you."

* * *

They left the highway just north of Huntsville, heading southwest on 518.

"We're close," Claire insisted when Austin pointed out the total lack of anything but Canadian landscape around them.

"Close to what?" he snorted. "The edge of the world?"

"We need to turn right soon. There." She pointed. "Is that a road?"

It was. After another thirteen kilometers of spruce bog and snow, they passed the first house. Then the second. Then a boarded-up business. Then, suddenly, they were in downtown Waverton—all five blocks of it.

"Park in front of the bank."

Braking carefully, Dean peered down at the thick, milky slabs of frozen water. "I don't know, Claire; it looks some icy."

"We'll be okay."

"If you're thinking of using my kitty litter to make it okay, think again," Austin muttered, climbing up onto the top of the seat.

"You mean because I'm only a Keeper with access to an infinite number of possibilities and wouldn't be able to get this truck moving without a bag of dried clay bits designed to absorb cat urine?"

"Essentially . . ." He paused to lick his shoulder. ". . . yes."

Lips pressed into a thin line, Claire reached into the possibilities and slid the truck sideways across the nearly frictionless surface, bringing it to a gentle stop against the slightly higher ice sheet that was the curb.

Dean released the breath he'd been holding and forced the white-knuckled fingers of one hand to let go of the steering wheel long enough to switch off the engine. "You need to warn me when you're after doing something like that," he said, still staring straight ahead as though he intended to keep the truck from ending up at the New Accounts desk by visual aids alone. "Sideways is not a good way."

"Sorry."

He turned to face her then. "Really?"

"No."

"Austin!"

"Just giving him the benefit of my experience. You've never been sorry when you do that sort of thing to me."

"When have I ever . . . ?"

"Plevna. December 12th, 1997."

"How was I supposed to know claws don't provide traction? It was an honest mistake."

"Uh-huh."

Yanking her toque down over her ears, Claire got out of the truck. "He scored the winning goal," she pointed out to Dean as she closed the door.

"How did you hold the stick?" Dean wondered, pulling on his gloves.

Austin's head swiveled slowly around. "I. Didn't."

"Oh." His hindbrain decided it might be safer to back away, making no sudden moves. He caught up to Claire by the corner of the bank.

"Someone set this fire," she said, looking up at the damage. "And that opened the hole." Hugging her own elbows, she shook her head. "There's a lot of nasty coming through for the size. This might take some time to seal up; can you keep me from being disturbed?"

"You got it, Boss."

"You haven't called me that for a while."

Their eyes locked.

"You haven't told me what to do for a while."

"Maybe I should start."

"Maybe you should."

A muffled "Get a room!" from inside the truck redirected their attention to the matter at hand.

"Excuse me, Miss!" Mr. Tannison, the bank manager, hurried toward his damaged building from his temporary office across the street, upstairs over the storefront shared by Martin Eisner, the taxidermist, and Dr. Chow, the dentist. "You can't stay there. Bricks could fall." He forgot about the ice until his front boot surrendered traction and he began to slide. Before he could steady himself on the truck parked in front of the bank, a large hand caught his arm and set him back on his feet.

"It's okay, sir. She's perfectly safe."

"She is?" Something about the young man made him feel like a fool for asking. He considered himself a good judge of character—well, he had to be in his position, didn't he?—and by voice, expression, and bearing, this stranger said, *I will have my withdrawal slip filled out properly before I approach the teller, I would never stand too close at the ATM machine, and your pens are sacred to me.*

"Yes, sir."

"Oh." The blue eyes behind the glasses made him think of contributions to retirement savings plans done monthly rather than left until the last minute. "You're not from around here, are you?"

"No, sir, St. John's. Newfoundland."

"Small world. One of my tellers is from St. John's. Rose Mooran."

"Does she have a brother named Conrad, then? I played Peewee hockey with a Conrad Mooran."

"No, not her brother, that would be her husband."

"Husband? Lord t'undering Jesus."

They spent a while longer discussing hockey and the relative size of the world, then Mr. Tannison patted a muscular arm, flashed a relieved smile, and hurried back across the street.

The clutch of eight-year-olds were a little harder to impress.

When Dean limped back to the truck, Claire was standing by the passenger door looking a little stunned.

"Is it closed?"

She nodded.

"What's wrong?"

When she held up her hand, her fingertips were dusted with black glitter.

"Char?"

"Demon residue."

*   *   *

"Once you're in the city, where are you planning on going, dear?"

Byleth stared out past the Porters' heads at the Toronto skyline, thrusting up into a gray sky like a not particularly attractive pot of gold at the end of a rainbow. "As far away from you as possible," she muttered.

To her surprise, Harry Porter lifted an admonishing finger toward her reflection in the rearview mirror. "That is quite enough of that, young lady. There is no call for you to be so rude. You will apologize to Mrs. Porter this instant."

"As if."

"Fine." At the first break in traffic, he moved into the right-hand lane and began slowing down.

"Harry . . ."

"No, Eva. She apologizes, or she walks the rest of the way."

Demons understood bluffing. Byleth folded her arms and waited.

When the car finally rolled to a stop, Harry put it into park and turned around. "Last chance," he said. "Apologize, or this is as far as we go together."

She tucked her chin into her collar and glowered.

"If that's the way you want it." He unbuckled his seat belt, got out, and opened her door.

When she stared up into his face through the blast of frigid air, she realized he wasn't bluffing. "You actually want me to walk. We're still miles away!"

"We're still kilometers away," Harry corrected.

"And I want you to apologize. It's your choice whether or not you walk."

It was cold outside. It was warm inside the car.

"Get back in the car and drive."

He merely stood there. She might as well have tried to command a rock.

"I'll hitchhike, then, and get picked up by a mass murderer, and then how will you feel when they find a broken bleeding body by the side of the road." It wouldn't be her broken, bleeding body, but he didn't need to know that.

Harry shook his head. "Not even mass murderers would stop for you. Not at these speeds. You'll be walking all the way."

"I don't want to walk!"

"Then apologize."

The car rocked as four transports passed, belching diesel fumes. She contemplated kicking Harry into traffic, but Eva would likely fall apart and be totally useless and although she knew how to bring plagues and pestilence, she didn't know how to drive.

"Make up your mind, Byleth."

"Fine." Anything to get her into the city where she could ditch these losers. "I'm s . . ." Her very nature fought with the word. "I'm sorr . . ." She had to form each letter independently, forcing it out past reluctant lips. "I'm sorry. Okay?"

"Eva?"

"Apology accepted, dear."

"Now was that so hard?" Harry asked, smiling at her reflection as he slid back behind the wheel.

"Yeah, it was."

"Don't worry. It'll get easier with time."

She was afraid of that.

*   *   *

"Excuse me." Braced against the movement of the escalator, Samuel reached forward and tapped the heavyset matron on one virgin-wool covered shoulder. "The sign says that if you stand on the right, then people in a hurry can walk up the left."

"There's no space on the right," she pointed out sharply.

"Then you should have waited."

"And maybe you should mind your own business."

"You shouldn't let the fear of being on your own keep you in a bad relationship. Your husband is controlling and manipulative, and just because he doesn't love you anymore, doesn't mean you shouldn't love yourself . . ."

The sound of her palm connecting with his cheek disappeared into the ambient noise. In the fine tradition of mall crawlers everywhere, those standing too close to have missed the exchange either stared fixedly at nothing or isolated themselves from the incident behind a loud and pointless conversation with their nearest companion. As they reached the second level and the heavyset woman bustled off to the left, Diana smoothed the tiny hole closed, grabbed Samuel's arm, and yanked him off to the right.

"What was *that* all about?"

Rubbing at the mark on his cheek, he looked confused. "I was just trying to help, you know, do that message thing."

"And what help is a message telling that woman her husband's a creep who doesn't love her anymore?"

"She knows that. Now she needs to move on."

"And *you* know that because . . . ?"

He shoved his hands in his front pockets and shrugged. "I have Higher Knowledge."

"Which gives you personal information on the life of a perfect stranger but neglects to tell you what a stoplight means?"

"Yes."

She'd never heard such a load of sanctimonious crap. "Just don't do that again, okay?"

"Sure."

"Did you know that with the price of those boots you could feed a Third World child for a year?"

Something in the gold-brown eyes compelled an honest answer.

"Yeah, I do."

"So . . . ?" Samuel prompted, smiling encouragingly.

"So why don't you mind your own fucking business, dude?"

"That's the guilt talking."

"Yeah?" A very large hand wound itself into the front of Samuel's jacket. "And in a minute you're gonna feel my fist talking!"

Diana handed the shoebox to the clerk and reached into the possibilities just in time to keep an innocent Bystander from committing mayhem on an angel—as justified as that mayhem may have been. Freeing Samuel's jacket, she shoved him out of the store and started things up again.

"I was just . . ."

"Well, stop it."

"But . . ."

"No. People like to have their moral failings pointed out about as much as they like to have their personal lives discussed in public by strangers." She tightened her grip and dragged him quickly past a couple playing what looked like the Stanley Cup finals of tonsil hockey. When she finally slowed and took a look at him, he seemed strangely restrained. "What?"

"Those two people . . ."

There were thousands of people in the Center, but she had a fairly good idea who he meant. "Yeah? What about them?"

"They had their tongues in each other's mouths."

"I didn't notice."

He snorted, a very unangelic sound. "They looked like they had gerbils in their cheeks."

"Okay." She had to admit she was intrigued by the image. "So?"

"So isn't that unsanitary?"

"Gerbils?"

"Tongues."

"Not really. And don't get any ideas—our relationship is strictly Keeper/Angel."

"I wasn't . . ."

"You were."

"I couldn't *help* it."

He sounded so miserable, Diana found herself patting his shoulder in sympathy. "Come on, we'll duck out at the next doors—a little cold air will clear your head."

"It's not my head."

"Whoa. Didn't I make myself clear? We're *not* discussing other body parts." If the last pat rocked him sideways a little more emphatically than necessary, well, tough.

The sidewalk outside the mall was nearly deserted. There was a small group of people huddled together at the corner of Yonge and Dundas, waiting for the streetcar, and a lone figure hurrying toward them from the other direction in what could only be described as a purposeful manner.

Hair on the back on her neck lifting, Diana stared at the approaching figure, then looked down at two identical snowflakes melting on the back of her hand. "Shit!"

"What's that smell?" Samuel muttered. He checked the bottom of both shoes.

"Forget the smell. Move it!"

She hustled the angel north, hoping that Nalo hadn't seen them. The older Keeper had no more authority over Samuel than she did, but something— the identical flakes that continued to fall, the way every car on the road was suddenly a black Buick, the street busker playing "Flight of the Bumblebee" with his lower lip frozen to his harmonica—*something* was telling her to keep them apart.

At the corner of Yonge and Dundas, Diana felt the possibilities open.

"Hold it right there, young lady!"

Grinding her teeth, she pulled a token out of necessity, shoved Samuel into the line of people climbing onto the eastbound Dundas streetcar, and told him she'd catch up later.

"But . . ."

"Trust me." She pried his fingers out of the down depths of her sleeve and, with one hand on an admirably tight tush, boosted him up the steps. "And try not to piss anyone off!" she added as the door closed. Staring back out at her through the filthy glass, he looked lost and pathetic, but she couldn't shake the feeling he was safer away from the other Keeper.

Wrapping herself in surly teenager, she turned, stepped back up onto the sidewalk, and folded her arms. "Don't call me 'young lady'," she growled, when Nalo closed the last of the distance between them. "I really, really hate it."

"Really? Tough. Now, you want to tell me why you were hauling ass away from me, or do you want me to make some guesses?"

They were alone on the corner—there'd be no help from curious Bystanders. Diana snorted and rolled her eyes. Not a particularly articulate response but useful when stalling.

"Your parents don't know you're here, do they? Don't bother denying it, girl . . ." An inarguable finger cut off incipient protest. ". . . you've got guilt rolling off you like smoke."

Perfect! True, if a tad trite. Diana could have kissed her. She widened her eyes. "You won't tell?"

"None of my business. I don't care if you're here to waste money, I don't care if you're here to see that boy you stuffed on the streetcar—oh, I saw him, don't give me that look—but I *do* care about what you've been up to since you got here."

"But I haven't done anything!"

"You stopped time, Diana."

Oops.

"I was trying to prevent a fight."

Nalo sighed. "Girl, I don't care if you were trying to prevent an Abba reunion. . . ."

"Who?"

"Never mind. The point is, you've been messing with the metaphysical background noise since you got here The whole place is buzzing."

"It wasn't me!"

"No? Then who?"

A black Buick cruised by, and Diana bit her tongue.

"Look, I spent half an hour on the phone with the 102-year-old Keeper monitoring that site in Scarbourgh who's positive we're heading toward a battle between the dark and the light, and I have better things to do with my time than convince the senile old bird we're not heading for Armageddon. Either tone it down or take it home, but stop screwing up my . . . what's that on your arm?"

Diana brushed away a little snow, taking the angel residue with it, and peered down at her sleeve. "Where?"

The older Keeper shook her head. "Must've been ice crystals." She tucked a cashmere scarf more securely into the collar of her coat. "I think I'd like to keep an eye on you for a while. You can join me for a bit."

Surrender seemed the only option, but she made a token protest regardless. "I can't afford the kind of restaurants you like."

"Honey, we're Keepers. We should be, if nothing else, adaptable."

"You buying?"

"I might be."

"Then I can be adaptable."

*　　*　　*

Distress bordering on panic pulled Samuel off the streetcar and across the road into a maze of four-story apartment buildings and identical rows of two-story brick town houses. He found the source of the distress crouched miserably at the bottom of a rusty slide and dropped to his knees beside her.

With gentle fingers, he brushed snow off her head.

She turned toward him, looked up into his eyes, and threw herself against his chest. "Lost, lost, lost, lost . . ."

"Shhh, it's all right, Daisy." He had to physically brace himself against the force of her emotions. "Don't worry, I'll help. Do you live in one of these buildings?"

Shivering, she pressed herself harder against him. "Lost . . ."

He could see where she'd entered the playground, but her prints were filling in fast. "Come on." Standing, he tucked two fingers under her red leather collar. "We'll have to hurry."

They weren't quite fast enough. The paw prints

had disappeared under fresh snow by the time they got to River Street.

"Now where?"

The Dalmatian looked up at him with such complete trust, Samuel had to swallow a lump in his throat. Dropping to one knee on the sidewalk, he held out his hand. "Give me your paw."

She looked at him for a long moment, looked at his hand, then laid her right front paw against his palm.

He reached into himself for the light.

* * *

"What was that?"

Diana kept her attention on her stuffed pita. "I didn't do anything."

"Did I even mention you?" Nalo swiveled around, her right hand combing the air. "Something shifted."

"It's not a hole."

"No, it isn't." She sat down again, eyes locked on the younger Keeper. "So I guess it's none of our business."

* * *

The glowing paw prints led him to a town house in the Oak Street Co-op. As they turned down the walk, Daisy pulled free and raced for the door.

"Home! Home! Home!"

The door opened before she reached it, and a slender

279

young woman rushed out and dropped to her knees throwing her arms around the dog. "You rotten, rotten old thing. How could you put me through that. Where-'ve you been, eh?" Brushing away tears, she stood and held out a hand to Samuel. "Thank you for bringing her home. We just moved to Toronto from New Brunswick, and I think she went out looking for our old neighborhood. She doesn't have her new tags yet." Suddenly hearing her own words, she frowned. "So, without any tags, how did you find us?"

Samuel grinned, unable to resist the dog's happiness. "We followed her prints."

"Her prints, of course." As a gust of wind came around the corner, she smiled out at him from behind a moving curtain of long, curly hair. "You must be half frozen. Would you like to come in and thaw out? Maybe have a hot chocolate, eh?"

He was suddenly very cold. "Yes, please."

"In. In. In. In." Daisy insisted on being between both sets of legs, but they somehow got inside and closed the door.

Her name was Patricia, her husband's name was Bill. As Daisy enthusiastically greeted the latter, Patricia took Samuel's jacket and led him into the living room. Left on his own, he felt a heated gaze on the back of his head. Slowly he turned.

"What is it?" The long-haired apricot-and-white cat turned his head sideways and stared at Samuel with pale blue eyes. "It's awfully bright."

"It's an angel," snorted the seal-point Siamese beside him, staring down the aristocratic arch of her nose. "Or a sort of an angel anyway. Someone seems to have messed up the design."

"What's an angel?"

"It's like a cat, only with two legs, minimal fur, and no tail."

"Oh." Confused but clearly used to taking the Siamese's word for things, he wrapped a plumy apricot tail around his toes. "It almost looks as if it understands us."

"It does. Don't you?"

"Yes."

"Yes?" Patricia repeated, returning with three steaming mugs on a tray. "Oh. I see you've met Pixel and Ilea." Setting the tray on the coffee table, she scooped up the Siamese. "This is really Ilea's house. She only lets us live here because we know how to work the can opener."

That was enough to distract Samuel from the heady scent of the hot chocolate. "Really?"

Rubbing the top of her head under Patricia's chin, Ilea purred. Some questions were too stupid to need answers.

* * *

"Turn here."

Dean glanced toward the boarded-up J. Henry and

Sons Auto Repair and then back to Claire. "There's a big batch of snow blocking the driveway."

"Park on the side of the road, then, and we'll walk in."

When Austin made no protest, Dean sucked a speculative lungful of air through his teeth and pulled as far off the road as he could. It was one thing to have Claire explain exactly what demon residue meant and another thing entirely when the cat faced a walk over snow in subzero weather without complaint. Things were clearly some serious.

He shut off the engine and reached for his hat. "Is it Hell again?"

"I'd like to think we'd have noticed that," Claire told him, chewing nervously on the thumb of her mitten.

"Well, I'd like to notice about a half a dozen garlic shrimp," Austin pointed out acerbically, "but that doesn't mean I'll get them, and let's face facts, there was a hole to Hell in Kingston for over forty years you Keepers never knew about."

"You didn't know about it either."

"Hey, I'm the cat. I do comfort when needed and color commentary. I don't deal with metaphysical rifts in the fabric of the universe, and I don't fetch. Live with it." His single eye narrowed. "Now let's get on with it before it gets any colder out here."

The snowbank blocking the driveway was about four-and-a-half-feet high but packed hard and easy to climb over. The snow in the parking lot was almost as deep and a lot softer.

"I'd better go first to break a trail," Dean offered. "You can follow me, Austin can follow you. Which way?"

Claire pointed. A line of footprints, strangely unfilled by blowing snow stretched back behind the building. "Angels walk lightly on the world, they don't leave footprints. Demons do. Demons want people to know they've passed by because you can't tempt people who aren't paying attention."

A side door, leading into a small office, was open. Streaks of demon residue crossed the crumpled lock.

"It was in here," Claire said softly, turning in place.

"No shit, Sherlock." Austin kicked snow off first one back foot and then the other. "Its prints lead right to the door.

The Keeper ignored him. "It took something from that hook, from the back of the chair, and from under the desk. Something that's been here for a while given how thick the dust is." Reaching into the possibilities, she filled the empty spaces with spatial memory. The translucent image of a pair of overalls hung from the hooks, a jacket draped over the back of the chair, and a pair of grimy running shoes lay half on top of each other under the desk. "Clothes?"

"Demons don't wear clothes?" Dean asked, unable

to resist poking a finger through the overalls as they disappeared.

"Yes, but I've never heard of a demon buying off the rack, let alone . . ." She waved a hand around the room and shuddered. "Granted they tend to be a little too fond of shoulder pads, but this is just not them."

"The footprints keep going back into the woods."

"Then that must be where the hole is, and if you say, 'No shit, Sherlock' to me one more time," she warned the cat before he could speak, "you'll be sorry."

Austin stared up at her, whiskers bristling with affronted innocence. "I was merely going to ask if that was where Summons came from, but if you're going to get snappy . . ."

"I'm sorry." Pulling off a mitten, she rubbed at the crease between her eyes. "The thought of a demon wandering around unremarked by the good guys has me a little tense. I'd better lead from now on," she added, walking back to the door. "If there's danger out in those woods, better a Keeper face it than a Bystander."

Although Dean didn't like it, he couldn't disagree and stepped out of her way.

"You *were* going to say 'No shit, Sherlock,' weren't you?" he asked Austin quietly when Claire had moved a few paces ahead."

The cat snorted. "Well, duh."

*   *   *

Claire picked her way carefully to the center of the small clearing, avoiding the worst patches of filthy snow. Squatting, she dragged her right mitt off with her teeth and extended her hand, fingers spread.

"What's all over the snow?" Dean murmured to the cat he held cradled against his chest.

Austin squirmed around to get a better look. "Darkness. When it took form, it flaked."

They watched Claire sift the air for a moment, then stand, frowning.

"This hole is tiny and old. It should have closed on its own and as far as passing a demon—it would have been like passing a kidney stone." She shook her head. "I could be days defining it well enough to close it."

"Gee, days spent out in the bush." Austin sighed and laid his head in the crook of Dean's elbow. "Words can't express my elation."

"You needn't get too elated," Claire told him, yanking her mitt back on. "And you needn't get too comfortable either, I'm going to need you."

"For what?"

"You get to play bad cop. Dean, maybe you should go back to the truck."

He took a deep breath and let it out slowly, wreathing his head in vapor. She was using the voice Diana referred to as more-Keeper-than-thou and, in his experience, that was never good. "Why should I go back to the truck?"

"We need answers, and we need them quickly. I'm going to gather up the darkness around the hole, and Austin's going to question it."

"The darkness?"

"It *is* substance; it should be coherent. But this is one of those 'the ends justify the means' situations and that's always tricky for the good guys." Reaching up, she broke a dead branch off an oak tree. "We'll pull more darkness from the hole. I can contain it in a circle, but it's going to want out, and you'll be the only thing it can use to break free."

"You'll be inside the circle?"

"I'm a Keeper. I can deal."

"And Austin?"

"It isn't actually possible to make a cat do something a cat doesn't want to do."

"But we try to keep that quiet," Austin added as he moved from Dean's arms to Claire's. "We learned a long time ago if people can hang onto the absurd hope that someday they'll train us to stop scratching the furniture, they'll keep handing over the salmon treats."

Dean squared his shoulder. "I'm not leaving you if you're going to be in danger."

"I'll be in more danger if you stay. And, you'll be in danger. If you leave . . ."

"I won't be able to help if you need me."

"You're fighting testosterone," Austin murmured into her ear. "Millions of years of evolution that says he has to protect his mate. You can't win."

"His mate?"

"Mate, girlfriend, old lady—all valid evolutionary terms."

"What?"

The cat sighed, his breath painfully loud up under the edge of her toque. "You know, if you watched more *National Geographic* specials and fewer after school specials . . ."

"You watch *National Geographic* to see lions mating!"

"So?"

Without the time to count to ten, Claire counted to three, looked into Dean's eyes, and reluctantly decided Austin was right. She couldn't win. If she convinced Dean to leave her, it would diminish him in his own eyes and, all things considered, further diminishing would not be a good thing.

"Okay. You can stay." His smile made the potential for disaster almost worthwhile. Deep down, she realized how completely asinine that thought was, but she couldn't seem to prevent a warm glow from rising. "Whatever happens," she murmured a moment later, leaning away from his mouth, "don't break the circle."

To Dean's surprise, the darkness gathered into a familiar from. Its legs were froglike and ended in three toes. Its arms, nearly as long as its legs, ended in three fingers and a thumb. Its eyes were small and black, and it appeared to have no teeth. Its fur and/ or scales changed color constantly.

Imp.

The last time Dean had seen an imp, he'd been scraping the lumpy mass of its pulverized body out from under a sheet of wallpaper. The last time he'd seen an imp alive, it had been dangling from Austin's mouth.

The tiny piece of physical darkness sat up, looked around, squeaked something that sounded very much like "Oh, fuck," and disappeared under Austin's front paws.

Claire squatted beside the cat. "Tell us everything that went on here, and I'll pop you back through the hole before I close it."

Faint defiant squeaking.

"Wrong answer."

Austin's tail lashed and the squeaking grew louder.

"You're lying," Claire sighed.

Indignant squeaking.

"I know, it's hard for you to tell the truth. But it's hard for Austin to keep his claws sheathed, too. You don't honestly think *they'd* lie to protect you?"

Reluctant acknowledgement. From the intensity of the high-pitched torrent that followed, the imp was clearly spilling more than name, rank, and serial number.

Shifting from foot to foot, Dean tried not to think about how cold he was getting. Maybe he should have gone back to the truck. Maybe he should go now. He'd just go in and tell Claire he'd decided to leave.

Go in?

The toe of his right boot rested less than an inch from the circle Claire'd sketched in the snow with the oak branch. Backing quickly away, he tried and failed to remember moving forward. *". . . it's going to want out, and you'll be the only thing it can use to break free."* But if the darkness could reach outside the circle, did that mean the levels inside with Claire had become dangerously high? Claire was in danger. If he loved her, he had to save her!

If he loved her?

No if. In a world that had become a stranger place than he ever could have imagined, loving Claire was the one thing he was sure of. As he realized that, he realized he was standing back at the edge of the circle. He had to do something to distract himself.

"Wow, this is really . . . tidy." Claire shifted her grip on the cat and turned slowly to look around the clearing. "Really."

Dean finished squaring up a pile of fresh cedar prunings and straightened. "Are you okay?"

"We're fine." Erasing an arc of the circle with the edge of her boot, she stepped clear. "I got enough information to close the hole. I know why it never closed on its own, and I know how the demon came through. But you're not going to like it."

He didn't.

"So you're saying that by making the angel *we* made the demon possible?" When Claire reluctantly nodded, he felt the blood drain out of his face. It was a distinctly unpleasant feeling.

Austin studied him for a moment, then looked up at Claire. "I hope you weren't planning on sex any time soon."

* * *

In spite of the cold and the approaching dusk, there were still hundreds of people surging back and forth between the lights at Bloor and Yonge. Most of them, heavily laden with consumer crap they didn't need, were tired, cranky, and desperately in search of one last bargain. Byleth had never seen anything so wonderful.

One hand clutching the dashboard as though she needed to anchor herself to the car, Eva shook her head. "I don't like just leaving you here."

"I'll be fine." She'd have been out of the car at the stoplight except the damned seat belt had jammed.

And it would be damned, she see to it personally. "Pull over anywhere."

"We're willing to take you where you're going," Harry told her as he maneuvered the car into a parking place on the south side of Bloor Street, just past Yonge. "Eva's right. I don't like just leaving you."

"I'll. Be. Fine." The stupid bulky coat was in the way. That was the problem. She squirmed around and yanked at the . . . there! A jerk on the handle had the door open. Byleth flung herself toward the world just in time to hear Eva say:

"I'd feel better if you took this money. It's not much but . . ."

Half out of the car, she reached back and grabbed the envelope without slowing her forward momentum.

"I wrote down our phone number. Call us if you need help!" Eva called after her.

That would be a cold day in Hell, Byleth decided shoving the envelope in her jeans—Twelfth Circle excepted, of course.

"That's certainly a generous offer, sweetheart, but I'm afraid you're making it to the wrong guy." He winked and patted her shoulder as he moved away. "Sorry."

Byleth made a mental note not to offer that particular temptation to men wearing eyeliner. Beginning to get cold, she moved into the nearest store and sidled through narrow aisles to a young man examining a portable CD player. "You should steal that, Steven," she murmured.

"Lifted one this morning," he told her absently, responding unconsciously to the dark aura. "Besides, right at this mo, I got so many disks down my pants I can hardly walk."

"That explains why your pants look like they're about to slide right off your skinny ass," she muttered.

"What's your damage?" Projecting tough guy, he shot her a look from under pale brows and folded his arms. "Santa not bring you any prezzies?"

Santa had never brought her any presents—her part of reality never having exactly welcomed the spirit of giving. And frankly, that sucked. In her whole entire life, Santa had never given her anything! Okay, her whole entire life was just under forty-eight hours long and the Porters had given her plenty, but that was so not the point.

The tough guy look vanished. "Oh, man, I'm sorry. I never . . . I mean . . . it's just . . ." Rifling his pockets, he pulled out a Santa Pez dispenser and held it out. "Here."

"What is it?"

Steven folded the head back, forcing out a tiny pink tile. "It's candy," he said when she hesitated.

Break Santa's neck, get a hit of sugar. Byleth crunched reflectively. *I can deal*.

"Take it."

"What's the catch?" Taking the Pez, she shifted her weight to one hip and looked him in the eye. "Did you want to have sex with me or something?"

His face flushed crimson, his ears scarlet. It wasn't a particularly attractive combination. Muttering something inarticulate, he scuttled away as fast as the CDs down his pants and the crowded store allowed.

Byleth was confused. A total stranger had just give her a gift and refused something he wanted in return. Crunching candy, she went looking for store security. Ratting Steven out would realign her world.

"Hey, there's a . . .

"I'm dealing with a customer." The harassed look-ing young women pushed past without really seeing her. "You'll have to talk to someone else."

". . . particular model has a greater range, you'll find . . ."

"That guy over there is shoplifting."

". . . that the battery may need to be recharged more often."

Byleth pushed between the two men. "Did you hear me?"

"In a moment, Miss. Of course our spare batteries are also on sale, so that could easily solve the prob-lem," the salesman continued, passing the cell phone over her head.

"What about those chargers that fit into your cigarette lighter?"

"Hey? Hello?"

"We carry them. I'm not sure whether we have any left."

"Why won't anyone listen to ME!" They were ignoring her. It was like she didn't exist—almost like, like she was actually a teenager! "This is MAKING ME ANGRY!"

"Hey! That's enough of that!" The burly security guard folded her arms over her imitation police blazer and glared down at the demon. "You're going to have to leave now, Miss."

Byleth folded her own arms. "Make me."

It shouldn't have been possible.

"Fine!" she screamed from the sidewalk. "Like I care!"

Reaching into the dark possibilities and activating the store's sprinkler system made her feel a little better.

* * *

"Summons?" Diana asked as Nalo paused, head cocked, listening to nothing.

After a moment, the older Keeper nodded. "Close, too," she said, climbing the last few steps and emerging back out onto the corner of Yonge and Dundas.

"Probably no farther than Bloor. Did you want to come with me?"

"Love to, but . . ." The sudden realization that it was almost dark cut off a fine sarcastic response. "Holy sh . . ." Nalo's lifted brow cut off the expletive. "I've got to get home!"

And I do have to get home, she reminded herself a few moments later, racing back down the stairs to the bank of pay phones in the subway station. But first she had to find an angel.

*　　*　　*

A little confused, Patricia held out the phone. "It's for you."

Samuel mimicked the motion he'd just seen Patricia make. "Hello? At the Oak Street Co-op at just up from the corner of River and Dundas Streets, town house four."

"How does it know that?" Pixel wondered.

"It has Higher Knowledge," Ilea informed the younger cat without opening her eyes. "It knows things."

"It didn't know us."

"So? Even Higher Knowledge has an upper limit."

Distracted by the cats' conversation, Samuel had to ask Diana to repeat herself, twice. Finally he nodded and handed back the phone. "My Keeper is going to meet me here."

"If it's all right with you," Ilea prodded.

"What?"

"Ask my soft, smiley can-opener if it's all right with her, you moron."

"Of course it's all right," Patricia told him when he'd relayed the cat's message.

"You're relieved I have a Keeper?"

A polite response was lost in the gold-on-brown eyes. "Oh, yeah."

Climbing up onto the streetcar, Diana felt her gaze pulled to the north. Something was . . . was . . . awareness trembled on the edge of consciousness. . . .

"Hey! Exact change!"

. . . and tumbled into the abyss.

* * *

Unrighteous anger kept her warm for a few blocks, but with the setting sun, the temperatures had plummetted. By the time she got to Yonge and Dundas, her teeth were chattering so loudly she almost couldn't hear the security guard kicking her out of the Eaton's Center. He walked away, scratching at a brand new case of head lice, but that was of little consequence when she was still out in the cold.

"You don't look very happy. Maybe I can help."

Byleth turned to find a middle-aged man standing very close. Under the edge of a sheepskin hat, his hair was graying at the temples, his smile was warm and charming, his eyes crinkled at the corners with sincere goodwill, his heart was blacker than hers.

"All right, let's get this straight," she snarled, tossing aside even a pretense of subtlety. "Thinking that I'm lost and alone in the big city, you're about to get all fatherly and offer me a place to crash. Over the next little while you'll addict me to heroin, then put me out on the street to quote, pay you back, unquote. You'll take every cent I make and control me with physical violence." He stepped back. She closed the distance between them. "Did I miss something?"

"I'm not . . ."

"You are so. But that's not the point. The point is you're trying to pull this bullshit on me." Her eyes narrowed and went black from lid to lid. "I've had a really bad day. I mean, like really bad. I'm not even supposed to *have* genitalia!"

"I . . ."

"You can take a walk in traffic, asshole!"

Emergency crews were scraping him out from under the streetcar when she realized she could have handled that better. She couldn't feel her feet, every muscle in her body had clenched tight, she couldn't seem to get her shoulders to come down from around her ears, and her stomach felt like it was lying along her spine. *Stupid, stupid, stupid. Next time wait until he's got you inside the apartment!* A quick examination of the gathered crowd suggested there wouldn't be a next time any time soon. "Isn't that always the way," she muttered miserably, "never a pimp around when you need one."

Manifesting the dark powers left her feeling wrung out and weak—it shouldn't have, but she couldn't manage enough energy to care.

"Hey, you look like you could use a place to stay."

"Well, duh." Turning, she came face-to-face with . . . "Oh, great. A God-pimp."

Leslie/Deter's lip curled. Pretty much all his understanding and patience had been used up earlier in the day when he'd gotten physical with his so-called friends. "Fine. Stay outside and freeze, then."

Since that was beginning to seem highly likely, Byleth grabbed his arm as he started to walk away. "You're supposed to be nicer than that. I'm not, but you're one of the good guys." When he continued to look annoyed, she sighed. "All right, I shouldn't have called you that. I'm so . . . sorry."

Harry Porter had been right. It did get easier. The implications made her knees buckle.

Leslie/Deter caught her, apologizing profusely in turn, and walked her toward the mission, explaining that after the meal they'd be hearing the word of God.

"Which word?"

"What?"

"Where I come from, we get a kick out of hearing the old guy try and say aluminum. . . ."

ELEVEN

The phone was ringing when Nalo got back to her apartment. The strident and slightly superior tone suggested she'd best hurry and pick up, or the next call would happen at a considerably more inconvenient time. So there. Some of the older Keepers had a theory that the entire telephone system had been touched by darkness just before the invention of call waiting and had grown increasingly corrupted ever since.

Kicking off her boots before she hit the carpet, she lifted the receiver and snarled, "I am not interested in changing my long distance service provider, but I will change you into something unpleasant unless you leave me the hell alone."

"Nalo?"

"Oh. Claire." Turning on the table light, she dropped onto the sofa. "Well, wasn't that a waste of a bad mood. What's up?"

On the other end of the line, Claire took a deep breath. "We've got trouble."

"Out there in River City."

There was cognitive pause, then: "What?"

Swinging her feet up onto the coffee table, Nalo sighed. "Never mind. And while I feel for your trouble, it can't possibly top what I've got going on right here."

"There's a demon loose."

"And then again . . ." The older Keeper stared down at the black glitter dusting her fingertips. "I closed a couple of holes it opened today."

"Are you all right?"

"I'm fine. It seems to be starting small—a little vandalism, a little urban renewal . . ."

"Urban renewal?"

"It convinced a pimp to walk under a streetcar. Hard on the driver but no loss to the city. There'll be cascading holes from the witnesses still to track down but, around here at least, it's been a low-key embodiment of darkness."

"That's a relief."

"And a bit of a surprise."

"Yeah, well, there's more."

"You mean the way we can't track it down because there's also an angel walking around big as life and twice as shiny?"

"How did you . . . ?"

"Know that? Well, I'd have to say that a piece of darkness walking around without any of us the wiser was the first clue, but I also ran into your sister today. . . ."

"Why would Diana hide the angel from another Keeper?"

"Why would Diana turn the vacuum cleaner hose into kudzu?" Austin snorted, kneading a pillow into shape. "Why does Diana do anything?"

"Because she's a pain in the ass?"

"That would be my guess," the cat agreed.

"Maybe she's embarrassed about her part in his creation," Dean offered.

"I don't think Diana gets embarrassed."

"Maybe she's taking him for a test drive." When both Claire and Dean turned to stare, Austin shrugged. "Well, pardon me for using a euphemism, but didn't Nalo say that from a block away she thought he was just a guy?"

"Diana wouldn't . . ." Claire's voice trailed off. "Okay, it's possible," she admitted after a moment's thought, "but she says she's a lesbian."

"No, she said she was a lesbian back in November. She could easily be a hemocyanin by now."

"I don't think that's . . ."

"The point is," Austin interrupted, "is that she's seventeen and subject to change without notice. And she's met a young man she can be herself with. Or have you forgotten how seductive that is?"

Claire looked up at Dean, looked past her reflection in his glasses, and sank into the blue of his eyes. "No. I haven't forgotten."

He reached out and stroked the back of his hand over her cheek. "I'm sorry I got you into this."

"We got into this together."

"Still . . ."

"Still need to get hold of Diana," Austin reminded them acerbically.

Claire reluctantly sat back and picked up her cell phone again.

"Yes, okay, I *should* have thought of how I'd get home *before* I went into the closet." Diana held the phone out from her ear, counted to six, then tried again. "Mom . . . Mom! I'm *not* being a smart-ass, I'm agreeing with you. And since there was money for a hotel room, not a bus ticket home, I'm obviously supposed to be here—no harm, no foul. Aren't you the one who always says, nothing happens to a Keeper by chance?" She winced. "Of course I listen to you. Yeah, okay, I didn't listen to that. Or that. Mom . . . Mom. Mother! I have to go now. I'll stay in touch. 'Bye. No. Now. Good-bye."

She hung up, leaned back, closed her eyes, and began rhythmically beating her head against the wall.

"You didn't tell your mother I was with you," Samuel pointed out from the room's other bed.

"No, I didn't."

302

"A lie of omission is still a lie, and a lie is the destroyer of trust."

"Why don't you just let me deal with that?"

"Banging your head isn't going to do anything but annoy the person in the next room."

She opened her eyes and glared at him. "There isn't anyone in the next room."

"But still . . ."

"Shut up."

"The phone's ringing."

"I'm beginning to think Claire was right about this whole joining the twenty-first century thing." Scooping up the receiver, she closed her eyes again. "Sorry, Mom, but nothing's changed in the last thirty seconds."

"It's not Mom. It's me."

"Oh, joy." Straightening, she mouthed, *It's Claire, so no background noise,* toward Samuel. "How did you get this number?"

"It's your cell phone number."

About to explain that she didn't have her cell phone with her, Diana decided that might be something she'd be better off keeping to herself. "Oh. Yeah."

"Diana, that angel you're hiding is blocking my . . . our, ability to find the demon that came through at the same time, so you've got to stop playing around and send it back."

"It's not an it, Claire, it's a him and . . ." The rest

of the sentence suddenly clicked into place. "Did you say demon?"

"Demon?" Samuel scooted to the edge of the bed, eyes wide.

Diana mouthed a stern, *"Shut up!"* at him so she could hear Claire's answer.

"Yes, a demon."

"That's so not good."

"Low-fat cheese is not good, Diana. *This* is bad. I don't know what you're up to with that angel, and I don't want to know . . ."

"Come to think of it, how do you know?"

"Nalo saw you with him and mentioned it when I called her, but that's not important. He's got to go back right now."

"No." Diana shook her head—an unseen emphasis from Claire's point of view but emphasis just the same. "Sending him back would be the same as killing him."

"You can't kill him, there's nothing to kill. He's a being of light."

"He's more than that."

"How can he be more than that? He's already a superior being!"

"Fine. He's less than that, then. He's a person, Claire." Who was attempting to eavesdrop on both sides of the conversation. A vigorously applied elbow solved that distinctly unangelic problem. Flashing him a triumphant smile, as he flopped around gasping for breath, she amended, "Okay, maybe he's not entirely a person, but there's a person *in* there."

"No."

"No, what?"

"No, you are not suggesting that a . . . a penis and a couple of testicles is what makes a man." Claire's tone laid a distinctly weird subtext under the words.

Wishing she had time to translate, Diana sighed impatiently. "No, I'm not suggesting that. But they've given him access to emotions and experiences genderless angels can't have."

"I'm happy for him, but there's a demon loose we can't find until the angel goes—therefore the angel has to go. And if he knew what was at stake, I'm sure he'd agree. Is he there with you right now? Let me talk to him."

"No."

Samuel poked her in the leg. "Your sister wants to talk to me?"

She couldn't lie to him. "Yes."

"So give me the phone."

"Not happening." Scooting out from under his arm, she crossed the room and glared at him from beside the bathroom door, the phone cord stretched taut between them. "One step in this direction and I'll lock myself in."

"Diana!"

"Claire!" Attention jerked back to her sister, she

rolled her eyes. "You don't need to yell. It doesn't matter if he agrees with you or not because I'd still have to kill him, and I won't do it."

"For the last time, you wouldn't be killing him!"

"Would."

"Stop being so childish. Listen, I can't get there tonight; the OPP have closed the highway north of Barrie because of the storm. But we'll be leaving *first thing* in the morning. This is serious. Send the angel back. Remember your responsibili . . ."

Diana jabbed at the power off button and pitched the phone across the room. "I do not need her to remind me of my responsibilities," she growled as Samuel rubbed his ear where the phone had clipped him on its way by. "If they knew you, they wouldn't be able to kill you either."

"I don't want to die."

"Good."

He sighed and spread his hands. "But there's a demon in the world, and if returning me to the light would expose the demon . . ."

"You have to say that," Diana interrupted. "And knock off the sacrificial pose, I'm not buying it." She threw herself down on the empty bed.

"Bouncing like that will destroy the mattress and the box spring."

"Who are you getting your Higher Knowledge from, Martha Stewart?"

"Did you know you can create a lovely mailbox

cozy out of a piece of felt and only six hundred dollars' worth of handwoven French taffeta ribbon?''

"What?" She squirmed around and stared.

Samuel grinned.

The corners of her mouth beginning to curve, Diana grabbed a pillow and heaved it at him. "Jerk!"

He wasn't sure why he considered that a compliment, but he did. "Diana, you have to send me back. I don't want to go, but I understand why I have to."

Squinting in the sudden glow, Diana sighed. Nothing like self-sacrifice to bring out the angel in a guy. If Claire or any other Keeper met him in this state, they'd send him back without even thinking about it. Easy answer—don't let Claire or any other Keeper meet him.

And how hard could that be? No Summons, no directions—no way to find them.

"Mom? Claire. When you were talking to Diana a few minutes ago, did she happen to mention what hotel she's staying at? Carlton Hotel, room 312. Thanks."

"That looks like room 81Z," Austin pointed out.

"I'd like to see you do better with an eyeliner on a condom wrapper."

"Well, it's nice you found something to use them for."

Dean reached across the cat and picked up the address. "I don't like this."

"But they're the only kind we've got."

"What? No!" Suddenly flustered, he dropped the packet. It bounced off the sniggering cat and rolled under the bed. "I meant, I don't like going to your mother," he explained, dropping to his knees and running his hand beneath the edge of the bedspread. "It seems, I don't know, sneaky."

"No choice." Claire folded her legs up out of his way. "First of all, Diana's confused. Secondly, I've dealt with nothing but angel or demon sites since it happened, which is telling me pretty clearly that this is my responsibility. Third . . ." Reaching out, she grinned and ran her fingers through his hair. ". . . there's just something about a man on his knees."

"Claire . . ."

"What?"

"Found it!" Straightening, he was about to toss the packet onto her lap when he frowned. "This isn't ours . . ."

"Eww."

Still glowing, although beginning to dim, Samuel lay back on the bed, hands under his head, and stared at the ceiling. "You know what I'd like to experience before I . . . go back."

"You're not going back," Diana told him absently. She paced the length of the hotel room one more time, examining and discarding another half-dozen bad ideas. The best she'd been able to come up with so far had involved rather more duct tape than she thought she could get her hands on.

"But still . . ."

"No."

"Pizza."

"What?" Either angels came with euphemisms high school didn't cover—which was highly unlikely—or that wasn't the experience she'd been expecting.

"And loud music."

"Why?"

He shrugged as well as he was able, given his position. "I don't know."

Well, she hadn't come up with any better ideas. "I could handle a pizza."

"I think I just want to eat mine."

"Oh, please, send me back now." Falling backward, Samuel groaned and rubbed both hands over a visibly distended belly. "Why did I do that to myself?"

Compelled to answer truthfully, Diana snorted. "I think you were showing off."

"Showing off what?"

"Beats me."

"I feel awful."

She dropped down onto the other bed. "What did you expect after a large with the works and half of my Hawaiian?"

"I wasn't expecting anything!" A mighty belch delayed part two of the protest. Startled but impressed, he waited until the echoes died down before continuing. "I just thought. . . ."

"Thinking? As if. You were being a guy." She squirmed back toward the pillows, propping them against the wall. "And speaking of, you're starting to smell."

"My olfactory senses have been working since I got here, thank you very much."

"Right. Rephrasing—you stink."

"I stink?"

Eyes rolling, she picked up the TV remote. "Don't take my word for it. Check the pits."

He lifted an arm. "I'm not supposed to smell like this?"

"No."

"Good."

"I'll show you how the shower works in the morning. After that last incident, I don't want you approaching new plumbing on your own."

"I thought I was *supposed* to urinate against the wall."

"Uh-huh." A quick flip through the available channels brought the expected result: there was nothing on.

"What was that?" Samuel heaved himself up onto his elbows. "No, not that. Back. Back. There."

Diana frowned. "It's a documentary on lions."

"What are they doing?"

She adjusted the contrast, but they were still doing it. "They're having sex."

"Kewl."

"You're disgusting."

Vaguely proud of himself, although uncertain of why he should be, he belched again.

*　　*　　*

Byleth hadn't expected to have so much fun. With a sense of Keepers too close for comfort, she'd planned on a low profile and a road trip in the morning. She'd listened to the praying, she'd eaten the meal, and she hadn't been able to stop a snort of amusement during the preaching.

So they'd asked her if she had a question.

Surrounded by teenagers pulled from the streets, Byleth stood—hands jammed into the pockets of her black jeans, weight resting on one hip, expression sullen—and asked, "If Lloyd leaves London at 6:00 p.m. on a train heading east going 90 kilometers an hour and Tom leaves Toronto at 6:15 p.m. on a train heading west at 110 kilometers an hour, when will they die in a fiery explosion?"

Eyes dark from lid to lid compelled the truth.

"I don't know."

"Why?" She threw the word onto the end of his sentence so quickly momentum kept the ball rolling.

"I never paid attention in math."

"Why?"

"I was fixated on Miss Miller's breasts."

"Why?"

"They were perky. What does this have to do with the text?" Leslie/Deter demanded, fingers white on the edge of the lectern.

"Nothing." The last thing she wanted to do was test the man's faith. That was the sort of inane probing the good guys got up to. "Boxers or briefs?"

"Egyptian leather thong."

Things went downhill from there.

* * *

Staring up at the exit sign, Claire listened to Dean breathe and waited for morning. Diana had gone too far this time. She hadn't been Summoned to the angel, or she'd have mentioned it—Summoned Keepers had the final say on any situation. Diana without a Summons meant Diana should be at home studying or whatever it was teenagers did these days. Piercing something maybe.

Claire hadn't been Summoned either, but as an *active* Keeper that only meant that she was already doing what she was supposed to be doing. The angel's physical form blocked any attempt to find the demon. Therefore, she had to return the angel to the light. QED—essentially, Latin for "so there."

Diana's personal opinions on the matter were irrelevant. Even more so than usual.

If functional genitalia defined personhood, then Dean . . .

She chopped off the thought before it could crawl out any further. Functional genitalia didn't define love either, and she loved Dean. In a relatively short time he'd become as essential to her life as breathing. She loved being with him, talking, laughing, traveling, cuddling, touching, kissing, caressing; turning her head, she pressed her face against the warm skin of his shoulder. He smelled so good, she wanted to . . .

Okay, that's it. Get up. Which wasn't, perhaps, the best chastisement under the circumstances. Sliding out from under the covers, she grabbed her robe off the other bed.

"Hey! I was asleep on that!"

"Sorry."

"I should hope so." Disdaining the jump, Austin stalked over the bedside table and curled up between Dean's legs muttering, "Angels, demons, impotence; I see no reason why the cat should suffer."

She woke Dean at five, and they were on the road by six-thirty. They would have been on the road an hour earlier, but when they went to check out, Dean discovered that the sleepy middle-aged woman behind the desk had once lived in St. John's right next door to a guy he'd played hockey with. The permutations took a while to work through.

Although the plows had been busy all night, it was still snowing lightly and the driving was treacherous. When it became apparent that Dean needed to concentrate on the road . . .

You'll find out what Diana's up to when we get there.

Could we deal with what happens after the angel's gone, after the angel's gone, then.

Claire, please shut up."

. . . she amused herself by watching a pair of frost fairies skating along the hydro lines. Matched double axles, a star lift, and a thrown triple salkow later, she popped in a tape of *The Nutcracker.*

"This is different." Austin climbed out from behind the seat and settled in her lap. "You don't usually like classical music."

"I know, but somehow it seemed to fit."

They stopped for breakfast in Huntsville.

"I should get gas," Dean observed as they pulled out of the diner's parking lot.

"I *got* gas," Austin moaned, head and both front paws draped over the edge of the seat. "I should never have eaten those sausages."

Claire folded her arms. "What sausages?"

"Did I say sausages? I meant, uh . . ." The windows rattled as his stomach made a sound between a gurgle and plate tectonics. "All right. I meant sausages; three plump juicy sausages. Slightly overcooked and containing bits of two items I couldn't identify. The kid in the next booth dropped them on the floor, and I ate them."

"When?"

"When Dean was explaining to the waitress how running the dishwasher at a higher temperature would keep the cutlery from streaking."

"Right. Then."

"Yeah, then. When you were studying the menu with such intense concentration."

Pulling up in front of the gas pumps, Dean shot her a quick look. "You were embarrassed?" When she nodded, he grinned. "Why? The waitress didn't mind."

The waitress didn't mind because he'd been smiling up at her and the combination of Dean's smile and accent and shoulders made most women and a goodly number of men between the ages of thirteen and death temporarily lose cognitive functions. He could have told the waitress how to get black heel marks off the floor, tomato sauce stains out of her apron, and greasy thumbprints off the napkin dispenser—all of which he'd done in the past—and she wouldn't have minded. In the past he'd never noticed the reactions he provoked, but something in the way he grinned as he got out of the truck suggested that had changed.

"So he's noticing people are noticing." Austin

twisted his head around until he could spear Claire with a pale green gaze. "So what?"

She watched Dean clean the windshield, carefully lifting each wiper blade and setting it just as carefully back in place. "So I'm not sure how I feel about it."

"About him noticing that waitress noticed him?" When she nodded, he snorted. "Don't worry about it. She made him French toast. You made him a man."

"But he really *liked* the French toast."

"And once you've dealt with the angel . . ."

"And the demon."

"*And* the demon—he'll really *like* locking me in the bathroom again."

"You think?"

"No. I'm just talking to hear myself." Belly sagging, he heaved himself up onto his feet. "Now open the door. There's a trio of sausages I have to introduce to a snowbank."

"I'd have thought that angels were more the early to bed, early to rise types."

Samuel heaved himself up into something close to a sitting position, blinked at the room in general for a few moments, and then reluctantly swung his legs out of bed. "Why?"

"I dunno. The whole sentiment is just so sanctimonious I figured it had to be one of . . . oh, man!" Diana clapped her hands over her eyes and rocked back in the chair. "Like I needed to see *that* first thing in the morning. I thought you were going to sleep in your underwear."

"This is what was under what I was wearing when you said that."

"Pardon me for not assuming angels would head out commando style." A quick look elicited a low whistle. "You ought to send Mr. Giorno a nice thank you letter."

His eyes widened. "It's doing it again!"

"Well, don't wave it at me!"

Ears burning, Samuel grabbed a pillow off the bed and held it protectively in front of him. "I'm not doing anything. It just . . ." He started to gesture, thought better of it, and resecured the pillow. "It just does that," he finished miserably. "I hate this body."

"Are angels allowed to hate?"

"Are we allowed to walk around with one of these?"

"You have a point."

He sank down onto the edge of the bed, pillow on his lap. "Like I need you to remind me."

Diana could feel the laughter rising. When she tried to hold it back behind her teeth, it escaped out her nose. Any chance she might have had at stopping it after that got blown away by Samuel's affronted glare. Nothing to do but ride it out. After a few minutes, she wiped her eyes, drew in a shaky breath, and managed a fairly coherent, "Sorry."

"Sure. Whatever." He glanced under the pillow.

"Anyway, you've taken care of the . . . Would you stop that!"

This time the apology came out in separate syllables as Diana slid off the chair.

Samuel sat and watched her flop about, indignation wrapped around him like a cloak. Finally, he stood and walked into the bathroom, every movement radiating injured dignity. "I'll figure out the shower on my own," he informed her reproachfully, reaching back for the door.

Wondering who he could possibly be reminding her of, Diana waved a weak hand in his general direction and fought to pull herself together. With the door closed, with her anatomically correct angel safely behind it, she staggered to her feet and dropped back into the chair. Her stomach hurt. She hadn't laughed so hard since the time Claire'd coughed half a cheese sandwich through her nose listening to one of Dad's old George Carlin albums.

Claire.

Suddenly it wasn't so funny.

Claire was on her way to Toronto believing she had to send an angel back to the light for the greater good. But, logically, emotionally, rationally, and every other ally Diana could think of, destroying a life couldn't be a part of the greater good.

There had to be another way to find the demon.

"All right . . ." She stood and walked purposefully over to the big mirror on the wall. Hands flat on the dresser, she leaned forward and glared at her reflection. "Let's do something radical for a Keeper. Let's actually think about the situation instead of just reacting to it."

Her reflection looked skeptical.

"Problem: there's a demon in the world, a big ol' walking around piece of darkness. And that's bad. We can't find it because there's also an angel in the world. Which would be good if it wasn't bad. We can't find the demon because of the angel. Because the big chunk of light that's Samuel balances the dark." She glanced over at the bathroom, then back at the mirror. "Except that the dark hasn't really been very dark, has it?"

Her reflection frowned in thoughtful agreement.

"You'd think that a demon would cause more havoc, wouldn't you? All the active Keepers should be scrambling to repair the damage it's caused, and I should have been Summoned to help. But that hasn't happened. Why? Why hasn't the demon caused more havoc?" She was close. She could feel it. "The demon is balancing Samuel. It hasn't caused more havoc because balancing means it's an exact opposite of Samuel."

Following the cord, she dove under the bed for the phone.

In the mirror, her reflection performed a truncated version of Deion Sanders' touchdown dance.

* * *

"All right. The demon's a fully functional teenage girl. We still can't find it while your angel is in the world. Yes, that narrows the search but not enough. Diana, I'm sor . . ." Claire let her head fall back against the seat as she powered down her phone. "She hung up on me."

"She's some set on saving that angel," Dean noted, carefully easing the truck around a blind curve.

"I know."

"Is there any chance she could be right?"

"No."

"You're sure?"

Claire sighed. "I'm a Keeper, it's my job to be sure."

Austin stretched out a paw, his claws sinking into Claire's jeans. "Far be it from me to point this out, but you seem to be forgetting something."

"I fed you. Although I don't see why, when you tried to kill yourself with sausages."

The claws sank a little deeper. "You're forgetting that Diana is also a Keeper."

"So?"

"It's as much her job to be sure as it is yours."

"All right, fine. So Claire can't find her, big whoop. That doesn't mean I can't." Euphoria having been shot down, Diana sat cross-legged on the end of the bed, reached into the possibilities, and jabbed seven numbers into the phone. "Local call," she muttered after the first ring. "I'll just deal with the demon before Claire clears Barrie, and she can stuff her . . ."

"Greenstreet Mission. Drop by and hear the word of God."

Diana opened her mouth and closed it again. Finally she managed a strangled, "The what?"

"The word of God." The young man on the other end of the phone sighed deeply. "And, no, it isn't aluminum."

"Okay."

"Can we help?"

"No. That is, sorry, I've got the wrong number." Hanging up considerably more gently than she had the last time, Diana stared across the room at her reflection. Her reflection stared back, equally appalled.

Higher Knowledge had told him that showers were both the cubicle or bath in which one stands under a spray of water and the act of bathing in same. It offered no help at getting the water the right temperature, but after a few false starts—and he would *not* give Diana the pleasure of hearing him scream—he worked it out.

Soaping up gave him the first chance to really examine the body he found himself in. Was he supposed to have hair in so many weird places? Why were his feet so big? If he hadn't actually been born, which he hadn't, why did he have a belly button?

And nipples—sure they added visual interest to the male chest but what were they actually for?

"These things really ought to come with owner's manuals," he sighed, reaching down to turn off the water.

The tiny room didn't seem significantly drier.

Shaking drips off the ends of his hair, he stepped out of the tub, slipped on the wet tiles, and suddenly found himself airborne.

Seventy-eight percent of all accidents happen in the bathroom, Higher Knowledge informed him as he landed.

"Samuel? Samuel, how many fingers am I holding up?"

"Why?"

"I have no idea, but it's what they always do in the movies when someone knocks themselves out."

"I'm not out." He blinked and tried to focus on what looked like three fat pink sausages. "I'm in the bathroom."

"No, you're not. I moved you to one of the beds."

"You carried me?"

"As if. I just, you know, poof."

"Oh. Poof. Was that the burst of light?"

The sausages disappeared and the edge of the bed dipped as Diana sat down. "No. I think that was when your head hit the edge of the tub."

"My head . . ." Movement brought smaller bursts

of light. Pain. He remembered pain. On the up side, it didn't hurt as much as catching himself in the zipper.

"There's a bump, but angels seem to be pretty tough."

"Yeah, well, soldiers in the army of the Lord and all that." He could feel her concern—her pain for his pain—and he kind of thought he ought to do something about it but he just couldn't seem to muster the enthusiasm.

"Samuel, I don't want to rush you or anything, but could you get over this a little faster. Checkout time is at noon, and I don't have enough money for another day—which clearly means we're not supposed to stay."

We. He felt a vague nostalgia for the time he'd spent on his own. "Maybe it means you're supposed to send me back to the light."

"Maybe you should just stay out of this."

"Sure."

Her eyes narrowed. "What's that supposed to mean?"

"It means my head hurts."

"Oh. Sorry."

The bed rocked as she threw herself off it. Samuel winced. "You want to hear the weird thought I had as I finished showering?"

"I guess."

"That makes me feel more human."

"What does?"

"The shower, I guess. It's the thought I had: That makes me feel more human. And then . . ." He waved a hand in the general direction of his head. ". . . this. Pain."

Diana snorted. "Got news for you, bucko. Pain is the general human condition."

"Then send me back. I don't think I want to be human anymore."

"Well, that's just too . . ." Her voice trailed off into thought. They couldn't find the demon because she was the exact opposite of Samuel. The exact opposite. Throwing herself back onto the bed, she grabbed his shoulders hard enough to dimple the bare skin. "I'm an idiot!"

"Look, I know it's unangelic of me, but I don't really feel up to dealing with your lack of self-esteem right now."

"What?"

"Stop shaking me!"

"Sorry." She pulled her hands away but continued looming over him. "I've just solved the problem. If you don't want to be in a human body, you don't *have* to be."

"I don't?" Pushing back against the pillow accomplished nothing much, but he didn't like the way her eyes were gleaming.

"No, you don't. I helped make you. My, for lack of a better word, power signature is a part of you.

That's why I can unmake you, but it should also mean I can transform you."

"Should?"

Ignoring him, she leaped up and spun around, arms outstretched. "You'll still be you but different. The demon copied this body, so without it, we'll be able to find her. It's simple."

"I won't be human?"

The spinning stopped. "No."

"But I'll still be me."

"Yes."

"What will I be?"

"I don't know. I'll undo the human seeming and the light will rearrange. Without Lena and her father to interfere, you'll self-define." Suddenly serious, she sat down and pushed her hair off her forehead. "I don't want to push you into this, Samuel, but it would solve all our problems."

It took him a moment to figure out her expression. When he realized he was looking at hope, he couldn't stop himself from smiling. Hope was, after all, one of the primary messages of the light. Maybe this was why was here. "Would my head hurt?"

"Different body. No reason why it should."

"Then let's do it."

Claire and Dean had opened the way for the light, but her crepe-paper snowflake hanging from the ceiling in the gym had held it together. Standing at the foot of the bed, Diana closed her eyes and reached into the possibilities until she could see Samuel lying in front of her. Slowly and carefully, she detached the parameters Lena and her father had placed around him. She took him back to what he had been in the gym, then wrapped the part that was Samuel in the possibilities and pushed him forward.

In the instant between Diana taking him back and shoving him forward again, Samuel thought he heard voices.

"So he's off the duty roster?"

"Let's just say he's on an extended leave of absence."

"Let's just say?" The first voice snorted. "Oh, easy for you, Gabriel. You're not the one who has to fill his post on the Perdition front."

"Bitch, bitch, bitch."

"Hey, there's a war on, you know. Or maybe that's something you guys in the band have forgotten."

And then there was only light, and a question.

If he wasn't an angel, and he wasn't a human, what was he?

Diana blinked away afterimages and stared down at the towel she'd thrown over Samuel's crotch. Whatever he'd become fit under it with room to spare. Fingers crossed, she bent down and flicked it back.

The marmalade tabby sat up and looked around.
"You're a cat."

"Well, duh. Didn't anyone ever tell you that angels were like cats only with . . ." He cocked his head, trying to remember just what it was Ilea had said. ". . . you know, differences."

Staggering back, Diana went to sit down on one of the chairs but, at some time during the proceedings, it had self-defined as a plant stand, and she hit the floor instead. It suddenly became painfully clear who Samuel had reminded her of as he'd made his reproachful way to the bathroom.

Austin.

TWELVE

Since Dean had politely but vehemently objected to her willing the truck faster, Claire let her head loll back against the headrest and closed her eyes. Extending her will toward Toronto, she slid past the permanently monitored sites, her passage noted only by the elderly Keeper at the site in Scarborough.

"Oh, sure, you can go by like a ship in the night, but you never write, you never call. A lousy birthday card would kill you? The best forty-two years of my life I give to you and you don't even remember my birthday. You got a memory like a cantaloupe."

"Excuse me?"

"Why? What did you do?"

Claire moved on into the possibilities a little faster. Keepers who essentially became the seal that stopped darkness from emerging out of an unclosable hole, became caricatures of their former selves. She'd narrowly missed becoming the youngest Keeper to ever hold such a position and shuddered at the sudden vision of herself at ninety-two in stretch capri pants and wedges, scarlet lips and crimson fingernails, badly dyed hair poofed out over way too much purple eye shadow—a cross between Nancy Reagan and Miss Piggy.

Didn't happen, she reminded herself. *Didn't . . .*

Wait.

Something was happening.

She heard voices . . .

"I'm warning you, Michael, don't touch the horn."

"Or you'll what? Blow me?"

. . . then a sudden flash of light threw her back into her body. She stiffened and moaned. The Summons hit a heartbeat later.

"As much as I'm happy you two are back into it," Austin muttered without opening his eye, "given that we're speeding down a snowy highway with a bunch of lunatics who've forgotten how to drive since the last time the frozen white stuff fell, don't you think Dean ought to keep both hands on the steering wheel?"

"I can feel the demon."

"I thought you were calling it Floyd. Ow!" He turned his head and glared at her. "Don't poke the cat, I'm old."

"So Diana came through, then?" Dean asked, making a mental note to ask about this Floyd guy when the cat wasn't around.

"I knew she would."

Austin snorted. "You thought she was going to destroy the world as we know it, bringing upon us the Last Judgment and roller disco. Not that there's a lot of difference," he added.

Somewhat redundantly in Dean's opinion. "Are we still after heading to Toronto, then?"

Claire checked the Summons. "So far."

They drove in silence for a few moments.

"The angel's gone, then?"

Curious about Dean's tone, Claire turned to face him. "Yes."

"And you can find the demon now?"

"Uh-huh."

"And when you find the demon, you can get rid of it?"

"I'm a Keeper. Of course I can get rid of it."

He glanced toward her and smiled suggestively. "No angel, no demon . . ."

"No problem." Realizing where he was headed, she returned his smile and stroked one finger along the top of his thigh.

"Is it just me," Austin asked, sitting up, "or are we suddenly moving a lot faster?"

The angel had changed.

Feeling suddenly exposed, Byleth ran into the only room in the mission where she'd be left alone—unexpectedly finding three other girls already in there sharing a cigarette.

The dominant member of the trio slid off the sink and turned to face her. "You want something, new girl?"

The part of her that was a seventeen-year-old girl wanted to protest that she'd just come in to use the bathroom and she wasn't looking for trouble. Then the rest of her pushed that part down and stole its lunch money. "I want you to leave."

"What?"

"Leave." Breathing heavily through her nose, barely holding all the parts together, Byleth reached into the darkness. "I want you to leave."

"Yeah? Well, I don't give a half-eaten rat's ass for what you want. I . . . What's that?" Pierced brows drew in and scowled at the dripping bit of flesh hanging from the tail in Byleth's hand.

"It's a half-eaten rat's ass. Take it and go."

Eyes locked on the partial rodent, the other two girls sidled by and out the door. In the complex hierarchy of adolescence, having a rat's ass conveniently on hand clearly trumped a pack of smokes and an attitude.

"What kind of retarded shithole do you come from?" their abandoned leader asked, taking an unconcerned drag. "That is so totally not what I meant. Now, me, I'm going to finish my cigarette and . . ." Her gaze locked on Byleth's nose. "I never saw you light up."

"I didn't."

"But there's smoke . . ."

"Get. Out."

"Hey, you're not the boss of me." Bravado winning over common sense, she flicked her butt toward the sink . . .

"NOW!"

. . . and was out the door before it actually touched the porcelain.

Byleth tossed the rat in the garbage and stared at her reflection. "Why is it so damned foggy in . . . oh." Like thousands before her, she found it a lot harder to stop smoking than to start, but, after an extended struggle, she managed it. Not that it mattered, her cover had been blown. She might as well walk around in a pair of horns, carrying a pitchfork—if that particular look wasn't *so* yesterday's demon. Without equal and opposite coverage by the light, she'd be easy to spot by any Keeper and probably most Cousins. Metaphysical alarms would be screaming, "Demon in the world!" and every Goody Two-shoes in the area not currently helping little old ladies across the street would be zeroing in.

She should have changed with the angel. He was as much tied by the stupid body he was wearing as she was. Therefore, he couldn't have changed on his own. He *so* cheated.

"Oh, yeah, he got a Keeper to change him so they could find me. Fine. You want to find me, Keeper, you'll find me!" A light wisp of smoke drifted out of both nostrils. It felt great. "If I'm going out, I'm going out big. No more just hanging around and irritating people." She spread her arms. "I'll open a hole of darkness so big it'll make the Home Shopping Channel seem like a cable network!"

Her reflection frowned. "It is a cable network."

"Shut up!"

"And you can't open a hole of darkness big enough to cause much trouble because the physicality of the body denies you access to that kind of power."

"I *am* that kind of power."

"Then you'll have to destroy the body. You'll cease to exist. Gone. No more reality than you can find in that stupid television program about those people on the island."

"What do you mean?"

"Read your lips. You'll be absorbed back into the darkness. No more you."

"Oh, like it's such joy to be a teenager." But it was better than being nothing at all, better than being a lesser part of a greater whole—actually it was remarkably similar to being a lesser part of a greater whole. Byleth chewed thoughtfully on the edge of a thumbnail, spitting bits of navy blue polish into the sink. If she could open a big enough hole, cause enough mayhem and destruction, she could maintain her identity even in the darkness where individuality depended on being more of a shit than the next guy—and not always metaphorically.

She'd have to open the hole quickly, before the Keepers found her, so she'd need a spot where at least part of the work had already been done.

"And I know just the place."

Unfortunately, her evil chortle fell flat as her reflection ignored her, concentrating instead on the dorky little flip ruining the right side of her hair.

"One, two, three, *four*. One, two, *three*, four."

"Are you all right down there?"

Samuel stopped counting and glared up at Diana, cream-colored whiskers bristling indignantly. "Why?"

"No reason,"

"I'm fine."

"Okay."

"This four legs walking stuff is a lot harder than it looks, you know."

Diana bit back a snicker as she pushed the elevator call button. "It couldn't possibly be. I think I should carry you," she added as the elevator arrived. "I've set it up so people's attention will slide right off you, but in an enclosed space you'd likely get stepped on."

"Something tells me I didn't think this transformation thing through," Samuel muttered as she scooped him up. Still, it felt surprisingly pleasant to be held.

He flicked his tail out into a more comfortable position as the door opened.

A small child stared up at them with widening eyes. "Kitty, Mama!"

"Yes, sweetheart," his mother agreed, as Diana moved past her, "a stuffed kitty."

"Who's she calling stuffed?"

"Kitty talks, Mama!"

"Toy kitties don't talk, sweetheart."

A small hand closed around Samuel's tail and pulled. "Ding dong!"

"OW!"

"Kitties don't ding dong either, sweetheart." Shooting Diana an apologetic smile, she grabbed her son's wrist with one hand and pried his fingers free with the other. A bit of fur came free as well. "And it's not polite to touch things that belong to other people."

"Especially tails!" Hooking his claws in Diana's jacket, Samuel swiveled around until he could stare down at the child, golden eyes narrowed to glimmering slits. "Listen to your mother, Ramji, because someday she'll die and you'll wish you had."

Ramji wrapped his arms around his mother's leg. "Kitty knows my name."

He was still wrapped around her leg when the elevator reached the lobby, and she crossed to the hotel's front door with a resigned shuffle.

"That's a kid who's going to need serious therapy

down the road." Diana shifted her grip. "What kind of an angel says something like that?"

"The kind that just got his tail pulled. Besides," Samuel continued after a few quick licks at his shoulder, "it's the truth and one day he'll thank me for it."

"One day he'll spend thousands of dollars being convinced you were a metaphor for toilet training."

"He grabbed my tail!"

"I know. I was there."

"You said people wouldn't be able to see me properly."

"He was a proto-person." She set him down in one of the lobby's over stuffed chairs and stepped back. "I'm going to check out. Stay there."

"Or what?"

"I haven't got time to go into it right now, but why don't you apply that Higher Knowledge thing to the joint concepts of can openers and opposable thumbs." As she walked over to the counter, she considered all the things he could have become and asked the world at large, more in search of sympathy than enlightenment, "Why a cat?"

The world at large offered no answers.

Left to amuse himself, Samuel did a little kneading, claws moving rhythmically in and out of the corduroy cushion covers. Shoulders up, head down, his eyes began to close as he moved in a slow circle. He didn't know what it was, but something about that yielding surface under his front paws created the most incredible feeling. Kneading harder, really putting his back into it, he heard a sudden loud noise and froze.

Two-stroke engine, single spark, gas and oil mix . . . oh, wait, it's me.

Which was when he spotted the other cat.

A marmalade tabby, it had a cream-colored bib and the same color markings around both muzzle and eyes. The darker stripes down tail and legs made it look as if it was wearing footie pajamas—the effect emphasized by the way the legs were still a bit too long for the body.

Samuel stared at it.

It stared back.

Head cocked to one side, Samuel took a cautious step forward.

It took a cautious step forward.

Hoping he wasn't rushing the introduction, Samuel leaned forward for a good long sniff.

The cinnamon triangle of his nose mashed flat against the mirror.

Leaping back, his back feet scrambled for purchase as he nearly went off the chair, only the barricade of Diana's legs saving him from an embarrassing fall. Blinking rapidly, he leaned against her knees, looked up at her, and said in what he hoped was a convincing tone, "I meant to do that."

"Okay."

"I knew it was a mirror."

"I believe you."

"Right." He took a few quick licks at the edge of a stripe. "So, where do we go from here?"

Diana sighed. "Home."

"But what about the demon?" Samuel demanded. "I'm not blocking it now. We should go after it."

"Yes, we should. But we can't." She dropped down onto the arm of the chair and scowled at her reflection, one hand absently rubbing the cat behind the ears. "I can feel that there's a demon out there, but I still don't know where she is. Which means some other Keeper has it sealed up. And, gee, I wonder which other Keeper?"

"Claire?"

"Good guess."

Samuel could tell Diana was upset, although he wasn't entirely certain why. "You don't know that for sure," he offered.

Diana snorted. "We—me and Claire—were responsible for you, which makes *us* responsible for the demon, which means *we* should have got the Summons, but since *I* didn't, *she* must have."

He frowned, ears saddling. "Then she must be able to handle the demon on her own."

"Well, duh. What?" she demanded of an eavesdropping Bystander, shooting him the look that had made her the terror of intramural field hockey back before the school board decided it might not be the best idea to give hormonally hopped up adolescents

338

weapons and carte blanche to break shins. "You've never seen anyone talk to a stuffed animal before?"

"Actually, no."

Holding his gaze, she reached into the possibilities. "You still haven't." Scooping up Samuel, she stood and headed for the revolving door. Outside, on Carlton Street, she put the cat down on a cleared bit of sidewalk.

"Hey! I'm in bare feet here!"

"You're a cat. That's the only way your feet come."

"Right. I knew that, but . . ."

As the pigeon back-flapped into a landing, Samuel whirled around and leaped. Had he been in the body longer, he would have had to have dealt with the small ethical dilemma of whether or not an angel could actually eat a pigeon he'd killed—not to mention the slightly larger health dilemma of whether or not anyone *should* eat a pigeon born and raised on the streets of Toronto. As it was, he hooked a tail feather, but the rest of the bird got away, dropping a large, white, hysterical opinion of the change on Diana's shoulder as it passed.

"Go on, chicken, fly! There's more where that came from!" He boxed the feather to the ground, flicked it up, and boxed it down again.

"Are you done?"

"One more time." Both front paws finally holding the feather captive, he smiled up at her. "Okay, I'm done. Now what?"

"First, you can stop being so cute."

"Actually, I don't think I can," Samuel admitted after a moment's consideration.

Diana sighed. "Swell. Do me a favor; if I ever talk baby talk to you, claw my tongue out."

"I don't think I can do that either."

"Not surprised." Bending, she picked him up and settled him in the crook of her arm. "Come on, it's the subway to the train station and the first train to London for us."

"That's it?" When she nodded, he looked thoughtful. "So essentially I became a cat in order to go home with you and live a pampered life devoid of responsibility while others take the risks and get the glory?"

"Looks like."

"Kewl."

The Bystander Diana'd adjusted in the hotel lobby never saw anyone speak to a stuffed animal again. Although his wife didn't believe in the disability, his children learned to exploit it early on by muttering constantly into the ears of plush toys when struck with the need to do something like fit a frozen hamburger patty into the DVD player.

* * *

"Yes, I have a car." Backed into a literal corner, panic rolling off him like smoke, Leslie/Deter saw no way out. "Why?"

Byleth smiled sweetly and moved a step closer. "Because I need a ride."

"No."

"If you give me a ride, I'll have sex with you." She probably wouldn't, but it seemed to be the best currency this body offered.

He swallowed and ground his shoulder blades into the wall, feet pedaling uselessly against the gray industrial tile on the floor. "No. I took the ch . . . chastity oath."

"The ch . . . chastity oath?" Her breasts flattened over a good portion of his chest. "Okay, if you give me a ride, I *won't* have sex with you."

"Deal!"

Nalo almost never went to Scarborough. As well as old Aunt Jen, it had another Keeper taking care of day-to-day metaphysical maintenance. Unfortunately, old Aunt Jen had taken a dislike to the man, and Nalo found herself in the unenviable position of comforter and confidante.

So here I am, back on the bus. Reaching into the possibilities, she adjusted the heat blasting out of the grille under the window—a minor technical infraction but preferable to dry roasting. *I know what Jen's thinking, calling me out here again. She's thinking she'll leave me that hole when she dies. Well, she can just think again. I don't give a damn about what's supposed to be, I'm not dropping my ass onto a hole in Scarborough for the next fifty years. The moment Jen passes, I'm hauling Diana out here and she can use that power of hers to slap the sucker closed and I don't care if she's got more important things to do because there isn't anything more important than keeping me out of Scar . . .*

Hellfire and damnation.

Her fingers closed around the cord, and she was up out of her seat before the sound of the bell reached the bus driver's ear.

"That's your car?" Pulling off a mitten, Byleth trailed her fingers along the gleaming black hood of the 1973 Firebird. "Who'd have thunk it—a God-pimp with a truly kewl set of wheels. Maybe I *will* have sex with you."

Eyes wide, Leslie/Deter jerked back. "Hey! You promised!"

Taking a deep breath, she leaned in and rubbed against the passenger door. "I know. But that was before I saw this totally demonic car."

"You want a ride or not?"

"Yessss. . . ."

"Then stop humping my car and get in."

The hair lifted on the back of Byleth's neck. She watched a city bus drive by, slow, and pull into a bus stop at the end of the block.

"Byleth?"

"In a minute. I've got to take care of something first."

The back doors of the bus opened.

She had to distract the Keeper or they'd never get away. Grabbing the first bit of darkness that came to hand, she tossed it into the small clump of preteens waiting at the light where it erupted into a sudden slush ball fight of epic proportions. She saw the massive handful of filthy ice and snow launched; she didn't wait to see it land.

"Let's go, Leslie." Dropping into the car, she slammed the door and reached for the seat belt. "Did I mention I was a demon?" she asked as they pulled into traffic.

His laugh carried distinctly nervous overtones. "I almost believe you."

"Really?"

"You're not like other girls. You're not even like the other girls we help off the street. You're not like any girl I've ever met. You're not . . ."

"I get it. Jeez. And thank you." She needed the reassurance as geeky as it might be.

It was getting harder and harder to touch the darkness.

As Nalo stepped off the bus, time slowed. She saw the slush ball approaching, the bits of rock and mud and ice standing out with unnatural clarity against the tiny bit of actual snow holding the thing together. She saw past it to the expression on the kid's face as he realized what was about to happen. She saw past him to a 1973 Firebird pulling away from the curb.

Then time sped up, and she didn't see anything at all for a few minutes.

Staggering forward, she clawed the slush ball from her face, reaching into the possibilities, past the pain and anger and certain knowledge that she was going to need to have her coat dry-cleaned again. Nalo had been a Keeper long enough that it would take more to distract her than a face full of frozen crap and the prospect of a twenty-two-dollar dry-cleaning bill.

But by the time she could see again, the car was gone.

The young man who'd exited the bus behind her, touched her lightly on one shoulder. "You okay, lady?"

"No. I have a sense of foreboding that can only mean darkness has found a way to corrupt the world, bringing down upon us a future of pain and pestilence. And I seem to have a piece of gravel up my nose."

"Bummer."

"Indeed."

Taking her seat on the half-empty subway, Diana did nothing to keep the other passengers from noticing the cat. Given the invisible walls that Toronto subway passengers erected around them in order to avoid interaction with potential crazies, religious lunatics, and lost American tourists, she could have been carrying a platypus on her lap and no one would have said anything. In fact, it very much looked as if an elderly woman in the other end of the car *was* carrying a . . .

"Hey, there's Doug!"

A talking cat, however, attracted a little attention.

"Hair ball," Diana announced, carefully tweaking reality. When everyone accepted the explanation—and no one took it as an instruction—she breathed a sigh of relief. "Keep it down," she muttered into the plush orange fur between Samuel's ears. "Unless you want to end up on late night TV hawking kibble between the psychics and those live girl phone things."

"1–800-U-CALL-ME," Doug added as he sat down beside them, having left a trail of cheap wine fumes the length of the subway car. "How's it going, Samuel?"

"Pretty good. Still haven't figured out the tail, though."

"It'll come. I see you're down to partial genitalia."

Diana closed her teeth on the comment she was about to make and took a closer look.

"Hey!" Samuel spun around and glared at her. "If you don't mind!"

"Sorry." *A self-neutering cat. Just what the world needs.* "And keep your voice down."

"No need, little lady. We're in my cone of silence."

Doug stirred the surrounding miasma with expansive gestures, the cuffs of two jackets and three visible sweaters rising up on thin gray wrists.

Breathing shallowly through her mouth, Diana reached into the possibilities. They showed no cone of silence but, on the other hand, street people were ignored so completely by the rest of the city's residents it amounted to the same thing.

"Any particular reason you decided to walk on the furry side, kid?"

"We needed to expose a demon."

"A demon? In the world?"

While Diana rolled her eyes and wondered why it was taking so long to get from College Street to Union Station where they could lose Samuel's fragrant buddy, Samuel explained the whole thing.

"A demon in the world," Doug restated, frowning thoughtfully. "Well, now, that does explain things. And here I was blaming that bottle of aftershave I knocked back this morning. So you exposed a demon, and now you're off after it, right?"

"Wrong," Diana told him—or more precisely told the space next to him. She was finding it hard to focus on his face, but that could have been because of the pale green strand waving from his nose. "We're off home. Someone else is off after the demon."

"Her older sister," Samuel added.

"And you got a few younger sibling issues with

that sister of yours, don't you? No need to deny it, it's dripping from your voice. Well, you know what I think?" He leaned conspiratorially forward. "I think that TV dinners go best with a nice Chardonnay."

"What?"

He blinked. "What did I say?" Diana repeated it and he sighed. "Whoa, train of thought got derailed. Toxic spills. Evacuate the women and children." He drew in a deep breath and released it slowly. Samuel flattened on Diana's lap, and it passed harmlessly over his head. "Okay. Let's try that again: I think you should go after that demon yourself. You have to save her."

"I what?"

"Save her. From your sister."

"It doesn't work that way. First of all, we don't interfere. Second, you seem to be a little confused about the good guys and the bad guys. And third, I don't even know why I'm talking to you about this."

"Because he's an angel," Samuel pointed out.

"Yeah, right, and I'm a model for Victoria's Secret."

Doug's eyes widened and he cupped both hands in front of his chest. "Hubba hubba!"

"Okay, that's it." Diana grabbed the cat and stood as the subway pulled into the King Street station. "I'm gone. We can walk from here."

"If the demon is an exact opposite of the young

man Samuel was, then isn't she as much of a person?"

Doug's quiet question stopped her at the door. Diana sighed and let it close in her face before returning to her seat which was, not surprisingly, still empty. "Yes, she is."

"And is your sister likely to take that into account?"

"No, she isn't." If not for an angel, then definitely not for a demon. "I think she's taking this whole thing personally. But Claire's being led to her, and I don't know where she is."

"Does she know she's being hunted?"

"She should."

"So, a demon in the body of a teenage girl knows she's being hunted; what would she do?" He leaned forward, eyes narrowed. "You're a teenage girl, think like a demon."

My cover's been blown, I know I'm being hunted, I know I don't stand much of a chance but I've been backed into a corner . . .

As though he were reading her mind, Doug nodded, the green strand bobbing emphatically. "You'll never take me alive, copper."

"If she's got to go," Diana said slowly, "she's going to flip Claire the finger on the way out, leaving behind the biggest possible mess for Claire to clean up."

* * *

The constant pound of the Summons changed tone and timbre. Claire shifted under her seat belt and brought both hands up to rub at her temples. There were times when being a Keeper resembled sitting next to the drum kit at a Moby concert. "It's moving east."

Glancing across the cab, Dean made a deductive leap. "The demon?"

Claire nodded.

"We aren't after heading for Toronto, then?"

"It doesn't feel like it."

"Nice to get some good news." He turned his attention back to the highway. "Going *through* Toronto's insanity enough."

"I never noticed any insanity."

"You're not driving." After his first trip through Toronto, Dean had decided that the Montreal reputation for having the worst drivers in Canada was undeserved. Sure, Montreal drivers all drove like maniacs, but at least they drove like maniacs who knew what they were doing. As near as he could figure, Toronto drivers had their heads so far up their collective arse they had to make it up as they went along.

"The biggest possible mess," Diana repeated as the subway pulled into Union Station. "Oh, my God! She's going to Kingston!" Grabbing up Samuel, she ran for the doors, paused, turned, and said, "Are you really an angel?"

Doug smiled. "Can't you tell?"

"No." The first whistle blew and she stepped out onto the platform. She *should* have been able to tell. Behind the closing doors, Doug spread his hands and bowed. Diana could see his lips move, but the roar of the old Red Rocket drowned him out.

He turned and waved as the subway headed north up the University line.

"I wonder what he said," she murmured, hurrying toward the escalators.

"Lex clavatoris designati rescindenda est."

"Good ears."

"I'm a cat."

"Only recently, so you can cut back on the attitude." Diana shifted the cat to her other arm, cut off an elderly Asian man, and raced up the narrow stairs, boots pounding against the metal treads. "And while I agree that the designated hitter rule has got to go, what does that have to do with him being, or not being, an angel?"

Samuel hooked his claws through her jacket. "Don't angels play baseball?"

"The Anaheim Angels. It's just the name of a team—I like so truly doubt there are actual metaphysical players on it."

"You sure?"

"No. And you know what? I don't care."

"Qui tacet consentit," Samuel muttered, as she stepped out onto the tiles and headed for the train station at a fast trot.

"Fac ut vivas! And stop showing off, I can't think of anything more annoying than a cat who criticizes in Latin."

"A cat who horks up a hair ball in a hundred-and-forty-dollar-pair of sneakers?"

"Tres gross. You win."

Leaning into the turn leading to a well-worn flight of limestone stairs, he smiled. "Of course."

"That was cutting back on the attitude?"

"What attitude?"

Taking the stairs two at a time, Diana realized why so many of Claire's conversations with Austin ended in unanswered questions.

"So why is the demon going to Kingston?" Samuel asked as they leveled out and headed across the polished marble floor toward the line for train tickets.

"She's going to reopen a hole to Hell. OW!"

"Sorry." Samuel fought his claws free of jacket, sweater, shirt, and flesh. "Are you serious?"

"No, I'm bleeding!"

"Hey, I said I was sorry, but you can't just mention Hell to an angel and expect no reaction."

"Fair enough." Diana slid in between the velvet ropes and prepared to wait for the first available sales agent. At the moment, all three of them appeared to be on break. "That's one powerful union," she muttered when reaching into the possibilities produced no visible results.

"Hell?" the cat prodded.

"Okay, short version of a long story: My sister and I closed this really old hole to Hell in the basement of a sort of hotel in Kingston before Christmas. Sealed the site, saved the world—yadda, yadda, yadda—but the place will still remember the hole, so reopening it will give the demon the biggest bang for the least buck. If she gets past the Cousin monitoring the site fast enough—and from what Claire told me about the dirty old man, she shouldn't have much trouble if she came fully outfitted—she'll have time to get the hole open before Claire catches up. We may not have to worry about Claire erasing her personhood because the rising darkness will completely overwhelm it."

"Not to mention overwhelm the world with pure unadulterated evil insuring that everyone on it lives short miserable lives of pain and desperation."

"Well, yeah. That, too."

THIRTEEN

"Now boarding at gate rorg, VIA Rail train number gonta sev to Nootival, with stops at Gaplerg, Corbillslag, Pevilg, and Binkstain."

"That's us," Diana declared, scooping the cat up off the bench as the station loudspeakers repeated the announcement in French.

"Hey, watch the whiskers," Samuel protested as she stuffed him into the backpack she'd bought at the station shop, heaved him up onto one shoulder, and hurried toward the gate. He peered out through the open zipper at the back of her ear. "And I thought we were going to Kingston on the train to Montreal."

"That's right: Binkstain on the train to Nootival."

"You're kidding?"

"Just try to look like luggage, would you."

The sudden blip of a police siren woke Austin out of a sound sleep. One moment he was lying between

Claire and Dean with a paw thrown over his eyes, the next he was up over the seat back and into the depths of his cat carrier muttering, "You can't prove it was me, anyone could have left that spleen on the carpet."

"You've got to admire his reflexes," Claire allowed, waving one hand through the contrail of cat hair.

"Do I, then?" Dean asked, gearing down and maneuvering the truck carefully to the narrow shoulder winter had left bracketing highway seven. "Sure. Okay, I guess."

Claire shot him a questioning glance, noted the muscle jumping along his jaw, and the distinct "man about to face a firing squad" angle to his profile. "You've never been pulled over before, have you?"

"No." He sighed and laid his forehead on the steering wheel.

It was a vaguely embarrassed no, but whether he was embarrassed because he'd been pulled over now or because he'd never been pulled over before, Claire couldn't tell. Some guys might be bothered by reaching twenty-one without a speeding ticket—or more precisely the story of how they got the ticket—but would they be the same guys who were bothered by un-ironed underwear? "Don't worry, I'll deal with it." She twisted around within the confines of the seat belt. "There's a demon out there; we haven't time to jump through hoops for the OPP."

"No."

This, however, was a definite no. An inarguable no. She watched Dean's chin rise as he rolled down the window and recognized his "taking responsibility" look.

"You don't do the crime," he announced, "if you can't do the time."

"What?"

"It's the theme song from a seventies' cop show."

"You weren't around in the seventies."

"I saw it at my cousin's. In Halifax. On the Seventies' Cop Show Network. He has a satellite dish," Dean added as Claire's brows drew so far in they met over her nose. "Look, it's not important, I just don't want you messing with the cop's head. I broke the law, so I'm after facing the consequences."

"You were doing one hundred ten in an eighty. It's not like you've been out robbing banks or clogging Internet access to I've-got-more-money-than-brains. com." Over the years, Claire had fixed a number of tickets while catching rides with Bystanders. Once, she'd attempted to convince a Michigan State Trooper that ninety-seven miles an hour on I-90 through Detroit was a perfectly reasonable speed. Poking around in his head, she discovered she hadn't been the first— or even the most convincing. "Dean, I'm sorry, but, as a Keeper, I have to say that getting rid of this demon has to be right at the top of our to-do list."

"It is."

"Good."

"Right after this."

"But . . ."

"Keepers police metaphysical crimes, right?" He caught up her hand and stared earnestly at her over her fingertips.

"Essentially, but . . ."

"How can I help you do your job, if I blow off this guy doing his?"

Her eyes widened.

"That's *not* what I meant." His glasses steamed up in the heat rising off his face. "It's not. It wasn't. Look, just let me deal with this. And then you can do what you want to make up the time." The sound of heavy footsteps drew closer. "Claire?"

"Okay," she muttered reluctantly. "But make it . . ."

"A quickie," Austin snickered from the depths of the cat carrier.

As he turned toward the looming figure of the OPP constable, Dean shot a glance behind the seat that promised a discussion with the cat in the near future. Claire didn't know why he bothered since Austin usually went to sleep right around the time Dean started talking about mutual respect, but she admired his persistence—futile though it might be. A cat's idea of mutual respect had nothing about it any other species would recognize as mutual.

"License and registration, sir."

The constable's accent was pure Ontario and Claire felt some of the tension leave her shoulders. Maybe it *would* be possible to get back on the road with a minimum of delay.

Dean struggled to get his wallet out of his back pocket, realized he was strapped in, and jammed his seat belt trying to open it. Pounding the release catch with one hand and yanking at the lap belt with the other, he flopped about, making it worse. With the theme song to "C*O*P*S" running through his head, he fought to keep from hyperventilating as he alternately pounded and yanked. He'd watched enough television to know that when the police thought they were being dicked around life got unpleasant for the perp.

"If you'd just relax . . ."

"Not now, Claire." Just relax and it'll happen. Just relax and don't think so much. Just relax and let nature take its course. After two nights of Claire telling him to relax, that word in her voice got him so anxious he wanted to scream at her to shut up.

"I think your lady's trying to say that the tension against the belt is causing the problem."

"Oh." He sagged back against the seat, pressed the release with his thumb, and pulled the belt free. Fully aware of Claire's pointed stare, he got out his license and registration and handed them over.

"Newfoundland, eh?"

"I meant to get my plates switched—and my license," he explained hurriedly, hoping it didn't sound like he was making feeble excuses for breaking the law, "but I wasn't certain I was staying."

The constable bent down and peered at Claire. "I see. You know a Hugh McIssac?" he asked as he straightened.

"Oh, no . . ."

He bent again. "Ma'am?"

Claire reached into the possibilities.

Five minutes later, they were driving east at a careful eighty kilometers an hour having received a stern although truncated warning that had included no references to hockey.

"Is it warm in here, or is it me?" Austin asked, dropping down onto the seat.

Claire gathered him up onto her lap and shot a worried glance at Dean. He looked as though he'd been carved from flesh-colored marble, the only indication of his mood a certain flare to the one nostril she could actually see. *If he doesn't say something before we reach that pine tree, I'll speak first.*

The pine tree passed.

Okay, if he doesn't say something between now and when we reach those blackthorn bushes by the side of the road, I'll explain.

A lunantishee looked out of the bushes as they went by and stuck a long, mocking tongue out at Claire.

Fine, if he won't talk to me by that next crossroad, he

can just sit there. There's no reason I should have to say anything. I was right. Because, after all, we're just on our way to catch a demon and that's so less important than a forty-five-minute discussion of a peewee game played back in 1979.

They crossed the crossroad.

Austin sighed. "So," he said, squirming around to face Dean, "who was Hugh McIssac?"

"A guy." Dean's teeth were locked so tightly together the words barely emerged, but innate politeness forced him to answer a direct question.

"A guy you knew back in St. John's?"

"Yes."

"Play hockey with him?"

"No."

Claire felt the burn rush up her cheeks at the clipped negative. *Oops.* There'd be no way to make this up to him. A sound caught somewhere between an apology and a whimper forced its way past her teeth.

Dean glanced at her and sighed.

"Against," he added grudgingly.

"Aha!"

"Oh, nice way to smooth things over," Austin muttered.

"So, if I hadn't stepped in, we *would* have been there another half an hour!"

Dean shook his head. "You don't know that."

"Because this would have been the time you cut the conversation short?"

"Yes!"

Claire folded her arms.

"Well, maybe."

She snorted.

"Okay, probably not. But that's not the point," he told her indignantly, slowing slightly to let a minivan pass. "You said you'd let me deal with it."

"I didn't change any of the police stuff. He had no intention of giving you a ticket."

"I'll never know that for sure, will I?"

"And there's nothing worse than girding your loins for a battle you don't need to fight," Austin interjected, climbing off Claire's lap and stretching out on the seat.

"You girded your loins?" Claire stared across the cat at Dean.

"No."

"No?"

"I don't even know what that means!" He sighed hard enough to momentarily frost the inside of the windshield. "I just wanted to handle it myself."

"You don't trust me?"

"Yes, I trust you. But you're some high-handed at times!"

"I'm a Keeper! And I'll have you know I'm no more high-handed than it takes to do my job. If you'd rather talk hockey than make love . . ."

"What?"

"We find the demon, I banish the demon, we find a private corner; isn't that the plan? Unless you don't want . . . Why are you pulling over? Dean?"

He put the truck into neutral, stepped down the parking brake, and pulled on the hazards. Then he turned to face her, one hand braced on her headrest, the other on the dash. "I want to make love to you. I want to make love to you so badly it's all I can think about. When I'm eating, when I'm driving, when I'm looking at you, when I'm not looking at you, when I'm talking about demons, when I'm talking about hockey—I'm still thinking about making love to you."

"And this is what you're thinking about when you're talking to me?" Austin demanded, rising up into the space between them. When Dean answered in the affirmative, he sighed and dropped back down again. "Well, that's really going to put a damper on future conversations."

Reaching out, Dean stroked the back of his fingers over Claire's cheek. "But I'm only thinking about making love to you because I can't actually make love to you. If I could, I certainly wouldn't be talking about hockey, I'd be . . ."

"Okay, that's enough. The cat does not need to know the details."

Without taking her eyes off Dean, Claire picked Austin up and dropped him behind the seat. Then she snapped off her belt and slid forward. After a moment she sucked Dean's lower lip away from his teeth and, when the suction finally broke, murmured into the swollen flesh, "Shall we find that demon, then?"

Dean's answer was essentially inarticulate.

Austin opted to stay out of the discussion entirely.

"Would you please stop doing that."

"Doing what?"

"Rubbing my car. It's . . ."

"Turning you on?"

". . . distracting me. I keep seeing peripheral movement, I think someone's about to make a lane change, and it's always you. It isn't easy driving this car in this weather in this traffic, and I'd appreciate just a little . . . HEY! YOU WANNA STOP VISUALIZING WORLD PEACE AND START VISUALIZING YOUR TURN SIGNALS! . . . consideration."

Byleth blinked, looked from Leslie/Deter to the SUV that had just drifted across three lanes of fast-moving traffic and back to Leslie/Deter again. "He didn't hear you."

"I know. But it makes me feel better. Helps me drive."

"Oh."

"It's just a way of releasing . . . TRY LEASING A CAR YOU KNOW HOW TO DRIVE, MORON!"

The car in question braked hard, swerved left, then

right, then hit a patch of ice, turned a complete three hundred and sixty degrees and settled safely on the shoulder. A half a kilometer of brakes squealed, dozens of steering wheels were cranked, sudden moisture caused two seat warmers to short out, and then it was over.

Byleth smiled. "He heard you that time."

Fingers white around the steering wheel, Leslie/Deter stared wide-eyed out at the surrounding traffic still moving miraculously to the east and beginning to pick up speed. "God saved us all."

"You think?"

"He reached down His hand to keep His children safe."

"No." Byleth frowned and shook her head. "I'd have noticed that."

"You can't deny that was a miracle."

"Hey! I can deny anything I want," she snarled, folding her arms and slumping down in the seat.

They drove in silence for a few minutes, then Leslie/Deter sighed and squared his shoulders. "You know, you're not as tough as you think you are."

Byleth glared at him past the lock of hair bisecting her face, her expression as much disbelief as anger. "You have no idea how tough I am."

"You think you're bad."

"I *am* bad!"

"You think it's cool to be all dark and dangerous."

"Hello? Hell to Leslie!" One navy-tipped fingernail

poked him hard in the shoulder. "I *am* dark and dangerous."

"I know why you do it."

"Oh, please . . ."

"It keeps people from getting close to you. Keeps you from getting hurt."

"*I* don't get hurt. I do the hurting."

"Essentially the same thing."

"If you think that having red hot pokers stuffed up your ass is the same as stuffing those same pokers up someone else's ass, you're dopier than I thought. And that's almost scary." Beginning to wonder why she hadn't considered the implications of being stuck in a car with a God-pimp for three hours, Byleth unhooked her seat belt and twisted around until she faced the driver, her eyes onyx from lid to lid. "Leslie, look at me."

"Not now, Byleth. I'm trying to keep the car on the road."

"I said, *look* at me."

"And I said, not now!" A glance in the rearview mirror showed the front grille of a transport and not much else. "Unless you really want to end this little journey upside down in the ditch."

She thought about that for a moment, her eyes lightening. "Well, no."

"Good." He leaned back, downshifted, pulled into the passing lane, and, engine roaring, shifted back into overdrive. They screamed past traffic and dropped speed only when they'd cleared the clump and had moved back into the right-hand lane.

Byleth closed her mouth with a snap. "That was *so* kewl."

Bright spots of color appeared on pale cheeks. "Thanks."

"Do it again!"

"Sure, next time I have to pass something."

"What? Like a kidney stone? Do it now!"

"No." Glancing over at her, his eyes widened. "Byleth! Do up your seatbelt!"

"Because you'll get a ninety-six-dollar fine and lose three points if the cops pull us over?" she sneered, her hands as far away from the belt as possible while still attached to her body.

"Because you'll get hurt if anything happens."

"Won't your god protect me?"

"It doesn't work like that."

"Tell me about it," she snorted.

He sighed and shook his head. "I've been trying to."

"I want you to know I'm only doing this up because I have to get to Kingston in one piece," Byleth told him as she dragged the shoulder belt down over her jacket, and shoved the clasp together as hard as she could. "I'm sure not doing it because you told me to. And I so totally don't believe you care if I get hurt."

"I do care."

"Why?"

"Damned if I know."

"Probably," she snapped, sinking down into the depths of the bucket seat, knees braced against the dash.

Samuel poked a paw out through the top of the backpack and tapped Diana lightly on the chin. "What's wrong?"

"Summons," she whispered. Although the train was crowded with post-Christmas travelers, they had a double seat to themselves—mostly because of the disgustingly realistic stain the possibilities had provided. She'd draped her jacket strategically, but talking to luggage would still attract Bystander attention.

"Okay." A quick shoulder lick to gather his thoughts and he had a plan. "Here's what we'll do: you deal with the Summons, and I'll go to Kingston and save the demon from your sister."

He looked perfectly serious. Or at least as serious as an orange cat in a green backpack could look.

"And just supposing I was insane enough to agree to that—how?"

"I'll think of something. I'm a cat."

"You're an angel shaped like a cat," Diana reminded him pointedly.

"That's what I meant, I'm an angel."

"Right. Fortunately, the Summons is on the train. I can deal." She stood, left her jacket lying where it fell and, turning reluctantly in place, attempted to pin down the feeling. It wasn't that she minded being Summoned, it was what Keepers did, after all, but since her wallet had been distinctly short of lineage money, and she'd had to spend her Christmas money to buy the train ticket, it didn't seem exactly fair. Either she was saving the demon on her own time, or she was working—which was it to be? "There! Is that the washroom," she added, smiling broadly down at the middle-aged man whose attention had been jerked away from his paper.

He shot her the look those over forty reserved for those under twenty and returned to a review of *Archie and Jughead,* the holiday's breakout movie. Diana hadn't seen it, but she strongly suspected George Clooney had been miscast.

The sound of claws in upholstery brought her shuffle toward the aisle to a sudden stop.

"Where are you going?" she muttered, bending so that her face was millimeters from the angel's, pushing him back under her jacket.

"With you."

"Why? You won't be able to do anything. I won't be long. Just stay here."

Samuel thought about it for a moment. "No."

"Why not?"

He seemed surprised by the question. "I don't want to."

"Fine." Grabbing the straps, Diana swung cat and

carrier up onto her shoulder, enjoying the muffled, "Oof!" rather more than she should have.

As it turned out, the accident site *was* in the washroom. Unfortunately, so was someone else. There were four people already waiting in line and judging by their expressions, not to mention the fidgeting, they'd been waiting for a while. Hoping she wasn't too late, that seeping darkness hadn't claimed a victim, Diana reached into the possibilities just far enough for safety—not quite far enough for voyeurism.

She couldn't quite prevent the astounded sputter.

The motherly woman in line in front of her half turned. "Are you all right?"

"Choked on spit. Hate it when that happens."

"I see." Still looking concerned, although her focus had shifted from concern for to concern about, she turned away.

The possibilities had shown two people in the bathroom. They'd already been there longer than they'd intended, and it seemed like they were going to be there for quite a while yet. Darkness had no intention of allowing a quickie, not when a delay would leave everyone involved so frustrated. Few things resembled a lynch mob quite as much as people waiting for a toilet.

As though Diana's thoughts had been her cue, the first person in line, an elderly woman with deep angry lines dragging down the corners of her mouth, stepped forward and banged impatiently on the door.

Which broke the rhythm and looked to delay things even further.

There seemed to be only one logical thing to do.

A few moments later, the couple emerged looking too totally satiated to be embarrassed by the amount of noise the finale had generated. Muttering in disgust, the elderly woman pushed past them, slammed the door, and shot the "occupied" slide home with such force it echoed throughout the car like a gunshot.

Moving Samuel to her other shoulder, Diana followed the line forward, jerking to a stop at the sound of a happy moan from inside the bathroom, closely followed by a muffled "Oh, yes. Yes! YES!" from the cubicle in the next car. Blushing scarlet, she reached back into the possibilities. She'd only intended to bring the original couple to a conjugal conclusion, not everyone who had to relieve themselves between Toronto and Montreal.

Although VIA *was* trying to get more people to ride the train. . . .

Diana caught herself on the edge of the toilet as the train lurched around a corner, barely managing to keep her head from cracking against the outer wall.

"Better wash your hands when you finish," Samuel observed from the sink. "You wouldn't believe what this place is covered with."

"I can guess."

Hooking a paw around a tap, he braced himself as the car rocked from side to side. "No surprise really, I mean, how can a guy aim when he's being flung around the room."

"How about sitting down?"

"Not manly. Don't put your hand there!"

"Eww. You're not helping." She erased the signature a Cousin had left behind and straightened. "It's not a big hole, but it's been here for so long it may take a while to close it down. I'll have to keep coming back—do it a bit at a time."

"You're going to attract attention," he pointed out, climbing into the backpack so she could wash her hands.

"As if. People don't watch other people heading for the bathroom."

"You think she'd try adult diapers or something."

"Yeah. Adult diapers."

Just past Coburg, heading into the bathroom for the seventh and hopefully final trip, Diana leaned down and smiled sweetly at the two young men who'd made their observation about adult diapers in carrying voices. "I'm on my period," she purred for their ears only.

They leaned away from her, appalled.

"Lots of heavy bleeding."

The blond turned green, his gold eyebrow piercing standing out in stark contrast to his new skin tone.

"Clotting even."

The brunet swallowed three times in quick succession and clamped a hand over his mouth.

"Sloughing off big chunks of uterine lining."

They exchanged identical expressions of horror.

"One more word out of either of you," she promised, "and I'll go into detail."

"Was that nice?" Samuel asked, emerging from the backpack as the bathroom door closed. "I mean, they were just being guys."

"Yeah, well, I am not an angel."

He sighed and shook his head. "You're not even a cat."

"Look, it's easy, stop the truck or I ruin the upholstery. Your choice."

Claire rolled her eyes as Dean began looking for a place to pull over. "You went to the bathroom less than fifty kilometers ago."

"And now I have to go again."

"Austin, we're in a hurry!"

"So am I."

Since the truck was now stopped, there didn't seem to be any reason to continue the argument. Opening her door, she watched Austin leap to the ground and disappear behind a young spruce.

After three minutes on the dashboard clock, she opened the door again and called, "Austin? Are you all right?"

"I'm old," his disembodied voice reminded her. "It takes a while."

"Be careful." She closed the door and sighed.

"Worried about him?" Dean asked gently, brushing a few snowflakes off her hair.

"A little."

"Seemed like some sigh for a little worry."

Noting the sudden spray of snow from behind the spruce, Claire glanced over at the clock and sighed again. "I just can't help thinking that there's got to be a more efficient way to fight darkness. There's a demon loose in the world and we're waiting at the side of the road for a cat to pee."

The certain knowledge that they were not going to be eating in his car gave Leslie/Deter the strength to hold his table against all comers. He looked up from two number fours, one supersized, a coffee, and a hot chocolate as Byleth approached, limping slightly, and demanded, "Are you all right?"

Byleth adjusted her jacket, smoothed her hair back into place, and shrugged. "I had to fight through a busload of old ladies to get to a stall."

Above the line of the black turtleneck, Leslie/Deter's pale face blanched paler still and he glanced toward the women's washroom as though he expected to see a blue-haired horde emerge brandishing American-made toaster ovens. "You didn't wait your turn?"

"As if. I'd still be in there." She looked around the rest stop, noting the lineup of elderly men at all three of the fast food outlets. "I know the baby boom is aging, but this is nuts."

"They're on their way home from a holiday trip to Casino Rama."

"You can tell that from looking?"

Byleth could feel him tottering on the edge of a lie, but in the end he shook his head. "No. It said so on their bus."

"Oh. Well, when I unleash Hell, old people will be among the first to go—because they don't run as fast," she explained when he made a strangled, wordless protest. "I mean, even demons with no actual legs can move faster than some old fart using a walker."

"I wish you wouldn't talk like that." He checked to make sure no one had overheard before squaring his shoulders under the black leather trench coat and meeting her . . .

. . . staring past her left ear. "I don't like it."

"Because of the God thing?"

"Yeah. Because of the God thing." His stance softened as he slid her food across the table. "It isn't funny."

She grinned at him over a mouthful of fries. "I wasn't joking."

"Byleth."

"Leslie. You know what I don't get," she continued. "You drive a really cool car, you've got that high-priced sort of Goth meets N'Sync look going, you're neither boxers or briefs so what is it with you and God? It's like, so geeky. You don't really believe you have a personal relationship with the big kahuna, do you?"

"Yeah, I do."

She put down her burger and took a closer look. He really did. It was . . . unexpected. And disconcerting. Pushing her hair back off her face, she glared at him from under lowered brows. "In my experience, a so-called personal relationship with God mostly involves criticism of lifestyle choices."

"Lifestyle choices?"

Her eyes went onyx. "I'm a demon."

Leslie/Deter's gaze skittered off hers, wandered the room for a moment, then slowly returned. His hands were trembling, but he swallowed and looked deep into the unrelieved black. "You don't have to be," he said.

And he believed that, too.

Byleth shoved her chair back hard enough to scrape the hard rubber legs across the tile floor with a noise that mixed fingernails on blackboards with the scream of a jammed fan belt. Half the people in the room winced, the rest put a hand to their better ear and shouted, "What?"

"Come on." She snatched her diet cola up off the table. "This isn't getting us any closer to Kingston."

Claire began to get fidgety as the main street of Marmora disappeared behind them.

"Are you all right?" Dean asked, reaching out to capture her hand.

"I don't know. Something's nagging."

He eased off on the gas. "Do you want me to stop?"

"Oh, sure," Austin muttered, stepping indignantly across her lap, "but when the cat has to pee, there's no sympathy."

"It's not my bladder, Austin, it's the Summons."

"I knew that."

"Of course you did." Pulling free from Dean's grip, she stroked her fingers along the brilliant white expanse of stomach fur, the familiar motion and answering purr smoothing out her agitation.

"Claire?"

"Right, the Summons. We need to turn south. Now."

Dean looked past her to the snow-covered fields and copses of naked trees passing on the south side of the highway. "Now?"

"Not exactly now. But as soon as you can." Claire drew the Ontario Map Book out of the glove compartment, found highway seven, followed it to Marmora and beyond. "There." Her fingernail tapped an intersection of two red lines. "Turn off on number 62 to Belleville."

"That where we're headed?"

"No, we have to go farther east, but that's where we'll pick up the 401."

"What's east of Belleville?"

Claire ran her finger along the double line. "There's Napanee," she told them, continuing to check the route, "but I don't think that's the . . ."

"Place?" Austin prodded rolling up onto his feet. Head to one side, he looked from Keeper to map and then followed a thin line of gray up to where it spread out against and disappeared against the gray upholstery on the inside of the roof. "What's that smoking under your finger?"

"Kingston." She closed the book with a snap.

"Kingston?" Dean repeated.

Claire met his eyes and nodded.

Austin sat down again. "At the risk of sounding clichéd, I've got a bad feeling about this."

"You know what I love about trains? When they stop between stations for stupid reasons, you can't get off."

Curled up in the depths of the open backpack, Samuel yawned. "Why would you love that about trains?"

"I was being sarcastic."

"I knew that."

"Sure you did." Diana glared out the window at the

cars moving by on the highway, one empty, snow-covered field away—her left foot tapping against the floor, right fingers splayed out on the window. "I could have walked over there and got another ride by now, but, oh, no, that'd be against the rules. If I'd been Summoned to Kingston, I could fix whatever the stupid problem is, but only attempting to prevent a gross injustice isn't reason enough. This is *so* lame."

"It's important you follow the rules."

She snorted. "That's something I never thought I'd hear a cat say."

"I meant you specifically."

"Oh, ha! I guess angels don't mind wasting time, the time we could be using to get there first and set a trap." Her right foot took over the beat from her left. "This so totally sucks." The weight of a Bystander's regard pulled her head up. The blond young man she'd previously terrorized was standing in the aisle staring down at her. "What?"

"Are you talking to your backpack?" he asked, leaning forward.

Diana closed the flap on the top of the big pocket. "Are *you* operating on more than two brain cells?"

"I just thought you had a . . ." He dropped his voice below the level of the ambient noise. ". . . cat."

"And what if I do?"

Glancing around, as though he were about to hand over state secrets, he shoved a piece of beef jerky toward her, managed half a smile, hurried away.

Frowning, she reopened the pack and offered Samuel the jerky.

"Did you let him leave?" he demanded, hooking it out of her fingers.

"I don't think he'll tell anyone."

"That's not the point," he protested. "The point is, there's always more than one piece in a package of beef jerky."

"Maybe I should just go offer myself to him to keep you from starving." Before he could answer, the train lunged about five feet forward, then began picking up speed in a less vertebrae-separating manner. "Finally! If that demon's raised Hell before we get there, I'm sending a nasty letter to the smoking ruins of the VIA Rail head office."

"Oh, yeah, that'll show them."

"So is there some place you want me to drop you off or what?" Leslie/Deter asked, as the car squealed its way around the tight exit ramp at Division Street. "If you're on your own, we have a mission in Kingston."

"I so don't care. Besides I know exactly where I'm going."

"Might be nice if the driver knew."

"Lower Union Street. Just off King." Byleth wet her lips in anticipation. "Place called the Elysian Fields Guest House."

FOURTEEN

"It doesn't look like it's open."

"That doesn't matter," Byleth said softly, staring up at the three-story Victorian building. The memory of darkness had left a grimy patina over the red bricks—a discoloration any eyes but hers would assume had been left by modern pollution. Well, the yellow-brown stains eating away at old mortar *had* been left by modern pollution, as had the patches of filthy, crumbling paint on the pale green trim, the white streaks from acid rain on the old copper roof, and the rather amazing amount of rust on every exposed piece of iron. She sighed and wondered why darkness even bothered.

"Maybe I should go in with you."

"Maybe you should mind your own friggin' business." She unlocked the seat belt and shoved open the door with the same angry motion, uncertain of just who she was angry at. *I ought to suggest that he put it in gear and then drive into something solid, but why waste such a cool car.* She considered telling him to park by the lake and walk out until he found a break in the ice. Or to jump off the top of a building. Or to take in a Britney Spears concert. Well, she might not be able to touch enough of the darkness to manage that last one, but all the rest were perfectly feasible. Standing on the road, still holding the car door, she examined her options.

Leslie/Deter ducked down far enough to see her face. "Be careful."

"Whatever." No point in wasting diminishing resources on such a loser, not when there was a world of dark potential at her back. Muscles straining, she pulled at the heavy door and was astonished to hear her own voice just as it closed. "Thanks. You know, for the ride."

Gratitude?

Eww.

Spitting wasn't enough to take the taste out of her mouth. This was so the last time she was manifesting in Canada.

Clutching her open coat more tightly around her, Byleth waited until the car disappeared around the corner before turning toward the house. The God-pimp was just the kind of guy who'd hang around to make sure she was all right. "As though he could do anything about it if I wasn't," she sneered, climbing over a ridge of snow and up the nine uneven steps to the porch. There was a door down an equal number of steps in the area, but a teenager breaking into the basement of a guesthouse might be noticed by the neighbors while a customer, even a young customer, approaching the front door would not—knowledge not from the dark end of the possibilities but overheard last night in the mission dorm. If things went her way over the next couple of hours, there were a few other bits of overheard information Byleth looked forward to trying out—although she wasn't entirely certain what a funchi, key caz star boi was.

The door was unlocked.

The old-fashioned brass knob turned silently.

There'd be a Cousin inside. A Cousin who'd have been able to sense her since this morning when that idiot angel had so unexpectedly changed. A Cousin who had to know she was close. Who could be waiting, ready for her, just inside.

I can take a Cousin.

Palms suddenly damp, she hesitated, wondering why she was leaking. She *could* take a Cousin. Couldn't she? At the precise moment she made form out of darkness, she could definitely have taken a Cousin, but for every moment after that, she'd been changing. Or, more precisely, the body had been changing her. Into what? That was the question. Suddenly racked with very undemonic insecurity, she froze.

I don't even know who I am anymore. This was such a stupid idea.

It took a cold wind blowing in from the lake to get her moving again. Freezing was fine as a metaphor, she decided, pushing open the door, but in the real world it sucked big time. So maybe she couldn't beat a prepared Cousin—no matter how pointless the whole stupid thing ended up being, it was infinitely preferable to spending another moment feeling like imps were jabbing icicles into her ears. She got enough of *that* back home.

It wasn't significantly warmer inside the guesthouse.

The lobby and the tiny office behind the long wooden counter were empty of everything except a rather pitiful looking desk and an old rotary dial phone. Either the Cousin whose presence permeated the building had set a trap closer to the memory of Hell, or he hadn't thought her much of a threat.

Byleth's fingers curled into fists and her mood flipped a hundred and eighty degrees, insecurity trumped by insulted pride. *That's just fine*, she snarled silently. *If you want a threat, I'll give you a threat.*

Tossing a disdainful glance at the hunter-green walls—so yesterday's color—she moved quietly down the hall, allowing instinct to guide her. After it guided her to the kitchen, which decidedly had never held a hole to Hell in spite of a rather eldritch pattern of grape jelly spilled on the counter, she started opening doors.

The basement wasn't that difficult to find.

Given the history of the place, Byleth could think of only one reason for the large metal door across from the washer and dryer, although reasons for it to have been painted turquoise escaped her. A few steps closer and she saw that it was ajar.

This, then, was where the Cousin had set his trap.

"Where to?"

Setting the squirming backpack carefully on the floor behind the driver's seat, Diana dropped into the cab and slammed the door. "The Elysian Fields Guest House, Lower Union just off King Street."

"That's downtown, by the waterfront?"

"Last time I checked." Given the building in question, that wasn't entirely a facetious statement.

"The Elysian Fields Guest House?" the cabby repeated thoughtfully, easing his car into the line of traffic leaving the train station's parking lot. "Bet that's a name that doesn't draw a lot of business. Might as well call it the Vestibule of Hell."

Diana smiled grimly at his reflection in the rearview mirror. "It's been considered."

" 'Elysian, windless, fortunate abodes // Beyond Heaven's constellated wilderness.' *Prometheus Unbound*, Percy Bysshe Shelley."

"Gee, and I can't imagine why my guidance counselors keep steering me *away* from an English Lit degree."

"I could also do you a great wanking piece from *Henry V*," he told her, changing lanes on Days Road, "but the city's not sanding as much as they used to and last night's snow is a bit packed in."

"I vote you pay attention to the road. You could even speed if you feel up to it."

"In a hurry."

"Definitely."

"Meeting a boy?"

"What happened to paying attention to the road?"

"Just asking." His reflection frowned slightly. "You got a cat back there?"

"No." It came out a little fast, but Diana thought it still sounded sincere. The last thing she wanted to do was mess with a Bystander's mind in a moving vehicle. Okay, not the last thing, but it was definitely in the top ten somewhere between seeing the N'Sync movie and having a root canal. "It's just a backpack."

"You think you could get it to stop sharpening its claws on the back of my seat?"

"If she opens the way . . ."

"It, not she. It's a piece of darkness given physical form, it's not a person."

Ducking back into the right lane to pass a Mazda Miata toddling along at a mere twenty kilometers over the limit, Dean shook his head. "Diana seems some certain there's a person involved."

"Diana also believes that The Cure is the best band in the world."

"They're decent," Dean acknowledged.

Trying not to feel old, Claire stroked a comforting hand down Austin's back, but whether she was comforting him or herself, she couldn't say. "It won't be that easy to reopen the site. There were three Keepers involved in closing it, as well as you and Jacques, and it's not that easy to find a hotel keeper from Newfoundland and the ghost of a French Canadian sailor in downtown Kingston on a Wednesday afternoon during the Christmas holidays."

"On a Saturday night in mid-January?"

"Not impossible."

"Demons have their own connection to darkness," Austin reminded her. "She won't need to reproduce all the factors."

"It," Claire reminded him. "And I know. But all the convolutions should slow it down."

"Should?" Dean wondered.

"Will. Why are *you* slowing down?"

"Exit ramp."

"Right."

"And there's a police cruiser on the shoulder up ahead."

"Let me worry about that." Reaching into the possibilities, Claire reset the radar gun to the Disney Channel. "You just drive."

There was no trap on or around the furnace room door.

Standing at the top of the stairs leading down to the bedrock floor, Byleth wet her lips and stepped forward. One step. Two.

No Cousin. So far, no Keepers.

"Oh, sure, ignore me all you want, but I'm not going away." The slight echo in the room made her sound more petulant than defiant. Definitely the echo . . .

On the bottom step, she paused, suddenly worried she was about to do the wrong thing.

"Wait a minute." The smack, palm to head, was a little harder than it needed to be. "I'm *supposed* to be doing the wrong thing." Stepping off onto the floor, she walked quickly to where the memory was the strongest and, before yet another mood swing could come along, dropped to her knees, placing her hands flat against the stone. The connection was there, but what should have been a rush of power revitalizing every dark molecule of her being was no more than a mere trickle of low-end possibilities it took forehead-furrowing concentration to feel.

WE'RE SORRY, THE NUMBER YOU HAVE DIALED IS NOT IN SERVICE. PLEASE INSCRIBE A PENTAGRAM AND TRY AGAIN.

"Oh, for . . ." Both palms slapped down hard. "I don't need a freaking pentagram, I'm a piece of you!" All the hair on the back of her neck lifted as her anger lent the connection new strength. They were listening down there, no doubt about it; probably arguing about who was going to take the call. "This isn't evil, guys, this is irritating. Do you want to be released into the world or not? I've got better things to do than sit around waiting for you to get your head out of your ass."

HEY! THERE'S NO NEED TO BE INSULTING.

Byleth sat back on her heels. "Got your attention, so apparently there is."

YOU'VE BEEN CORRUPTED BY THE WORLD.

WE HARDLY RECOGNIZED YOU.

Hell sighed. THEY GROW UP SO FAST.

"Look there's a Keeper coming . . ."

WE FEEL ONLY YOU.

BECAUSE THERE'S NO ACTUAL HOLE, IDIOT.

OW.

Didn't miss that, Byleth remembered. "The point you're not listening to is that we don't have much time so like pull it together into one voice, would you, and tell me how to reopen this thing."

In the long pause that followed she had the strangest feeling Hell was about to ask if she was sure, if she really wanted to wrap the world in a shroud of darkness and pain. All the world, including the Porters and that axworthy guy in the music store and

Leslie/Deter and his car. Which was ridiculous because Hell as a general rule could care less about the opinions of and/or motivations of those who offered it a chance to release chaos.

She bit her lip almost hard enough to draw blood. *Was* she sure?

ALL RIGHT, HERE'S WHAT YOU HAVE TO DO. . . .

Too late anyway.

"It doesn't look like it's open."

"That doesn't matter," Diana told him, handing over the last of her Christmas money. "The guy who runs this place is a Cousin."

"Ah, yes, family, where they always have to take you in. 'A happy family is but an earlier heaven.' John Bowring."

"And this particular family is trying to prevent an earlier Hell." Backpack on her lap, she slid out the door and straightened. "Keep the change."

" 'There is a certain relief in change, even though it be from bad to worse.' Washington Irving."

Smiling tightly, Diana slammed the cab door. "Get a life," she advised as he drove off, then she turned and raced up the porch stairs, ignoring Samuel's muffled protests as he banged against the small of her back. Once inside, she dumped him out on the counter and watched incredulously as he raced to the end, flung himself to the floor, charged across the lobby and halfway up the stairs, spun around, returned at an even higher speed, launched himself back onto the counter, across to the desk, to the windowsill, and back to the counter again.

"What was that all about?" Diana demanded, hoping no one had heard.

"I figured out the legs," Samuel told her proudly. Turning around, he caught sight of his tail out of the corner of one eye and pounced.

"This is so not the time," she sighed as he spun about like a furry, orange, and not terribly coordinated dreidel. "The demon is in the building. Can't you feel the dark possibilities opening?"

Head spinning, Byleth struggled unsuccessfully to make sense of the information Hell had just passed through their tenuous link. "Let me guess," she muttered peevishly, wishing she could rub both throbbing temples, "those instructions were translated from the Japanese by someone whose first language was Urdu."

CLOSE.

"They don't make any sense!"

THEY DON'T? After a moment Hell cleared its throat in a vaguely embarrassed sort of way. UM, THAT'S BECAUSE THEY'RE ACTUALLY THE INSTRUCTIONS FOR HOOKING UP THE CABLES BETWEEN A DVD PLAYER AND A DIGITAL TELEVISION.

"Would they make sense if I *had* a DVD player and a digital television?" she snapped.

NOT REALLY, NO. HANG ON, WE'LL TRY
AGAIN.

"That Cousin who's supposed to be here . . ."

"Augustus Smythe."

Samuel's fur felt as though someone had been
standing on a nylon carpet stroking him the wrong
way and he had to keep fighting the urge to run up
the walls. "He's not here."

"You can't smell him?"

"Oh, I can smell him. But he's not here."

"He's probably bleeding in the basement," Diana
decided, wincing as the cat dropped to the floor with
an emphatic double thud. "The blood of the lineage
is the fastest way to open a dark hole."

"At least we know she hasn't got it open yet."

"Actually, we don't know that for sure because my
brilliant sister never bothered to remove the dampening field around the furnace room." Leading the way
to the basement door, Diana zipped her jacket back
up, wondering why it was so cold. "Okay, full stealth
mode until we see how far things have got. We don't
want to spook her into destroying herself."

"Or the world."

"Yeah, that too."

Having hit every possible red light since they got
off the highway, Claire was considerably less than
happy as she reached into the possibilities to change

the light at Division and Queen. "It's almost as though something was trying to prevent us from reaching the guesthouse in time."

"Gee, I wonder what that could be," Austin said dryly. "Or maybe we just should've left the highway at Sir John A. MacDonald Boulevard like I suggested, thereby missing the downtown traffic."

"Nothing personal," Dean told him, accelerating through the intersection and not even slowing as Claire changed the light at Princess Street, "but it's some hard to take driving suggestions from a cat."

"Why?"

"You don't drive."

NOW GO RIGHT.

"My right or your right?"

YOUR RIGHT.

"There?"

OH, BABY . . .

"Oh, stop it," she muttered, unamused. She'd been pouring all the darkness she had left in her into the stupidly convoluted pattern that sealed the hole, and although she'd thinned it to a thread, it was nearly gone. There might not be enough, even though she could now feel Hell trying to force its way to her from the other side.

"They'll be sorry." It was meant to be a snarl. It sounded more like a whine. "They'll *all* be sorry."

*　　*　　*

"Who'll be sorry?" Samuel asked, whiskers tickling the edge of Diana's ear.

"Standard teenage riff when attempting to destroy the world," she explained, crouched down and peering around the edge of the furnace room door. "So what happens if you two touch? Do you blow up? Like matter and antimatter?"

"I don't think so."

"You don't know?"

His tail lashed. "Hey, I just got here four days ago. You're the one maintaining metaphysical balances in the world, not me."

"Well, since this is my first angel/demon crossover, you'd better wait here. We're trying to save her, not lose you both."

"What are you going to do?"

"Convince her that there's another way." She straightened, pushed the turquoise door completely open, and stepped over the threshold.

There was no reaction. Not from the demon. Not from Hell.

Must be really concentrating.

One step. Two.

Maybe I should just try and knock her off the site.

Three steps. Four.

Then I sit on her until she listens to me.

Five steps. Six.

Just wish I knew what to say.

Seven.

The black-haired girl kneeling in the center of the bedrock floor, palms pressed against the stone, looked up, onyx eyes locking on Diana's.

Say something, you idiot. Claire can't be far behind you.

"Whassup?"

Byleth stared at the girl on the stairs in disbelief. "Oh, like that is *so* over. Take one more step, Keeper, and I punch right through to Hell." Which was total bluff; she'd gone as far as she could, it was up to the other side now.

WORK TOGETHER, GUYS! TOGETH . . . STOP THAT!

Clearly, she'd have to stall.

"Send me back now, Keeper, and this is the path I'll take. You'll be opening the hole for me."

"Diana."

"What?"

"My name is Diana, after a great-aunt my mother was sucking up to. I think she was angling for this totally ugly soup tureen. Got a 1915 chamber pot instead. Frankly, I didn't see much difference. Old ugly is still ugly." Two quick steps and Diana was standing on the floor, thankful for the thick-soled winter boots that partially blocked the emanations from Hell.

WHAT PART OF TOGETHER DO YOU NOT UNDERSTAND?

"Hardly your real name," Byleth snorted. "You wouldn't give me that kind of power over you."

"Why not?"

393

"Duh. Because I'm what I am and you're what you . . ." The onyx eyes blinked. "You did. Are you terminally stupid?"

"No. I hate being called *Keeper*, like I'm an earring or something. And you are?"

"Busy."

"Yeah, and rude. Do you have a name or what?"

"Byleth." She hadn't intended to tell but there was power in trust as well. "Not that it matters," she snorted, fully aware that the Keeper had been able to read the thought from her face, "only Demon Princes actually have names, I just borrowed this one."

Diana shrugged. "Seems solidly yours now."

"No way!"

"Way. You must've noticed how the form you're in has changed you. If all you were was darkness, you'd have had this hole open by now and I'd be talking to you with my head up my ass."

"I'm not sure you aren't," Byleth snarled.

"Nice. The point is, you're not just wearing flesh, because of the way you created yourself, you're wearing a fully functional human body, and it's corrupted you the same way it corrupted . . ." She resisted the urge to glance over her shoulder toward the basement and Samuel. "Well, you know who."

"You're the bitch who changed the angel and exposed me!"

"Yeah, yeah, sticks and stones. Now, shut up for a minute and listen; we don't have much time!"

Byleth's lip curled. "Because all Hell is about to break loose."

"Because my sister is right behind me."

"Ooo, another Keeper! I'm *so* scared."

"You should be. It's her seal you can't get through, and she could deal with *you* in a heartbeat."

"It doesn't look like it's open."

"That doesn't matter." Although the sidewalk and the steps had been shoveled, the driveway and parking lot beyond it had not. Dean pulled up as close to the curb as the snowbanks allowed. "I kept a key."

"Dean, boy, well done." The cat beamed at him as Claire shoved open her door. "It's nice to know that even the most over-ethical has a tiny streak of larceny."

"Mr. Smythe asked me to keep it."

Sighing, Austin jumped down to the top of the snowbank. "So much for that bonding moment."

"Byleth, you've become a person, and while you're not Miss Congeniality, you're not significantly different from at least half the kids I go to school with."

"And that's a good thing?"

"Actually, no, it's just a thing and that's what I'm trying to tell you, take away the darkness and there's a person with the same potentials as anyone else, and that person deserves a life. I want to help."

"Yeah, right. You're a Keeper, you're supposed to stop me."

Hands on her hips, Diana exhaled emphatically. "Look, if I was supposed to stop you, I've have done it by now. Stopped you, sealed the site, and gone for mocha latte. I'm not here as a Keeper. I wasn't even Summoned, I paid my own way with, I might add, money that could have been better spent on a new snowboard."

"I should've known you were a boarder." Her eyes narrowed on either side of the strand of hair. "I so don't see the attraction in careening down a hill in a stupid hat."

"I so don't see the attraction in black clothes and bad poetry, so we're even. Come on! You specialize in lies, you must know that I'm telling the truth. Have I touched a possibility since I got here? If you can't sense that, Hell can." Diana gestured toward the floor, keeping the movement as neutral as possible. This would not be the time or place to accidentally trace a sign of power in the air.

Door. Running footsteps. Another door.

Samuel was up on the shelf over the washing machine before the first set of boots appeared on the basement stairs. It was a pure cat reaction and by the time he realized he should have warned Diana, it was too late.

He recognized Claire immediately; not only did she emanate Keeper almost as loudly as Diana did, but there was a distinct physical similarity between the sisters. Beyond that, they shared the intensity that came from knowing they could, singly or collectively, explain British humor. Not to mention save the world. Unfortunately, Claire seemed as intently determined to send him back to the light as she was to send poor, confused Byleth back to the dark, and that made her someone he had to avoid.

Dean, who followed Claire down the stairs only because she held both handrails, refusing to let him by, seemed like the kind of guy who could be depended on to open the door seven or eight times an hour and pass down a sausage or two to keep a cat from starving.

Close on Dean's heels, Austin stopped suddenly and turned, mouth slightly open. His one-eyed gaze swept over Samuel's shelf like a pale green searchlight and kept going as though he'd noticed nothing.

Samuel wasn't fooled. *He knows exactly where I am. What do I do now?*

There was nothing he could do except tuck in his paws and wait, hoping the possibilities would give him a chance to redeem himself.

"All right, so you're here because you *want* to help me stay me. Big whup. I'm here for the same thing." Under the red sweater, Byleth squared her shoulders, wishing she could stand and stare this Keeper down but unable to lift her hands from the rock until the link was completed. "When I release Hell, I'll gain the kind of notoriety that'll keep me real no matter how things turn out."

Diana sighed. She recognized bravado when she saw it. It was, after all, something she saw every day at school and occasionally in the mirror. Squatting, so that their eyes were level, she looked deep in the black depths and asked quietly, "Are you sure you want to do that?"

Was she sure? Confused, Byleth wondered how Diana's question could sound so much like the question she'd thought she heard back before Hell decided to cooperate. Maybe . . .

Maybe it wasn't too late.

Then the possibilities opened.

Claire entered the furnace room at a run, not having slowed in any significant way since she'd left the truck. She saw the demon kneeling in the center of the floor, hands pressed against the stone and knew what was happening. When the darkness in the demon reached through the pattern sealing the old hole and touched the ultimate darkness on the other side, all Hell would break loose. Which was an expression Claire had grown heartily tired of.

Banishing the demon down its own power stream and sealing the breach behind it would solve the problem nicely. A few minutes spent reinforcing things, and all but one of the embarrassing complications rising out of Dean's first time would be taken care of and the other Keepers could just go back to saving the world instead of hanging about in meta-physical chat rooms speculating about her love life.

Halfway down the stairs, she reached into the possibilities.

Her focus split between the demon and the anticipa-tion of dealing with that one remaining complication, she didn't see Diana until her sister surged up out of a crouch, whirled around, and caught her power, stop-ping it cold a full three feet from its target.

The room, the house, and a three-block radius grew so quiet no one dared drop so much as a single pin. The point midway between the Keepers began to crackle and hum.

"I can't let you do this, Claire," Diana announced dramatically. "It isn't right."

Claire closed her mouth so forcefully the crack of her molars impacting could be clearly heard. "What are you doing here?"

So much for dramatic announcements. "What's it look like I'm doing, doofus? I'm stopping you."

"From doing my job!"

"From doing the wrong thing!"

"Says who?"

"Says me!"

"Diana, I'm warning you, get out of my way." Claire's voice had begun to hold more fear than anger. The last time Keeper had fought Keeper, the fight had occurred on the exact same spot and it had ended with one Keeper lost to darkness. "I was Summoned to deal with this thing!"

Diana squared her shoulders. "Then deal with the thing part and leave the rest of her alone."

"It's not a her! It's a demon! Stop being so stubborn and look at its eyes!"

"I've looked *into* her eyes, which is more than you've done, and I know what I've seen."

"You've seen what it wanted you to see."

"You are so wrong. I saw what she didn't want me to see. I saw someone who, from the moment she found herself in that body, made excuses to act against what she perceived as her nature. To act like a person. Okay, a kind of bitchy not easy to get to know I wouldn't trust her to watch my backpack, kind of a person but a person. And you have no right to destroy that."

"She's seduced you!"

"What? The lesbian thing and a cute girl in a tight red sweater? Sure, I've noticed, but I no more let every beautiful woman I meet seduce me than you let every beautiful man." Glancing over Claire's shoulder, she smiled up the stairs. "Hey, Dean. And," she switched a burning gaze back to Claire. "You just called her she."

"That's totally irrelevant!" It didn't matter how much power she pulled, her little sister effortlessly pulled more. "Diana, listen to me. So far the dampening field has contained this little rebellion of yours, but once it gets out . . ."

"Little rebellion of mine?" Diana rolled her eyes in disbelief. "Claire, I'm serious about this. *This* is serious."

"And you don't seem to recognize how serious this is." Older sister clearly wasn't working, Claire switched to older Keeper, her voice cold. "You are betraying everything you're supposed to protect!"

"Hey, Earth to stick up her butt, I'm protecting what I'm supposed to protect! I'm protecting a person from darkness. And you."

The air began to buzz and, between the Keepers, grow distinctly brighter.

Just inside the door, Dean had to squint to make out Diana's face and could only just barely see the back of Claire's head. "Claire, she's making a lot of sense. Why not shut this down and listen to her?"

The temperature began to rise.

"She wasn't Summoned, Dean. This goes against everything we are."

Diana stamped her foot against the floor in frustrated emphasis. "Claire! We're not slaves to what we are. We're as free to make choices as anyone, and I know I'm doing the right thing."

The vibration started in the center of the light and worked its way through the room.

"You'll open the hole yourself in a minute!" Claire warned.

"I'm just standing here, you're the one throwing power."

"Hello? Does anyone care what I want?" Byleth demanded.

NO.

"I do." Austin came out from behind Dean's legs and walked slowly down the stairs, the energy in the room fluffing him out to twice his normal size. He brushed against Claire's legs as he passed and looked pointedly at a drift of orange cat hair on Diana's jeans, then sat down just outside the old pentagram's center. "So tell me, besides the latest Cure CD, what do you want?"

"How did you . . . ?"

He smiled at her. "I'm a cat."

"But . . ."

"Let it go," Dean advised from the top of the stairs.

Byleth looked at him, realized he was nothing more than human but, more importantly, nothing less than human, looked at the two Keepers, looked at the cat, and sighed. "All right. Fine. You want to know what I want? I don't know, okay?"

"You don't know?"

"What, are you deaf?"

"Sounds human to me," Austin declared as though that settled it.

"Well?" Diana demanded, spearing her sister with a dark gaze. "We haven't got time for DNA evidence. Which one of us blinks first?"

Claire could feel Dean behind her, even through

all the building possibilities. This was more than a Summoning, this was her chance to fix things between them. Balance of good and evil aside, if she didn't banish the demon, they'd be condemned to long nights of playing cards with a cat who cheated.

"Claire, please?"

She had no intention of looking into the demon's eyes, she knew too well how darkness worked, so she looked into her sister's instead and saw Diana honestly believed in what she was doing. It wasn't defiance, it wasn't sibling rivalry on a grand and possibly explosive scale, it was, plain and simple and totally unexpected, an attempt to do the right thing.

But I was Summoned to deal with the demon.

Would it be enough to destroy merely the demonic?

"Maybe," she said softly, "we're both right."

Feeling her eyebrows singe, Diana smiled, relieved. "I can live with that. Byleth?"

Byleth screamed.

LET THE GAMES BEGIN!

"Break her contact!" Claire commanded, gathering up the possibilities as Diana released them.

They had no more than a heartbeat before Hell reached her. "How?"

An orange blur raced past before Claire could answer, slammed into Byleth's chest and, in flash of both black-and-white light, knocked her over backward.

"She's clear!"

AND SO AM . . .

Claire hit it first with all the power that had been building against Diana's block.

NOT YOU TWO AGAIN!

Then Diana slammed the power from the block against it.

WE ARE THE HEART OF DARKNESS; YOU CANNOT PREVAIL.

"Can too."

"Diana, don't argue with Hell."

Together, they backed the heart of darkness down the narrow path, denying the possibilities it represented one after the other, until finally they shoved it right back where it had come from . . .

THIS IS REALLY STARTING TO PISS ME OFF.

. . . and sealed the hole tight.

I'LL BE BACK!

AND I'LL BE BEETHOVEN.

SHUT. UP.

OW!

* * *

Dropping to her knees beside Byleth, Diana scooped Samuel's limp body into her arms and peered anxiously into golden eyes. "Are you okay?"

He tried to focus on her face. "I, I can't feel my tail."

"Sorry." She shifted her knees.

"Oh, yeah. That's better."

"He's fine." Austin laid a paw on the younger cat's flank. "That was a brave thing you did, kid."

"It was a dangerous thing," Claire corrected, untangling herself from Dean's embrace and coming to stand over them. "Who are you, and where did you come from?"

Diana sighed. "Chill, Claire. His name is Samuel, and he's with me."

A set of claws pressed into the sleeve of her jacket, releasing a puff of down. "I am?"

"Aren't you?"

He rubbed his head against her face. "Yeah, I am."

Claire opened her mouth to demand more information, but the look on Austin's face stopped her. She smiled and shook her head. "Welcome to the family, Samuel." When Diana glanced up, startled, the smile vanished. "You, however, are still in deep trouble."

"I was . . ." About to say right, Diana glanced past Claire to Dean shaking his head warningly and said instead, ". . . wrong. I was wrong to defy an older Keeper in such a way, but there wasn't time to for anything else. I'm not sorry I did it, but I am sorry we had to clash like that." Settling Samuel against her chest, she held up a hand. "Friends?"

"I'm still mad at you."

"I know."

"This is bigger than taking my bra to school for show and tell."

"It wasn't that big a bra."

"Diana."

"I know."

Claire looked down at their clasped hands, unable to remember the actual moment when their fingers had linked. "This is going to take more than an apology."

"Then tell me what it's going to take, oh, older, wiser, shorter Keeper."

"Stop it." The corners of her mouth twitching, she released her sister's hand. "You were right and you know it, and there's no need to be so irritating about it." Before Diana could disagree, she dropped to her knees on Byleth's other side. "Let's just take care of this little problem before she wakes up and puts us through all that . . . indecision again. I won't go so easy on you the next time." But the heavily mascaraed eye pried open was pale gray and the rest of Byleth's body was equally darkness free. "That's strange. Samuel knocking her free of the site so unexpectedly must have dragged the rest of it out of her."

When no one offered any better explanation, Claire sat back on her heels and spread her hands. "So. What do we do with her now?"

"Why don't I carry her to a bed and we all spend some time thinking about it?" Dean asked, stepping forward. "You two don't always have to have instant answers."

"Obviously you haven't read the handbook," Diana snorted.

Claire ignored her with the ease of someone who'd

spent seventeen years living with a cat. "That's a good idea, Dean. I'm sure we can come up with something once we've all detached a little."

"I'll be after putting her in my old room, then." He slid his arms under Byleth's shoulders and knees and lifted her easily. "It's closest."

Rising with Byleth's body, Claire reached out and pressed her hand against Dean's cheek. "I'm sorry I didn't keep my promise to banish the demon."

He smiled. "I'm after feeling it's not going to matter."

"You think?"

"I do."

"Yes!"

"Code?" Diana asked, watching her suddenly cheerful sister follow Dean and his burden up the stairs.

Austin shook his head. "You don't want to know."

"Uh, Austin, about Samuel."

"What about him?" He gave her the sort of look that was usually accompanied by small feathers around the mouth.

Suddenly unsure, Diana set the orange cat on his feet and stood. She had a feeling she'd need all the advantage height could give her.

"He knows," Samuel told her before she could decide how to answer. "He knows what I was."

"Will you tell Claire?" Diana asked the older cat, hoping he couldn't sense how anxious she was.

"After what we went through with Byleth, if she found out what Samuel was, she wouldn't want him around. She'd be worried it could happen again."

"Hey, it's none of my business how you two crazy kids got together," Austin snickered, starting up the stairs. "And I think Claire's going to have plenty of other things to do for the next little while." Halfway up to the basement, he turned and glared into golden eyes following close behind, looking concerned. "If you so much as insinuate I'm too old to be doing this, I'll notch those virgin ears of yours."

"I wasn't going to."

"You're a terrible liar."

"Sorry."

"So you should be, kid. So you should be."

Claire was waiting for them at the foot of the basement stairs. "Dean's just digging out a blanket. Diana . . ."

"I thought we worked through this?" Diana demanded, folding her arms and lifting her chin defiantly, working the "best defense is a good offense" line. "Look, I know it was your Summoning and I shouldn't have gotten involved, but you've got to admit you were working from your own agenda here and not seeing what was so obvious to me. If I hadn't stopped you, we'd have lost all the potential Byleth represents."

"I'm not arguing." Her tone was so mild Diana

braced herself. "I was only going to ask if Mom and Dad knew where you were."

"Mom and Dad?" It took her a moment to realize the implications. "Oh, no. I got so into stopping you and saving Byleth, I forgot to call." Patting her pockets, she remembered she'd left her cell phone behind. "Nuts! I'll have to use the phone in the office."

Kicking aside the cashews, she raced up the stairs two at a time with Samuel at her heels.

Claire and Austin followed a little more sedately.

"You're not going to go on and on to her about this little incident, are you?"

Claire shook her head, smiling contentedly. "No need. I'll let the pros handle it."

Exiting into the first floor hall they heard a desperate, "But, Mom, I meant to call!" and then giggling.

Cat and Keeper exchanged puzzled looks.

Giggling?

Before they had time to investigate, the only other door in the hall swung open to reveal a small Victorian elevator. Dean and Jacques had repaired it in the fall but when, on the inaugural trip, they'd boldly gone where no elevator had gone before, Claire'd declared it off limits until she was able to study it. Unfortunately, she'd been Summoned away before she had the chance.

A short, gnomelike man stepped out, arm in arm with an elderly bottle-redhead of formidable proportions. Matching his and hers lime-green bathing suits under open parkas and a trail of fine white sand suggested they'd just been to the beach. They stopped short at the sight of Claire and Austin.

"Augustus Smythe? Mrs. Abrams? What . . . ? Where . . . ?" Realizing that shock could keep her stuttering questions she didn't want the answers to all afternoon, Claire managed to pull herself together. "Never mind. Not important."

Snorting hard enough to nearly flip his mustache, Augustus Smythe stepped forward. "About time you got here."

"It is?"

"I should think so. We're on a commuter plane to Toronto in two hours and then it's off to sunny Florida."

"Florida?"

"We have a nice little condo in a seniors building only a block from the ocean." Mrs. Abrams wrapped both hands around Augustus Smythe's upper arm and beamed. "You'll have to come down and see us some time, Connie."

"Claire." This was all just a little more than she could cope with right now.

"Don't contradict," Smythe warned her. "It's rude. And what's more," he continued, turning his scowl on his companion, "she can't come see us, she'll be here."

"No." Claire raised both hands. "I'm not . . ."

"You are. You're the new Keeper for this whole

region. Check your damned e-mail on occasion, why don't you. There you are, McIssac, I wondered where you'd got to. Figured you wouldn't be far."

"Mr. Smythe? Mrs. Abrams?" Dean's astonished gaze slid off the shelf of lime-green supported bosom exposed in the open parka and wandered around the hall, unsure of where it was safe to alight.

"Hello, dear boy. My, you're looking well."

"Thank you, um, you, too."

She released her grip on Augustus Smythe's arm just long enough to wave at the elevator. "We've been working on our tans."

"No time for chitchat." One hairy-knuckled finger jabbed toward Dean . . . "McIssac here will run the guesthouse." . . . then changed direction to jab at Claire. "You'll take care of the metaphysical from Brockville to Belleville with this as your base. He needs to be more than your love slave, and this area needs a permanent Keeper. Your cat looks like he could use a few less nights sleeping rough, too."

"He's never slept any rougher than a Motel Six," Claire protested.

"It was awful," Austin sighed.

"No doubt."

"Just wait a minute." Her urge to grab Augustus Smythe's arm aborted when he turned to glare. "Keepers my age don't get tied to one place."

"Times are changing. Thanks to modern communications, modern transportation, and spandex, Keepers can get to sites before they grow big enough to be dangerous."

"I've closed dangerous sites!"

"You dead yet? Then don't argue with me. A century ago, you'd have beaten considerable odds to be alive at your age. But now, fewer Keepers die, more Keepers are alive, the lineage can cover more of the world safely and still have what resembles a life. It's basic math. Your sister'll probably spend her first few years closing sites no one's been powerful enough to close until now. If she doesn't blow herself to kingdom come first."

It sounded good. But there had to be a catch. "So eventually the world won't need us."

"Did I say people were getting smarter?" He turned to Mrs. Abrams. "Did you hear me say that people are getting smarter?"

She beamed down at him. "I surely didn't, puddin'."

"There, see? The dumb asses in this world will always need someone to clean up after them. You're just getting a chance to live happily ever after while you do it. We'll get changed and out of your way. Coming, Mags?"

"Coming, puddin'."

"That was surreal," Austin observed as the two turned the corner into the office and then disappeared into Augustus Smythe's apartment.

Strangely uncertain, Claire looked around at the

guesthouse—stopped looking around when her gaze got to Dean. "You want to stay, don't you?"

He shrugged. "It's your choice, Boss."

"Our choice."

About to defer, he suddenly shook his head. "Then, yes. I want to stay."

"Because you want to be more than my love slave?"

"I never said that. Just promise me something," he added after a moment, capturing her face in both hands and holding it far enough away from his that he could look into her eyes. "Never call me puddin'."

Claire shuddered. "I think I can safely promise you that."

"Hey!"

They moved apart again as Diana and Samuel came down the hall.

"Was that who I think that was?"

"Yes."

"With . . . ?"

"Yes."

"Why?"

"They're moving to Florida together, Dean's taking over the guesthouse and, if Augustus Smythe is to be trusted, which, of course, he isn't, I'm now covering a specific area . . ." She patted one of the hunter green walls almost fondly. ". . . based around this very building."

Diana's lip curled. "Oh, man, that's such a happy

tie-up-all-the-loose-ends ending I think I'm going to hurl.''

"Take a number," Austin advised.

Claire ignored them both. "What did Mom say?"

"That I did the right thing and we'll talk about the rest when I get home."

"Well, she actually said," Samuel began and broke off as Diana glared.

"So what do we do with Byleth long term?" she asked, pointedly changing the subject. "She could live here with you, you've got the space. I think you two would make wonderful parents."

Dean blanched. "Uh, better idea." He pulled out a crumpled envelope. "I found this in her jacket pocket. It's got the address and the phone number for a Mr. and Mrs. Harry Porter and a note that says 'if you ever need us, call.' "

"I don't know," Claire began.

He handed her the envelope. "The 'i' has been dotted with a little heart."

"Oh, yeah. They deserve each other. Although . . ." She sighed, frowning at the little heart. "I still don't like the thought of releasing even an ex-demon into the world."

"She'll be going to high school," Diana reminded her grimly. "Anything demonic she managed to do in the short time she was here, she'll more than pay for."

"Good point." The envelope changed hands again. "She's your project, Diana, you can do the honors."

"Okay, but I'm doing it from the phone in Dean's old apartment, I *so* don't want to run into Mr. and Mrs. Scary Old People again." Pivoting on one heel, she scanned the hall. "Samuel?"

Just as she started to worry, he emerged from the elevator, jaws working.

"Come on, we're going to go ruin Byleth's life. What are you chewing?" she asked as they started down the basement stairs.

"Someone left a piece of calamari in that little room."

"Eww. Don't eat stuff you find on the floor."

"I'm eight inches tall. My options are kind of limited."

As their voices faded, Claire moved back into Dean's arms, slipping her hands under his coat and grinning at his reaction to the temperature of her fingers. "Now that Hell's back out of the picture, you really have to put a furnace in this place."

"I know. Claire, I was wondering . . ."

"Natural gas is probably cheaper."

"Not that . . ."

Her hands dropped lower. "Just as soon as we get rid of everyone."

"No. Well, yes. Wait a minute." He caught hold of her wrists while he was still capable of stopping her. "The angel, is it gone, then?"

She nuzzled his neck. "Not exactly. Diana turned him into a cat."

"Samuel?" Shoulder blades pressed into the wall, he detached enough to look down at Austin.

"Samuel," Austin told him. "But Diana thinks Claire doesn't know, so keep it to yourself."

"Why?"

He shrugged and wrapped his tail around his front paws, managing to somehow look like a small, furry, one-eyed Buddha. "It's an older sister thing. In an effort to keep a small piece of the high ground, Claire needs to know things that Diana doesn't know she knows because Diana is so much more powerful. Keeperwise."

"Okay. But couldn't this whole thing . . ."

"No, he's no more an angel now than that girl's a demon. They canceled each other out when he knocked her away from the hole."

"Did he know that would happen, then?"

"Does it matter?" Claire asked.

"I guess not."

"I wouldn't worry about him," Austin said soothingly. "He's a cat."

"Which means?" Claire demanded from inside the circle of Dean's arms.

"Which means—and do you have to do that in front of me?—that he's still a superior being."